# THE  STONE CHILDREN

*To Jamie Best Wishes Always,*

8/10/05

# THE STONE CHILDREN

**By**

**C. J. MORRIS**

*C. J. Morris "Cliff"*

ISBN 1-58597-314-9

Library of Congress Control Number: 2004117916

A division of Squire Publishers, Inc.
4500 College Blvd.
Leawood, KS 66211
1/888/888-7696
www.leatherspublishing.com

*This book is dedicated to my brother, Bradford, whose optimistic outlook is inspiring, and who greets each day with courage and perseverance in spite of physical challenges.*

# 1

JUST A BIT more … one more pull … and the hub should be locked down tight. Frank Stone yanked on the wrench. The worn nut fought all efforts to twist snugly on the stripped spindle. The old John Deere was being cantankerous again. He kept this plowing relic in the field turning sod and belching diesel exhaust with a combination of spare parts and a few choice words. Blasted machine … if it doesn't fall apart, it'll end up killing me, he thought; yet he was accustomed to the frequent repairs.

Frank wiped black sweat from this thick white forehead. The headband of his bright red Cornhusker ball cap looked as if it had been dipped in 40-weight oil as he pulled it over his brow and gazed up at the clear afternoon sky. He shifted his position on the stubble-churned ground between six-foot-high tires, then threw the wrench into his catchall toolbox. He'd done this kind of repair a half-dozen times a week, more often during planting time.

How could he know at that moment, involved in a routine chore on such a calm and sunny day, that within the hour he would be dead. No more long walks to the back door, hanging his dusty denim jacket on the nail over the washing machine. No more ice-cold 7-Ups from the antiquated Frigidaire while five-year-old Melissa ran to his side waiting to be lifted into the air. It all happened so quickly. It was especially hard on his wife, Sandra, who found him.

Farming in Nebraska was always hard. So much to do. Never

enough time to get it all done. Up before dawn, in the fields until long after dusk after the fading rays of a fallen sun flickered away.

Only Sundays were a tad less stressful. Frank would take the family to church, all loaded down in their only vehicle, a once white '83 Ford F150. He'd play catch with the boys in the afternoon. Still, it seemed, there was always farm work to do, like mending fence or chasing down a stray cow. And the livestock feeding never ended. When it concerned their meals, the farm animals didn't take kindly to the idea of taking Sundays off.

Frank walked around the tractor, rust spots checkered faded green paint. It wasn't leaking any fluids. He opened the engine cowling, checked the hoses and looked for new problems that might cause delays in the field. Better to double check everything now. After all, the tractor was really getting old. Three growing seasons passed under its wheels even before he bought the privilege of making payments on the beast. This year would mark the eighth it had helped him bring in a crop. It always needed attention, like it just didn't want to work without being shown it was fully appreciated. But it had seen him through … all the plowing, seed drilling, fertilizing and cultivating. Then when harvest came the old tractor got to rest in the barn while the combine took over. Frank pulled his mind back to the job at hand. The tractor was ready to work, and he needed to get this fallowed field plowed before nightfall.

Mother Nature was already whispering to Frank Stone about his age and the ravages of farm work on his body. His face was weathered far beyond his 38 years. He never wore gloves, the black earth permanently embedded under his nails. His enormous hands were calloused and cracked, yet tender and strong. He played with his youngest children, the Little Ones he called them, and tossed them into the air as though they were pillows, catching them with the care afforded china dolls, their landings in massive arms as soft as a goose-down feather bed.

His brow was heavy, his hair sun-bleached and thin. Deep lines etched the corners of his mouth and eyes. The land he loved had claimed his features; the elements made him appear a man nearing 60. But his heart was invigorated daily by his farm and family.

Tractors in general, and this one in particular, start forward with a jump. It's the power take-off, and it jerks the huge rear tires with a powerful low-ratio engagement that's designed to snap the machine out of mud or loose sand. When a disc or plow is attached, this feature drives the implement immediately, insuring that all of the field will be worked.

Frank knew all of this, being prepared for the sudden jerk of the power take-off was just part of driving a tractor. He knew all the quirks of the aged machine, how it made tighter circles turning left than it did turning right. He'd been able to deal with everything it threw at him — until today.

He climbed onto the open-air rusty metal seat which bounced on a leaf spring like the head of a jack-in-the-box. The farm-weary mechanical beast chugged to life as Frank turned the ignition key. It built up RPM, then roared under the hot afternoon sun. Dust sifted in the air. Frank scratched his back with a long stick as the mixture of sweat and chaff-laden dirt made him itch.

A hazy dryness hung over the topsoil. Yet, the upturned ground behind the plow revealed furrows of rich, moist black Nebraska earth. Robins, killdeers, meadowlarks, doves and starlings all dropped from the sky for the easy pickings of worms and grubs and pecked through the freshly turned sod discovering other previously hidden morsels.

Frank looked about. All around him was the treeless expanse of miles and miles of prairie. Except to the east, a quarter of a mile away, his house and home, nestled in a pocket of elms and cottonwoods and farm buildings. The green of the trees, which buffeted the house from frequent winds, gave a dash of color to a horizon of brown dirt. He could see hay spilling from the open loft where Chrissy set up a nursery for a litter of newborn kittens, and the special rock pen Danny built to house his prized fair pig. The tire swing hung motionless from the giant oak in the front yard. All appeared quiet and serene, but he knew Sandra was inside fixing dinner. He smiled to himself. All the time and effort it took to buy this place and bring his family to the country was worth it.

He turned on the seat to check the plow, to make sure it was clear of all obstructions. Everything looked in order. As he turned back around to the front, he slipped from his half-cocked position, his hand grabbed air, his balance tilted to the rear. Had the tractor been off, or in neutral, he could have easily righted himself by grabbing a tire or anything else nearby. But the tractor was ready to go. His foot slipped from the clutch. The machine lurched forward, and Frank Stone tumbled into eternity. He landed on his head, bounced off the connecting shaft and onto the ground. The six-ton plow, with its razor-sharp discs, steel wheels that dig into, pull up and turn over the soil, rolled over him. Four of the round blades hit him. His intestines were laid open to the frying heat and drifting dirt. His right leg was severed across the shin with a slice as smooth as a surgeon's incision. Frank Stone lay dead on the ground of the farm he loved so much, and the tractor kept chugging unattended across the field.

* * * * *

"You make it look so easy," Freddie moaned. "I always miss the bag or twist up my feet."

"I've been practicing," Danny beamed. "My dad's been helping me every night. There's nothing more important than the pivot when you're playing second."

"I know. I wish I could get the knack like you. Can't get my feet right. I'll probably have to go back to the outfield."

Ever since Danny Stone had moved to the country, he and Freddie Stalnaker had been the best of friends. No other kids around this area, none close to their age anyway. Each school day they made the mile and a half walk together after the bus let them off at the corner marked by old man Shaw's limestone fence. And each afternoon as they walked to the split that led to their separate farms they had plenty of time to talk.

"Big game tomorrow," Danny said.

"You have a big game. I doubt if I'll even get to play."

Freddie's crystal blue eyes cast dejection from under a shock of golden hair. He slouched as he walked, hands in his pockets, dragging his worn-out baseball shoes behind him in the dust.

Danny gave his friend an understanding smile. "Sure you will. We'll work on your fielding some more, before and after the game. You'll make a great infielder some day."

"You really think so?" Freddie stopped and stood erect. He really liked Danny and looked up to him. Besides, Freddie was an only child. If it weren't for Danny, he'd be stuck out on these rolling acres with no one to talk to but his pet dog.

"Sure! The more grounders you shag, the better you'll get," Danny said.

"Yeah, I know. But I don't have anyone to hit me grounders. My dad thinks it's all a big waste of time. All he wants me to do is finish my chores and stay out of his way."

Danny started to turn north up the split toward his home, but he stopped and turned back toward Freddie. "I'll help you out. My dad has chores for me; we all have that … but he still likes to play baseball with me. Guess I'm pretty lucky."

"You sure are. My dad's okay and all, but all he ever talks about is farming."

Danny stood and watched his friend walk south down the split. What Freddie said gave him a warm feeling inside, the compliments about his baseball playing, the way he compared their fathers.

Danny continued down the dirt road at a quicker pace. He'd had a great afternoon of baseball practice. He'd have to tell his dad and Sam all about it.

With a flip of his finger he knocked off his emerald green cap to let the dry breeze ruffle his thick brown hair. He tried to juggle his cap, ball and mitt as he walked, but all three quickly ended up at his feet. He smiled his wide gapped-toothed grin as he bent over. Big for his 15 years, his mother commented almost daily how it seemed he was growing another inch every week.

The falling sun turned from yellow to orange. It was still light enough to see, and he searched the fields for clouds of dust to signal where his dad was plowing. There were none. Maybe he'd decided to come in early today. Great! Chance for a game of 500 before dark. He was hungry and excited and began running the final yards to the house.

But then, in an instant, Danny knew something was out of place. Something was different about the farm house and its surroundings. A strange feeling gnawed in his stomach. Four strange cars sat in the driveway alongside their truck, nice shiny cars from town. And everything fell silent, even the incessant chirping buzz of the field crickets escaped his ears.

Kiko, his black and white Labrador mongrel, sauntered to his side and walked on in with him. The dog was old, long past his hunting days, just a familiar relic resting his hours away on the porch. But even the dog seemed to sense that something had changed.

Christine usually fed the chickens about this time each evening, but Chrissy was not in the yard. Nor was Melissa anywhere to be seen, dragging her matronly doll, Mrs. Leatherwood, by the arm as she played in the tire swing or chased the chickens about.

Danny petted the old dog a few strokes atop the head and scratched him behind the ears. He knelt beside Kiko and squeezed the dog's head gently into his chest. Then he tossed his ball and mitt on the wooden planks of the farmhouse porch.

Through the curtains Danny could tell the house was flooded in light. Every bulb in the place was aglow, which cast eerie shadows into the yard. Danny knew people were in the house, yet even as he stood by the back door, he couldn't hear a sound coming from inside.

The kitchen was empty as he entered, no dinner had been

prepared. Several ears of corn lay untouched in the sink, a mixing bowl beside it full of sifted flour, a half-dozen eggs on the counter. Danny walked into the living room. As he came through the dining room, low volume sobbing became audible. He appeared in front of them all. They had been waiting.

Danny recognized the preacher seated with his wife at the far end of the couch. The old worn divan, muddy squares of brown fabric with gaudy orange stripes, threw everyone who sat on it deep into its cratered cushions. Ordinarily, he'd be embarrassed to see company in their living room on the mismatched assortment of rag-tag furniture, but all the eyes fixed on him held his attention.

The Reverend began to rise, but his wife pulled him back. Sam sucked on his thumb, seven years old and sucking his thumb, his eyes buried in Chrissy's chest as she shook with silent sobs. Melissa huddled the same way on their mother's lap. Sandra Stone was not comforting her youngest daughter in any way. The doll lay on the floor. Of all the sights before him, the doll on the floor was the most disconcerting. Melissa always had that doll in her grasp.

Freddie's mother was there, seated next to his mother and Melissa, stroking the little girl's hair. Mr. Doren, who farmed just down the road and helped his dad during harvest, stood next to the fireplace. When their eyes met, the short bald-headed neighbor turned his gaze away.

Other faces in the room he recognized, but they all looked so pitiful, the same … all quiet, sad faces with lifeless eyes. His head spun as a knotted lump rose in his throat.

Danny looked into his mother's eyes; eyes that did not focus back on him, eyes as blank and glassy as those of a cow. The lump that had been in his chest began to grow and ache. The eyes he gazed into were no longer the eyes of the mother he knew. The bright, happy windows into his mother's loving soul were now clouded and veiled. Her eyes appeared as those of a deer caught in headlights, expressionless milky globes, unconditionally surrendered.

Her radiant auburn hair was bound in a scarf; her cheeks

streaked with tears. Deep within her apron her hands were tightly clasped and concealed. She seemed physically shriveled, emotionally withdrawn, her outgoing personality totally receded.

Sandra Stone had always been so radiant and positive. Even when she scolded her children, it was with a glint in her eye. She was never too serious about rules and discipline, choosing instead to spread her love and attention evenly, and let her husband deal with more serious breaches of behavior. There was always a smile near her lips. Only her rough, red hands gave any indication of all the hard work she did around the farm. She had followed her husband willingly when he decided to move the family from Kansas City. She knew farm life would be difficult, but she agreed it would be a good place to raise children.

Danny thought his mother was beautiful. Her sunny disposition made her seem that way regardless of what anyone else thought. Even on bad days she was encouraging, like the day a coyote got in the chicken coop and killed them all, and the day termites were found in the crawl space, and $600 they really didn't have had to be spent to treat the house.

She sang when she worked in the kitchen, and often in the evenings. She always read a bedtime story to the Little Ones. One day Sam fell from the tree swing and broke his arm. Through all his howling and screaming, she gave Danny a wink and her special smile to let him know all would be okay, everything would work out. Today that wink and smile were gone. Things had changed, now she needed him.

Danny felt his heart pounding. Panic mixed with a strange sadness as new emotions rushed through his body. He moved to his mother and knelt on the hardwood floor in front of her. He took her hand and brushed his cheek over it.

He spoke directly to her, but the recognition wasn't there. "Tell me what happened," he said in a soft voice as he fought to keep the words from cracking. A well of tears stung his eyes.

Five-year-old Melissa turned her face toward him. Her lower

lip quivered, she tried to speak but couldn't. A moan erupted from her precious face, a bubble of saliva sprayed from her mouth. She wheeled her face away, back into the refuge of their mother's warm breast.

Danny took his little sister's hand. The weight of seconds grew until he was sure he'd die from sheer suspense. "Talk to me, Punkin. What happened?" He knew the revelation was going to hurt. A part of him didn't want to know. For a brief second he knew the foolish bliss that comes from not knowing … the paradise of ignorance. But not knowing was driving him crazy. He knew a shock was at hand. Melissa turned back, her swollen eyes and runny nose confronted him. "Daddy's dead," she cried. Through red, tear-filled eyes she looked at him, pleading, begging that he tell her the words she spoke were not the truth. "Daddy's dead."

# 2

SANDRA STONE'S OLDER sister, Lois Devon, drove down immediately from Omaha. In her mid-40s the woman possessed the same laughing smile that Sandra had before the accident. She was single, twice divorced, and now lived alone. She kept her second husband's last name because she liked the sound of it. Lois was a city person, everything was at your fingertips there. Only the sudden tragedy compelled her to make the trip "out to the middle of nowhere."

The funeral service was brief. About 40 attended: farmers and their wives who knew Frank and the family. The casket wasn't opened. The girls, Chrissy and Melissa, sat huddled together sobbing while Sandra stared blankly at the far wall in front of her.

Danny remained as strong as he could. He was now the man of the family. He sat next to Sam and rolled a song book over and over in his hands. He struggled to think about things far away from the funeral parlor. He fought to keep his composure. When the organist played *How Great Thou Art,* he almost tore the song book in half trying to rein in his emotions. He didn't know exactly why, he just didn't want to burst out crying. He knew if he started he'd never be able to stop. He just couldn't believe his dad was gone.

All Danny wanted to do, all he could think of, was to sit tight in the varnished mahogany pew and look straight ahead. Beside him, Sam's hands were clenched, his knuckles bone white as he gripped the edge of the bench, his chin buried in his chest. The small boy pressed his body next to Danny. A slow organ requiem droned while the funeral director placed a single flower wreath of white lilies interlaced with yellow goldenrod directly behind the casket.

Danny saw his school buddy, Freddie, seated with his parents. Freddie did not look his way, his head was down, his eyes preoccupied with his own lap. Many of the people Danny knew through his dad from throughout the county were there, all somber-faced and as mute as statues.

Melissa clung to her dolly, absently adjusting a white cotton baby blanket around its face. Christine was choking and sobbing. Danny held her hand firmly to try and lend some comfort.

The funeral chapel felt so sterile and unreal; a chamber for the dead filled with the lifeless. Up at the front a thin walnut pulpit stood in front of heavy crimson drapes. The death bier was opposite the podium drenched in an eerie amber light. You could have heard a field mouse run across the floor. Except for the almost imperceptible shakes that accompanied Chrissy's sobs, the audience was as motionless as set concrete.

Sandra Stone was devastated; her children and friends knew it. They couldn't snap her out of it. Everyone had been trying to cheer her up for days. Melissa cried herself to sleep the past three nights without her mother ever taking notice of her youngest child.

Chrissy tried to fill in, carry on the household routine as though nothing serious had happened, tuck the Little Ones into bed each night. But everyone was dealing in their own way with the painful realization that life had changed. No one escaped the hurt.

As the minister spoke, Sandra Stone, wife of departed Frank, never indicated that she heard a single word. When Chrissy looked to her for comfort, she looked back at her daughter as though she were a stranger. For the past several days the bleary-eyed 11-year-old Chrissy sat on the edge of the bed she shared with Melissa. After the Little Ones were finally in bed, with silent sobs she rocked herself into an exhausted sleep.

As the minister finished speaking, the funeral director stepped to the end of the pew where the family was seated. He made a hand gesture and led them to the front. Everyone moved in slow motion. Danny tried to concentrate on the stability and movements of his mother. Chrissy wept on his shoulder. He closely watched the Little Ones, too.

The close-up sight of the hand-rubbed walnut casket drove a hard lump into his throat. It lay before them in the surreal light, gleaming brass medallions along the side with inlaid silver clip handles and red velvet seams.

Sam began crying. His grief was not subdued as the usher in the back of the chapel could clearly hear his wails. Tears streamed down Sam's cheeks as Danny knelt beside his little brother. Sam's throws of despair increased with each passing second; his entire body racked with anguish. "Daddy, Daddy," he wailed. Danny hugged him close while bowing his head, fighting to keep his own composure. A knife in his chest would not hurt any worse. And there, for more than ten minutes, next to the casket of his father, Sam cried and cried and cried.

\* \* \* \* \*

"Honey, things are all going to work out. You wait and see if I'm not right," Lois spoke in an upbeat vein as the group of mourners walked from the gravesite to awaiting cars. "You'll all just have to move back to the city."

"I feel tired," Sandra spoke into the wind, the comment directed at no one in particular.

"Of course you do, sweetie," Lois replied. The family boarded a polished black Cadillac provided by the funeral home. "I'll stay as long as you need me. With these four beautiful children helping you, everything will be back to normal in no time."

Danny resented his aunt's trite statements. She didn't seem to see what was going on, or to be experiencing the grieving of the moment. She was friendly enough. Maybe at a time like this it was good that someone wasn't so depressed and gloomy. But deep inside Danny didn't think her gabby nature was helping any of them cope with this terrible event.

"Do you know of a good place to eat in town?" Lois asked Danny. "Let's all go and have a really delicious lunch."

"I'm not hungry," said Melissa.

"Neither am I," seconded Chrissy.

Lois glanced around the Caddy and realized that she was out-voted. "I understand. We'll just go back to the farm."

\* \* \* \* \*

The days that followed were totally dreary. Routine chores were all but neglected. Necessary activities were undertaken with agonizing will power and the conditioning of rote memory. Danny couldn't get his mother to talk. She'd sit in her room and stare at the wall. He'd have felt much better if she'd done something ... anything, look at old photographs, wring her hands, cry all day into her pillow, but she did nothing more than sit and stare.

Danny and Chrissy cared for the Little Ones. Chrissy cooked; Danny did the chores that had to be done with help from Sam. None of them went to school.

True to her word, Lois stayed at the house, but she became more restless with each passing day. She did her best to get Sandra to come around, but all the coaxing and consoling came to no avail. With the children, she'd talk about the big wheeler-dealer real estate developer she worked for in Omaha. Always lighting a cigarette every other moment, she patted the Little Ones on the head every time they came near, as though they were pet poodles waiting for a treat. With Danny and Chrissy she acted more adult, more in tune and considerate of a family in mourning. but you could never be sure with her ... sometimes she'd talk softly to her sister, other times she acted like they were back in school deciding whether to take in a movie or go to the malt shop.

The two women had not actually grown up together. Lois was almost ten years older than Sandra. However, they did look remarkably alike. Both were tall, about 5'9", slender, with dark brown hair. Their similarities ended with their physical resemblance.

Lois didn't care for the country life one bit. She couldn't see how anyone could stand to live on a farm. Lois liked to be around people. She liked the convenience and entertainment choices of the city. In the eight years the Stone family had lived in rural Nebraska, Lois had never made a trip out to visit them — until now.

Her voice was about all there was to be heard in the house in the days following the funeral. One day while talking with Sandra in her bedroom Lois discovered a strong box. It contained all of the important family papers, and she went through them to help Sandra put the business side of things in order.

\* \* \* \* \*

A week after the funeral the four children gathered behind the barn. The intense pain of the funeral had subsided; their youth and optimistic outlooks promoted emotional healing. It was time to have a family meeting, for those who could participate — their mother wasn't up to it — and for those who were invited. They really didn't know Aunt Lois. She really wasn't family. The whole thing was spur-of-the-moment, an unspoken consensus that a discussion was in order, without having the slightest idea what was on the agenda.

"I guess I'll have to learn how to drive," said Sam without batting an eye. Danny knew how, and had been allowed to drive around the farm for some time.

"You do, huh," said Danny. Melissa giggled.

"Sure … of course, why sure."

"You hardly know how to ride a bike," said Chrissy, her long, limp blonde hair billowing in the breeze.

"So?"

"Well, you're not old enough, that's so."

"I can learn."

"I'll teach you how to drive the combine. You could do that," Danny said as he stroked Sam's head. The top of the little boy's head didn't even reach Danny's chest.

Sam craned his eyes up into the sun and smiled. "Oh, boy. that's great. Can we practice now? Can we?"

"Later. First we've got to divide up chores, and do them. No more putting things off until Dad tells you twice ..." Danny caught himself. The others had their eyes glued on him. For a second, he couldn't speak, couldn't think of what to say next. Danny swallowed, then cleared his throat. The slip of the tongue caught him unprepared. He almost succumbed to an impulse of self-pity, but he fought it off. "... Tend to all the animals, too, and the house, the cooking and cleaning. Me and Sam will finish up the plowing."

"Do you think we'll have to move?" asked Melissa from out of nowhere. Only five years old, she always seemed to see the heart of any subject. Her questions were often quite poignant. Chrissy knelt at her feet and looked her in the eyes.

"No, honey. We won't have to move — not anytime soon. Mama likes it here. Danny can keep things going." Then 11-year-old Chrissy looked up at Danny, her eyes searching for confirmation of the statements she'd made.

"That's right. We're staying right here," Danny said. But his words didn't ring true to him. He really wanted to go. It would be fine by him to get off the farm. Sell the place. That would give them enough money to get a house in some city, or at least a real town. Leave this tragic incident behind.

Danny wanted to play baseball and pursue it as a way to get a college scholarship. Maybe that would lead to a major league contract. He wanted to live in the city. Maybe this would be his ticket off the farm. He hated the price that had been paid, the sudden death of his dad, but it had already been paid. His dad was dead and nothing he could do would ever bring him back.

"Okay," Danny said, "let's divide up chores."

"I'm in the house," said Chrissy. "I'll keep cooking and washing the dishes. Aunt Lois hasn't cooked anything yet. I doubt if she will, or even knows how. Only time she comes in the kitchen is to get a glass of water or to put out her cigarette in the sink. Ask her to quit smoking so much in the house."

Danny nodded.

"Melissa can take over feeding the chickens. Sam can take out the trash, and feed Belle and Booty," Chrissy continued.

"Sell those cows. I won't have time to feed them every day," said Sam. "I'll be working the combine."

Danny laughed. "There's nothing to cut till fall. You'll have plenty of time to practice driving the combine."

"Don't you like fresh milk?" questioned Chrissy.

"Have Melissa do it."

"I'm in charge of the chickens. I'll take care of the kittens, too." Melissa saw a fuzzy white face poke through the barn slats, followed by another kitten with a tan face and black ears. The baby felines heard voices behind the barn and began scooting through the building's cracks — six of them in all, tumbling into the daylight all covered with straw.

"Big deal," said a perturbed Sam, growing downright indignant. "I'm going to work in the fields. I'm not spending no time feeding a bunch of stupid-looking, lazy milk cows."

"Now, Sam," said Danny as he glanced at Chrissy, "we all have to pitch in. We have to change things up so that all the chores get done."

"Have her do it," Sam said, pointing again at Melissa.

"I'm in charge of the chickens," she repeated, her brown eyes glaring, standing toe-to-toe with her brother two years older than herself, but exactly the same height.

"I ain't feeding no pen cows, or cats. Them ain't farm animals.

They're just pets." Then he pushed Melissa out of his face.

"Sam!" Chrissy jumped up with a start.

But instantly the brief war of wills was over. Melissa wasn't hurt. If anything, Sam was the emotional loser, and he hung his head. "I want to work in the field," he mumbled. It was not like him to get confrontational with Melissa. He was her protector, yet she often led when they tried new things together or went exploring. Whenever they tussled, Melissa held her own, often getting the better of him.

Sam was upset about his absent father. Farming was the only endeavor Sam had ever seen the man engaged in, and that was good enough for Sam. At age seven, he had been thinking about what he would do as a farmer for a long time. Now Danny had dangled an enticing carrot in front of him — learning to operate the combine. It was just what Sam wanted, and he'd lost his head.

Danny saw that all was back to normal and he continued. "I was hoping to show Rufus at the fair, but we'll probably have to sell him. Mom's going to need all the money she can get."

"Oh, you don't have to sell him, Danny. You've raised that pig this long — he was the best of the whole litter," said Chrissy, with an empathetic note in her voice.

"I'm just thinking. I don't want to sell him, but the fair is still several months away."

"I'll help take care of him," volunteered Melissa.

"I'll help when I'm not in the house," said Chrissy. She looked at Sam and said, "Danny's not going to have much time to work with Rufus now. He has to finish plowing. We could all work together and get him to the fair. How's that sound?"

She looked around. "Will you help, too, Sam, when you're not too busy? Could you help with Rufus when you're not in the fields?"

Sam looked up at the others and smiled. He knew what was going on. He looked into their faces and saw their eyes bright, suppressed grins growing at the corners of their mouths.

"Sure, I can help," Sam said. "We'll make Rufus the top prize pig at this year's fair."

With that they all let out a cheer, and Danny threw Sam high in the air. His dad had liked to throw him up in the air. Each time he fell back to earth, caught in strong arms, his eyes were wide with astonishment, his breath short with a twinge of fear. Every time Sam was safely caught, and so it was with Danny. Sam loved it. A short, dangerous thrill ride. Sam's face beamed with a broad smile as Danny lowered him to the ground. The four children let out with another whoop, twice as loud as the one before.

\* \* \* \* \*

A few days later Lois loaded her Thunderbird with three suit-cases and took Sandra into town to see the doctor. Lois said they were going to Fremont. Danny knew of the town, but didn't know how far it was from their farm just outside of Albion, Nebraska. He didn't know how long it would take for them to get there, and Aunt Lois made no mention of when they might return.

For days Lois suggested that Sandra see a professional. It both-ered everyone that Sandra would hardly eat, and she never cried. She'd speak maybe three sentences a day; she wasn't changing her clothes. The children worried and agreed with their aunt that their mother should visit a physician other than the family doctor in Albion.

The moon was high in the sky when Lois returned that night. Danny was stunned that she was alone. Chrissy too was right at the door when Lois walked in, searching her aunt's face for an explanation. Lois sat down and gathered the children around her in the living room.

"Your mother realizes she needs some rest under a doctor's care," she said as she looked at each child in turn, probing for the understanding she needed from them to explain the situation. "She's checked herself into the hospital."

"Is she okay?" asked Chrissy, quite concerned.

"She is fine physically, but her mind needs rest. We can all get sick, but you know with rest and medicine you can get well. Isn't that right?"

Sam nodded reluctant agreement, as did Melissa, her chin buried in Mrs. Leatherwood's hair.

"How long will she be there?" Danny asked as he began to think of important questions.

"As long as it takes … maybe a month or more. The doctor recommended it, and your mother is doing this as her own choice."

"But why so quick? Why didn't she come back and tell us goodbye?"

"She wanted to start getting better. She wants to get back home as soon as possible to be with all of you. She wants to be her old self again. Look … she wrote a letter."

Lois opened the single sheet of typing paper as all four children huddled around to see. Danny read the letter, then handed it to Chrissy, who read it several times, then passed it down to the Little Ones. Sam could read some; he pointed at each word as he read slowly out loud. Melissa's attention hung on every utterance to make sure the message hadn't changed since the previous reading.

*Dear Melissa, Sammy, Chrissy and Danny,*

*I love you all very much and I want to be with you. I want us to be a family, especially now that your father is gone. I want to be a good mom, and to do that I must get to feeling better. I want to get well so I must stay in the hospital for awhile. Aunt Lois will take care of you, and we'll be back together very soon.*

*Love, Mother*

It was their mother's handwriting for sure. Danny knew that as soon as he saw it.

"I'll be looking to you for help," Lois said to Danny as a serious tight-lipped expression came over her face. But her eyes conveyed excitement with her darting glances. Danny felt odd and knew he was receiving mixed messages. Lois said the same thing to Chrissy, then headed to the kitchen to smoke a cigarette, leaving the letter with the children, who read it over and over again.

Soon Danny followed to the kitchen. Chrissy was close behind, and she heard him say, "Why didn't you mention this yesterday? Going to the clinic is one thing, leaving Mom there is another. Did you know all this was going to happen?"

"No, I did not. This was the doctor's recommendation."

"I just don't understand …"

"You don't understand what, young man? You understand that things are different now that your father is absent, don't you?" Aunt Lois looked at him with a fierce stare as though she had to prepare for trouble. But Danny was stiff, confused, disconcerted and incapable of a strong response.

"Look, the world does not revolve around you. Your mother is human, too. She has needs and she's doing what she thinks is best for this family. That means getting treatment now before she has a total breakdown."

That word, *breakdown,* unnerved Chrissy and she stepped back into a corner of the kitchen.

"What's her phone number?" Danny asked.

"You can't call her."

"What's her address?"

"I have it here. She's at a facility in Omaha. You can write her all you want."

"What about the farm?" Danny's head was spinning. Every second more unanswered questions swarmed into his brain. He threw up his hands. "I can't run this place by myself … without Mom being around."

"I've taken care of that, too," Lois said, with a deliberate emphasis and spacing in her words so that the two oldest children would not mistake her meaning. "Get all your things together. Tomorrow we're moving to another farm."

"We can't move," protested Danny. He knew he'd heard her

say it, but it floored him. He couldn't believe it. "What about the animals?"

"They'll be moved, too. It's a working farm. Everything will be the same. When your mother is out of the hospital, you'll all move back here."

"I don't want to leave," said Chrissy.

"I don't want to leave either." Danny began to pace as he spoke. "What about school? We can't just leave school."

"School's almost over for this year. No teacher is going to hold you back for missing a few weeks. You'll all be back here when next school year starts." Lois tried to reason with him. She thought of putting both hands on his shoulders and speaking directly to him, but she thought better of it. He was as tall as she, and certainly stronger. At the moment he didn't look very happy. "This is what your mother wants."

"What do you mean she wants? She didn't say nothing in the letter about leaving the farm."

"I can't stay out here with you all summer," Lois retorted. "I have to get back to my job … and don't try and tell me you can all take care of yourselves. It's not going to happen that way. If you don't come with me, I'll call the sheriff and you can all be split up into separate foster homes."

"I don't want to get split up," Chrissy said meekly. She'd been listening intently to every word of the conversation, and lines of ominous concern were written all over her face.

"Where do you plan to take us?" asked Danny.

"It's a farm just like this one over in the next county. You'll love it. You can even take your dog. The people who run the place will love to have you, and they have plenty of room. Their name is Jameson."

# 3

IT WAS A solemn, quiet drive to the new farm. A muggy warm haze hung over the fields as the sun grew hot in a cloudless sky. The Thunderbird was loaded with just the bare essentials the children would need to stay awhile at the new home.

As the unofficial leader, Danny felt added pressure of this sudden departure into uncertainty. It was like going to summer camp without a definite date to return home. His thick brown hair fluttered in the air passing through half-opened windows, his rich brown eyes dark with contemplation.

In a day or two, according to Lois, the boys would go back with this Mr. Jameson and get their farm animals. Chrissy and the Little Ones huddled in the back seat as Danny sat up front. They watched as farm after farm flew by, the bushes and small trees that lined the roadside ditches flashing past in a blur of dust and swirling leaves.

Kiko sat on the floor, his head of ragged ears and baleful eyes resting in Sam's lap. Lois hadn't wanted to bring the dog on this trip. She didn't care for the mutt in her car, but she knew the children wouldn't come without it. No one had anything to say. The only sound was the hum of the tires rolling over sun-baked dirt.

In a little over an hour they were there. Lois was right about one thing, the place did look a lot like their own home. A long drive ran up one side of the property leading to a frame garage that leaned slightly to one side. The house was two-story wood, painted all white. There was even a tire swing hanging from a giant tree in the front yard. But it had been there awhile, unused, a frayed rope suspending a dried-out old tractor tire coated with crud.

Lois began hollering as soon as she opened her car door. Danny saw someone open a door inside the screened-in back porch, but no one came to greet them. He helped his siblings from the car, and they made a line according to age next to the Thunderbird.

"Come on, come on. You don't have to be so modest and all. This is your new home," Lois encouraged as she headed through the back way. She disappeared for a few minutes, then reappeared with the Jamesons.

The woman walked a half-step behind her husband. Lois introduced her as Beth. She was thin, downright skin and bones, wearing a dingy cotton dress with an apron she was continually wiping through her hands. She took a moment to meet the children, shaking each one by the hand with a stiff locked elbow as though she didn't want to get too close. Her hair was a short and stringy washed-out blonde. She seemed pleasant enough as she asked each child their name, but as soon as she was finished she stepped back behind the man and lit a cigarette.

Mr. Jameson's name was Ralph. "So this is the brood," he said with a nervous chuckle as he stepped forward. "Bet you've all had a long day." The way he spoke and quickly warmed to the sound of his own voice seemed to indicate he'd rehearsed his speech. "Want you to know we got lots of room for you. Sorry to hear about your pa. Got chores to do around here, of course," he pointed to Danny with a grin, "but we hope you think of this place as yours while you're here."

Ralph was wearing a plain white V-neck T-shirt. His huge gut protruded below the shirt. He tugged on his belt and hiked up his pants, but his gut was showing again in less than a minute. Bags were noticeable under his eyes. Any hair on his head was invisible, if existent. His arms were hairy, tan and thick, but it was the middle of plowing season and Danny was struck by the sight of him wearing house slippers. "Ma, let's show 'em the penthouse," he said with another nervous chuckle.

The children followed Beth into the kitchen through the screened-in porch. An unpleasant odor hit them as soon as they were inside. Unwashed dishes sat in a strainer. Dried jelly, a cup full of cold skimmed-over coffee and bread crumbs littered a Formica dinette table. As Danny was the last one in, he overheard a rising conversation near the Thunderbird between Ralph and Lois.

"What's with this dog? You didn't tell me about no dog."

"Had to bring it, it's their pet. It made it a lot easier. They might not have come if I hadn't said yes to Kiko."

"What else haven't you told me? This here Kee–ko ain't going to do nothing but eat … can't do no work. I didn't agree to pay out no money, you know."

"You don't have to pay out nothing, just keep them together. Take the oldest …"

"Danny?"

"Right. Take him to help you get the livestock. You can make money off them, too."

"What they got? I like rabbits," Ralph said.

"A whole bunch of chickens … some pigs. No rabbits, that I know of. A cow or two, I think. Don't know if it's the kind you get milk from or butter or cottage cheese." Lois started to laugh. A dribble of spit came out of her mouth and she lit her cigarette. "I don't know nothing about those animals. You're the farmer."

"Cottage cheese, that's good," Ralph said. And they both laughed at the top of their lungs.

The house wasn't all that big. Once the children were standing in the living room the whole house felt stuffy and claustrophobic. The first floor consisted of five rooms, the kitchen and dining room side by side in the back. A bedroom and the living room were in front. Tucked between the kitchen and the bedroom was a bath.

A straight stairway directly aligned with the front door went through the ceiling to the two bedrooms above. There were no closets upstairs. Between the bedrooms was a bathroom with a toilet next to a porcelain Victorian tub with decorative claw legs. The tub was partially rusted and full of layers of dried soap scum.

For some reason there was no upstairs sink. There was also no hot water on the second floor. Cold water pipes ran next to the chimney, but in the summer the fireplace was never lit, therefore no hot water. There was also no air conditioning. The children would soon learn how fierce the collection of heat in the attic could be. By noon each day the upstairs was stifling hot, and it was often several hours after dark each evening before it was bearable to go to their rooms.

Danny petted Kiko and looked around outside while Sam and the girls took their things upstairs. There were two beds, actually one queen size mattress with frame and one without. The three of them pulled one mattress into the other room for the boys. A few strong orange crates lay about that could be stacked as a shelf or two. An ancient coat rack with a broken rib stood in the corner. Two folding chairs rounded out their furniture … no tables, no nightstands, no dressers and no mirrors.

Chrissy went over to the vertical bedroom window, peered through holes in the plastic shade, then raised it. The emerald green back yard lay before her, lush in thick grass badly in need of mowing, flowering goldenrod flowers growing in waves. From her vantage point, she could see the rows and rows of rabbit pens and an endless vista of farmland that disappeared into the horizon.

If the four of them must live here for awhile, she knew that they could get through it. She had confidence in Danny and faith in herself. Certainly, Aunt Lois was doing the best she could for them under the circumstances.

Chrissy had always been a quiet girl, much like her father. Her dull blonde hair, with bangs, cut long and straight, created a concealing border to a reserved face. Her hazel eyes conveyed more meaning than her sparse words. Chrissy Stone was an intelligent introvert who loved to read books to herself, and children's stories to Sam and Melissa. She especially enjoyed writing in her diary and penning friendship poems on special paper to imaginary heroes.

At age 11 Chrissy was a resourceful girl who had learned from the strong example of her mother. Following the funeral Chrissy tried her best to brighten her mother's outlook. The death of her father tore out a part of her heart; the depression of her mother threatened to tear out the rest. When her efforts proved fruitless, Chrissy's soft eyes would well up, opaque with wetness. Salty eyelids failed as dams against the sorrow. And in a place where no one else could see, Chrissy's tears would fall in torrents over tender cheeks. She promised herself that she would make sure the family stayed together until her mother was well. Until they were all living together again.

\* \* \* \* \*

Within days it became evident what Ralph and Beth did out on the farm — nothing.

Ralph was an army pensioner, a career supply sergeant E-6. He and his wife had been out on the flat land for two and a half years. His property holdings totaled 120 measly acres ... and one house. He'd fallowed out all his ground last year because he hadn't wanted to mess with it. This year he said he was going to seed it all to dry land winter wheat and harvest whatever grew. With the good top soil in these parts and just one or two decent rains, a man could bring in a pretty good crop by leaving the yield to Mother Nature. But you had to at least plow, seed and fertilize the land. Danny would believe that Ralph was going to plant a crop this year when he actually did it — not until.

During the winter Ralph worked part-time at the corn mill in Madison. The rest of the time he went to Leigh or Creston to play pool with his beer-drinking buddies.

There was only one endeavor involving work that Ralph actually enjoyed. He devoted time and care to the maintenance of his rabbits — their meat and fur provided a healthy supplement to his pension income.

All of the children took to the delicate, fuzzy animals, and each of the Little Ones adopted a pet. Melissa's was a snow-white pink-nosed powder puff she called Angel. Sam named his rabbit Digger. Melissa and Sam acted as though their newfound friends would be around as pets forever and ever, just like Kiko. Danny and Chrissy couldn't find the heart to tell them the truth.

Within weeks Chrissy was doing all the cleaning around the place, not that any had been going on before. Chrissy was also expected to take care of the meals, certainly for her and her siblings, and make some extra for Ralph and Beth. Most often, however, Ralph would stick up his nose at whatever she'd prepared and grab a beer from the fridge.

Beth didn't eat much herself, but she could lay fire to better than three packs of cigarettes each and every day. She watched a lot of TV, which she controlled whenever a program she liked was on, which was most of the time. One afternoon Danny wanted to watch the last two innings of a major league baseball game. Beth would have none of it because her afternoon movie was about to begin. She got all flustered and red just at the idea that she might miss the start of her show, her arms moving wildly back and forth as though she were about to wrap herself up in her own arms. Beth got her way.

Ralph made all the trips into town. Seemingly every day Danny was saddled with more and more chores — maintenance on the vehicles, cutting tree limbs, mending fence, and the rabbits. He had to water and feed them twice a day, plus clean the pens. He spent four to five hours a day just tending to Ralph's rabbits.

The Little Ones were allowed to run about as long as they stayed out of the adults' way. No one was allowed to leave the farm even though the nearest town of Madison was less than ten miles away. Danny wanted badly to play summer baseball, but after asking several times he gave it up. Ralph would have nothing to do with hauling him around for baseball practice and games.

They didn't hear from their mother, either by telephone or mail. They did receive one brief note from Aunt Lois that said their mother was improving, but the anxiously received correspondence was poorly short on specifics. Chrissy had them all sign selected letters she had written, and she helped the Little Ones compose letters of their own.

Several times a week she gave letters to Ralph to be mailed. She gave letters to Beth, too, in hopes that some of them would find their way to the post office. But still, they never heard from their mother.

June became July. Although the situation was resented by all, from their standpoint it was still bearable. Except for the nights Ralph came home drunk and slapped Beth around. Danny would huddle the others upstairs as they listened to the yelling and Beth's screams. Objects flew around the lower floor, dishes exploded; once the dining room window was busted. The next day Beth usually sported a black eye or an ugly welt.

\* \* \* \* \*

Danny tolerated all of the burdens of living with the Jamesons ... the stink, the cramped quarters, the hours of chores without pay, even the bland diet. But Saturday mornings bothered him the most. He could hardly make himself get out of bed. Just thinking of Saturday mornings almost made him ill.

For it was Saturday mornings that Ralph's beer-drinking buddies from the mill came out to the farm and made a production of killing the rabbits.

Regardless of how long or hard he'd worked the day before, they always made him help. He'd have to hold the critters up by the hind legs or smash them in the head with a baseball bat. Someone would immediately cut off their heads with a razor sharp knife and someone else would skin 'em. The usual kill was 30 to 50 rabbits each and every Saturday morning. The rabbit skins and meat brought in extra money for Ralph, but for all the mess and trouble Danny didn't see how it was worth it.

Maybe it was. Danny didn't really know. It was just that the entire production made him nauseous and disgusted. And Ralph seemed to enjoy it all. It wasn't just the money, Danny thought, Ralph also enjoyed killing those poor defenseless animals.

Today Danny was consumed with more anxiety and dread than usual, because today, Sam's adopted pet Digger was in the killing pen. Ralph didn't care if you called one of the rabbits a pet or not. When it got to be 10 weeks old, it was going to be harvested along with the others. Melissa's Angel had already experienced the fate that Digger faced today. She had cried for hours, the best comforting efforts of Chrissy disregarded, and she was angry at Danny for days. She blamed him for her pet's demise, her sad five-year-old eyes looking at him with a "why did you do it" stare. It broke his heart. He didn't want to deal with similar looks and emotions from Sam.

Danny pulled on the filthy ragged overalls he kept just for this gruesome detail, and a yellow raincoat slicker covered with splotches of dried animal blood. Ralph's buddies began getting liquored up as soon as they arrived, usually by nine, and they'd start hollering around the yard, slapping each other on the back. Much of the carrying-on was an extension of Friday night drinking, and the men acted as though they were about to do battle with a mighty enemy. Danny saw it as a mob scene, a handful of over-the-hill loners working up the nerve to slaughter a bunch of harmless animals.

The rabbits bustled nervously in the holding pens, sniffing and hopping over one another in a continuous stirring motion. By 9:30 the day already felt excessively warm and muggy. Danny was overcome with dread. He knew exactly which rabbit was Sam's pet; yet he had absolutely no idea of how to save it.

Danny's job this day was to take the rabbits from the pens and hold them up by the back legs to be clubbed, one swift whack on the back of the head with an old splintered bat. A man he knew only as Singer was the clubber, and the guy was always ready for another, seeming to thrive on the activity. He'd grin widely on his backswing, and his eyes would light up. Danny could see black holes in his teeth and orange crescents along his gum line.

When Danny got to Digger's pen, he saved him for last, then just left him there and went on to the next pen. At first no one noticed. But soon the rest of the carnage was finished, pelts stretched out on boards, meat in ice chests, a pile of fresh rabbit heads in a pile behind the garage where Kiko and a convention of stray cats enjoyed a gourmet meal of warm rabbit guts.

Then Singer spoke out. "What about this one? Boy says he wants to keep it."

Ralph had been working at the other end of the line, his mind elsewhere. He walked to the pens wiping blood from his hands and wrists. When he saw the single rabbit, he shrugged his shoulders and threw a pointed finger toward the pen. "Kill it! Let's get a move on."

Danny moved in front of the pen door. "I want to keep this one," he said looking straight at Ralph.

"That tain't happening, boy. We don't have time for that crap."

"I'll buy him from you," Danny said quite evenly.

Ralph cocked his head and walked closer to the 15-year-old. Their eyes remained locked on one another. "Look, you know the rules, boy. This tain't no petting zoo. These things are raised to be sold, you know that. Meat gets tough when they get older than they are now."

"How much do you want for it?"

Ralph had to think. Agreeing on a price actually meant giving in to the kid. He didn't know if he wanted to do that. His friends were here; he had a reputation to think of.

"Fifty dollars," Ralph said flatly.

"What … no way. Be reasonable, Ralph. It's for the Little Ones.

Just let me have one, just one. I'll keep it out of the way. I'll take care of it."

"Whatcha gonna do, take it upstairs and make it comfy in your bed?"

The men began giggling. "Yeah, and you can dress it up and play dolls with it," Singer blurted out. Ralph shut him up with an impatient wave of his hand.

Ralph got really serious, and stuck his nose right in Danny's face. Danny had to swallow. He could smell the booze on the man's breath. Ralph began to speak in a guttural whisper, each word measured and chosen for effect.

"Look, you sawed-off, good-for-nothing … this is my farm. It was a mistake letting you bunch of rug rats on the place. It tain't worth the nickels and dimes I'm getting for all the aggravation the four of you cause me."

Danny knew that was a lie. More work was getting done since they arrived than this farm had seen in years. "Let me have the rabbit," he interrupted.

"No! Hell no!"

Danny tried to block the pen, but Ralph threw him away from the door. If anything, Ralph was strong, and at 250 pounds he outweighed Danny by almost 100. In less than a minute Singer and another man had dispatched Digger. Danny righted himself in the dirt and watched the end to Sam's pet from his knees. He didn't understand why Ralph couldn't give in on such a simple request. He hadn't realized that some men were so different from his father. As Danny walked to the house, he heard more snickers behind him. He hung his bloody clothes on a tree limb near the back door. His primary concern was Sam, and what he could do to ease the effect of the unpleasant news.

Danny proceeded to the upstairs bathroom and the old porcelain tub with the decorative legs. He filled the tub with cold water and washed as quickly as he could. As he stepped out and grabbed a towel, a knock came at the door.

"I need in," the voice had a pleading tone.

"Come on in, Sam. I'm almost through." The seven-year-old tottered in, still half asleep, his sandy hair stuck up straight in the air. Sam's broad high forehead, like his father's, was the first feature people noticed about him. His chin was small now, but if it followed suit, it would be large and wide when he grew up. The boy was usually easy-going, often quiet like Chrissy, yet more determined than she when he set his mind to something.

"Is there anything to eat?" Sam asked as he stood over the toilet.

"I think Chrissy is cooking up some pancakes. That's about it." Danny knew his little brother enjoyed his pet. He hoped he hadn't gotten so attached to the rabbit that he would carry on like Melissa when he found out what happened. Danny shook the thought from his mind. "But if you want anything to eat you're going to have to beat me to the kitchen," Danny said as he pulled on a pair of faded blue jeans. Sam looked up at Danny, then he jumped to the door. Both boys barreled out of the bathroom and pounded down the stairs.

In the kitchen Chrissy turned pancakes in a giant black skillet. She glanced Melissa's way as the younger girl played with a plastic bottle of Log Cabin syrup at the table. Chrissy's cotton dress was unwashed and hung limply over her toothpick frame. This morning her hair was still uncombed. In many ways, she appeared as a miniature high plains pioneer woman slaving over an open fire. Her face didn't express her astute awareness; it looked void of energy, unless her lips were letting through a smile. That wasn't often. Her dour expression did not change as the two boys rushed into the room. She glanced sideways toward Danny; she knew what was going on outside and what it meant. He looked away as their eyes met.

"Put on some plates, and Kool Aid," she said in a monotone.

Danny seated Sam next to his younger sister. Mrs. Leatherwood was propped up on the corner of the grease-inlaid, gouged wooden table that rocked back and forth as Melissa played with the bottle of syrup. Danny checked the refrigerator for some bacon or sausage to go with the pancakes. There was none. There wasn't any milk either, just a leftover plate of brisket and a pitcher of stale tea.

Beth hadn't gotten up yet. When she did, the first thing she'd go for would be a smoke. That would probably be around noon. She'd start reading one of her romance novels, or turn on the TV, but she might stay in her room all day. Ralph wouldn't be back either. With his friends around they'd go back into town, do some serious drinking and play pool all afternoon. They'd laugh about the rabbit incident. Ralph wouldn't miss the opportunity to tell others how he showed up that snot-nosed kid and killed the animal he was trying to spare.

"So, how did it go today?" Chrissy asked, still standing at the stove.

Danny ignored her question. After Melissa's pet had been killed, he had promised himself that things would be different. He probably should have talked to Ralph ahead of time, before his friends were around, before he was all liquored up. He rubbed his backside; it was going to be sore for awhile where Ralph pushed him down.

The Little Ones dove into their breakfast plates. Two things they had plenty of to eat around the place was butter and maple syrup. Each of them had eaten more than a few meals of butter-smothered and syrup-covered rabbit steaks. The menu left a lot to be desired. Danny watched intently as the Little Ones ate, and Chrissy cooked more pancakes for him.

When Sam finished, Danny motioned him over. He put his hand on Sam's shoulder and said, "I've got some bad news for you, partner." As he looked into Sam's trusting blue eyes, he almost lost his nerve to go further.

"Digger's gone …" It was all he could get past his lips. The attentive boy waited for more. Danny pulled him onto his lap. "Ralph decided to send him in with the others … do you understand what I mean?"

Sam nodded reluctantly, but Danny could tell he was still waiting for more, more information as to why his older brother was so tense.

"Danny, just tell him what happened. It wasn't your fault," Chrissy said.

"I don't want to 'just tell him what happened.' "

"He's got to learn."

"They killed your rabbit, too, just like they did Angel," Melissa blurted.

"Melissa, be quiet," Danny said. He hugged his little brother. "I tried to stop them."

Sam just sat in Danny's lap, his soft cheek against his brother's chest. He didn't get upset, he took the news like a trooper. Like Chrissy and their father, it was hard to read exactly how Sam felt. After a few minutes he got down from Danny's lap and poured himself a tall glass of grape Kool Aid. They all watched him drink it down.

"I understand," he said without emotion, and walked from the kitchen. Sam's stoic lack of expression worried Danny the most.

"Stay away from people who belittle your ambitions. Small people always do that, but really great individuals make you feel that you, too, can become great."

— *Mark Twain*

# 4

THE HEAT OF August was suffocating. Danny tilled Ralph's quarter section of dry, nostril-choking sod to get the ground ready for fall planting, but Ralph changed his mind. No explanation, just decided he wouldn't buy the needed seed and fertilizer. Danny didn't worry about it; he didn't really care what Ralph did on the farm. As much as anything the hours and hours of chores kept his mind off of more unpleasant thoughts.

Still there was no word from their mother. Chrissy wrote daily to the address Lois had given her in Omaha, but for one reason or another, after all the letters she had written, there was still no response.

Neither Ralph nor Beth had mentioned enrolling for the new school year. All of them except Melissa had already attended school, and now she was old enough for kindergarten. With no word from their mother and no arrangements being made to attend school, Danny knew something had to change. He hadn't come to this place to live forever.

Also, Ralph's temperament grew more volatile each day. He and Danny almost came to blows on several occasions. Ralph complained about Kiko constantly just to have something to moan about. The pet was never under foot, and the children tended to all of his feeding and care, but Ralph often threatened to "blow that bag of fleas full of holes."

Ralph didn't care if the children had milk. When the opportunity to sell Belle and Booty presented itself, Ralph had the cows delivered to a nearby farm and pocketed the money for himself.

Ralph was a control freak; creating a scene was his way of getting attention and intimidating the children at the same time. He'd stick up his nose at Chrissy's cooking, sometimes he'd throw it all out the back door and make the kids go hungry. Even Danny couldn't figure what brought on these outbursts where Ralph would punish everyone and never say a word as to why he was upset. Ralph acted like Danny was a personal farmhand at his beck and call. Danny didn't mind working, doing his share, but whenever Ralph started cussing him out he'd slow down on the job. Once, Ralph hid Mrs. Leatherwood from Melissa and threatened to tear the doll apart.

The blackest day at the farm arrived in the form of the Jones Packing Company truck from Madison. Without so much as a word to Danny, Ralph sent his prize show pig into town to be slaughtered. The fair had come and gone, but Rufus had remained at the farm. The children had begged and pleaded to be allowed to go to the fair to enter Rufus in the competition. But Ralph would have none of it. The more they asked to go to the fair, the more he relished saying no. For all his work with the pig, Danny received nothing. Ralph didn't really need the money; he sold Rufus for a fraction of what he was worth, and he kept all the money for himself.

A few weeks later the final straw finally fell upon the farm. School had begun for other kids, but not for them. It happened on a Monday morning after Beth had driven the oil-burning Tempo into town. Danny, tired and dirty, had been working the barn since sunup. As he walked into the house and came to the steps leading upstairs, he saw Ralph on the upper landing, peeking into the bathroom.

"What are you doing up there?" Danny shouted.

Ralph jumped at the sharp sound.

Danny shot up the stairs, pushed past Ralph and glanced into the bathroom to see for himself. There in the tub, now covering herself and slipped down into the water, was Chrissy.

Danny slammed the door shut, his temper boiling. "Get down," he screamed as he stood locked-nosed glaring at Ralph.

Ralph was stunned from being caught, his knee buckled as he fell back a step and a half, paused, then started to back up. "Piss on you, kid." Danny's instincts recoiled in an immediate reaction. He threw a kick, the inch-thick heel of his hunting boot caught Ralph under the chin. The retired Army noncom ejected off the steps and flew in slow motion down the staircase, over the landing. Ralph landed on his back with such a thud on the living room floor that a rumble rolled through the walls of the house.

Danny sprang to go after him as Ralph lay in a heap for a moment, rubbing his chin, a trickle of blood seeping from the corner of his mouth. Halfway down the stairway Danny stopped. Ralph got up and disappeared from view, headed toward the kitchen. For a carved slice of time, so many individual breaths, the entire farmhouse was wrapped in total silence. Maybe this hairy pervert was ashamed and had run off to rationalize his behavior and lick his wounds.

No … Ralph was not a man to take a whipping and just forget about it. Within seconds, he was back at the foot of the stairs, swinging a solid ash Louisville slugger above his head, bellowing at the top of his lungs. Danny could see the blackened sweet spot on the baseball bat where dried rabbit blood stained the wood. "Come down here, you damn punk," he cried repeatedly as he hit the low landing with the bat, splintering the lowest step with mighty hacks.

The staircase was too narrow for Ralph to ascend and protect himself from a blindside attack at the top. He remained at the bottom, challenging Danny to come down, working himself into a hotter rage by the second.

"You ungrateful piece of crap, get your ass down here and fight."

"Kiss my ass," Danny taunted back, "you pitiful excuse for a man."

Ralph blew! He beat on the wooden step at knee height until it exploded into kindling, then he started on the step above it. Chrissy huddled with Melissa in their bed. Sam was outside when the commotion began, and he knew to remain clear of the fray.

"I'm going to kill you ... you punk."

"Want me to tell Beth?"

Ralph hurled an ashtray up the steps with the force of a catapult. It cracked the plaster wall and reverberated around the upper landing. Ralph followed the throw by launching a ceramic Easter Island figure toward Danny that shattered into a thousand pieces when it impacted. Ralph stood and glared killer eyes up an empty stairway. His sides were heaving. A few seconds of spitting and guttural noises passed, Ralph's mumblings droned with ominous undertones. Time seemed to pull up short, and then Ralph slammed the bat against the floor.

"I want ALL of you assholes to get out. You're through. I ain't nursing no more ungrateful damn kids." He panted, his hands on his knees, drawing air forcefully into his over-taxed lungs. "Get the hell out! You ain't sleeping here no more." He bent over and took another deep breath. "I'm leaving for now ... but I'll be back." Ralph spoke directly up the steps. "Get all your crap and clear out. If you're still here when I get back, someone's going to the hospital. I don't want to ever see you again." And then he said, with a cutting, heartless bite to his words, "I hope you never see your crazy mother again."

The back door slammed shut and the pickup started with a hesitant chug. Then each of them, holding their places like statues, ears pricked to the sound of Ralph's departure, could hear tires spinning as sand and gravel shattered against the house. Within seconds the roar of the truck engine faded away.

"Okay, let's go. You heard the fat son of a ..."

"Danny ... you don't need to talk like he does," Chrissy said, still hugging Melissa.

Danny was pumped — frightened — excited. "We don't need

you," he shouted toward the window.

"Danny, where will we go? We can't just leave."

"We have to. You heard him. I can't fight him. I would have now, but he'll be ready later on." Danny began to calm down. "He's a coward, he'll bring some of his friends back here. We've got to go."

"Oh, Danny," Melissa said with fear in her eyes.

"Don't be afraid, Punkin. You want to see Mama again, don't you?" He looked into Chrissy's eyes too. "I've already been thinking about this. We can do it … we can find Mom and get back home. We can do for ourselves … get things back to the way they were before …" Again his voice caught, but he walked closer to the bed and reached out his hands. "You want to do that, don't you?"

The girls nodded tentatively. If Danny said something was possible, then they were willing to consider it, but this was all happening so fast. The idea of leaving someplace familiar, even if they hated it, was a strange idea indeed.

Chrissy looked closely at Danny, searching his face for clues. Only a short moment passed before the concern on her face ebbed away and her jaw locked. She hugged Melissa again and helped her from the bed, then she jumped to the floor and announced, "Yes! We can do it."

Okay then, get your important things. Let's go."

They heard rapid light footsteps coming up to the bedrooms. "What happened?" Sam shouted.

"We're getting out of here. We're leaving," Danny replied. "Ralph was looking at Chrissy while she was in the tub."

"Danny, you don't have to tell everybody," Chrissy said.

Danny didn't even give her a glance. The incident, the fight, the threats from Ralph were all history as far as he was concerned now. He had much more important matters on his mind.

"Get all your warm clothes," he directed Sam. "I'm going to the kitchen to load up on food. Chrissy, help them with their packs, okay?"

In the kitchen Danny tried to think of not only what they would need, but what they could best use. What did this sparsely stocked room have in it that they could carry and use? They might be on the road for several days, maybe more. He wanted to do this. He could take care of his brother and sisters, and it was high time they were reunited with their mother. Certainly, she was better by now. Even if she wasn't, they needed to see her, and she needed to see and touch them.

Chrissy threw every stitch of clothing Melissa had stuffed in two orange crates on the bed, and quickly searched through it. She had Melissa pull on her blue leotards, then bundled her in three knit sweaters over a cotton blouse. Next came a gray pair of sweat pants which Chrissy tied snuggly over the little girl's hips with a cord belt. Over that came a pair of Sam's old khaki trousers.

Melissa had one coat, a light brown mohair, Sunday-go-to-meeting, thigh-length garment with white buttons in the front. Chrissy tucked her pigtails inside a pink woolen stocking cap, tied the straps under her chin in a bow, and patted her on the shoulders. The little girl looked like she was ready to attend church at the North Pole in the numbing cold of an Arctic winter.

Likewise, she layered Sam in underclothes, bright red long underwear emblazoned with the logo of the Kansas City Chiefs, three T-shirts, a long-sleeved flannel shirt, two pairs of pants, and his favorite blue denim overalls. He had a hunting cap with earflaps and one coat — the only jacket he ever wore — his sky-blue, down-filled Future Farmers of America nylon jacket.

The rest of their warmer clothes they stuffed into the bottom of three canvas school knapsacks. While Chrissy dressed, Melissa found Mrs. Leatherwood's ankle-length gray wool overcoat, and she buttoned it up on the doll. Sam's eyes made a quick check of the two upstairs rooms that had been their sleeping quarters for better than three months. He made a face — there was nothing here he wanted. He ran downstairs with one of the backpacks, leaping over the disintegrated lower steps, toward the kitchen where

Danny was rummaging through the pantry.

Danny took all of the crackers, bread and chips in the house. He found a half-jar of peanut butter, a package of soft tortilla shells, a block of cheese and a tin can with the paper label missing, but he was pretty sure it was Spaghetti O's. He put a pan of water on the stove to hard-boil all the eggs, a total of 16. To top it off, he found a can of tuna fish and another small tin of sardines, and a box of kitchen matches. Whatever space remained in the knapsacks he'd pack with rabbit steaks and freezer-burned venison killed the previous year.

"Look around the house," Danny told them all. We're going to be doing a lot of walking. I don't know when we'll get a ride. I only know what way we're headed."

He saw the determined look on Chrissy's face. They were in this together now. No turning back. They were leaving this house with all its abuse and hard work. They would keep the Little Ones with them and, somehow, some way, be reunited with their mother.

Ralph's an idiot, Danny thought. He doesn't realize how good he had it. Danny wasn't about to leave without everything they could carry and use. He put his hunting knife on his belt, then ran upstairs, dressed warmly and packed extra clothes he felt he'd need. Then he bounded back down the stairs to Ralph's bedroom, took a .12 gauge shotgun leaning against the wall inside the closet, and all the shells he could find.

When he appeared back in the dining room, they were all ready for him. Their anxious eyes waited for him to lead the way. Melissa clung tightly to Mrs. Leatherwood. Danny bent down and kissed her on the cheek. He hugged Sam and tightened the shoulder straps of the pack harnessed to the boy's back.

"Are you ready?" he asked as he gazed directly into Sam's wide eyes.

"You bet! Let's get the hell out of here."

"Sam! Don't be talking like that," Chrissy scolded.

"Let's go." Danny led them out the back, the screen door

slammed shut signaling their departure. They headed straight south, away from the road, out past the barn.

"Towns are in this direction," Danny said, pointing in front of them. "When we get to one we'll find someone to help us."

Melissa glanced back and shouted. "Wait ... Kiko's coming. Wait for Kiko."

Of course, Kiko would follow them. In the fury of the past hour Danny had forgotten entirely about the dog. Kiko would want to go wherever they might go.

"Come on, boy," Danny shouted, "you come and take care of us."

They were on their way, traveling to an unknown destination. It was early afternoon as they began their slow march, four un-protected children and a mangy old dog. As a group their size was so small as to be almost invisible. They walked past the farm's outbuildings and headed over barren plowed fields of black earth.

The autumn air smelled clean and fresh. The children's brisk pace made them feel invigorated and alive as though they were enjoying a weekend hike through a meadow. But Danny realized he'd forgotten to listen to the radio for a check of the weather. Furthermore, if he'd done some real planning instead of just a vague intention of leaving the Jameson farm, he could have de-vised a harness for the dog to carry some of the load.

They kept walking hour after hour as the sun moved steadily toward the western horizon. The Little Ones were keeping up well. Danny alternated carrying each one of them on his shoul-ders as much as he could, switching the shotgun from hand to hand. Much of the time, Chrissy was forced to carry two back-packs.

Soon the orange sun would set and they would need to find a place to stop for the night, but there was no shelter in sight. Bar-ren plowed ground surrounded them except for patches of sparse weedy stubble. Far, far in front of them was the outline of trees, but that probably signified a farmhouse. Danny knew that an occupied farmhouse was not what they wanted now, not just yet.

They needed to keep walking, as long and as far as they possibly could travel the first day. If Ralph had come home and changed his mind, if he had friends with him and decided to come after them, their only hope would be having a lot of distance between them. They continued walking even as dusk fell, and minute by minute the red-streaked golden ball of sun settled out of sight. Danny was determined to continue on. They would stop and rest as much as necessary, but he wasn't going to remain in one place all night. He got the others to join him in singing songs, songs their mother loved to sing. Yet, even as the rising moonlight lit their path, Danny's feet and legs were growing tired.

The moon was directly overhead when Sam began to complain. Danny took Melissa off his shoulders and knelt beside his little brother.

"I'm hungry, Danny," he said in the toughest voice he could muster. Moonlight reflected from his alert eyes. Sam knew what they were doing, and he was doing his best not to slow them down. Danny had to smile.

"Sure, buddy. We can take care of that right now." He filled a soft tortilla with peanut butter, took a bite and gave the lion's share of the makeshift sandwich to Sam. Then he made another for the girls. Within a few minutes they were back on their journey.

Finally, in the early morning hours, Danny had to stop. Continually he had been carrying either Sam or Melissa, and the extra 60 pounds or so had worn him out completely. He didn't have any idea how far they had traveled. They stopped along a row of scrub brush trees near a pond with no buildings of any kind in sight. There they set their packs between the scraggly tree trunks to block the cool wind. With the Little Ones in the middle, they all nestled together and slept soundly until the crack of dawn. Kiko circled the mass of exhausted children several times, then he too found his resting place. The dog stopped at the feet of his youthful masters and stared out into the darkness one more time, his nose checked the air, his ears twitched in the silence; then he lay down and added warmth to the sleeping children as he kept watch.

* * * * *

After seven rings the phone was answered. "Hall-o?"

"They're gone." There was a protracted pause on the line, followed by a distinct rush of air blowing into the receiver.

"What do you mean gone? The children?"

"Yes."

"Where?"

"I don't know where."

"Then when, Ralph?"

"Yesterday afternoon. Beth and I weren't here at the time. We searched all evening into the dark."

"Oh, my God. Nothing can happen to those kids." The exclamations were followed by another wheezing exhale of breath into the phone. "I thought you were going to take care of them?"

"I tried, but have you ever been around four kids at the same time ... in a house no bigger than this one? It tain't easy." His tone was matter of fact, as though he were telling Lois what he'd had for breakfast.

"But I need more time. Their mother still isn't ready to take them back. Jeez ... this is terrible."

"Time for what?"

"It doesn't matter. So, what happened?"

"They all just run off. I don't know where or why."

"Okay ... okay. Call the local authorities. Have them do the footwork, but you've got to get them back. Call me the second you hear something."

# 5

MADISON COUNTY DEPUTY Sheriff John Ranther read the name on the mailbox. His squad car moved slowly up the farm-house drive, as the car fell and rose in a series of potholes. A light gray Ford Tempo sat beside a beat-up Chevy pickup. The bed of the truck was full of trash, sun-faded beer cans, discarded tubes of axle grease and spilt motor oil. Several torn bags of rabbit feed mixed with the oil formed a thick crud that held tight a rusty tow chain. Ranther knocked on the back screen door. He adjusted his gun belt and searched his shirt pockets for a pen. Hadn't ever had a kidnapping around here since he'd been on the force, he thought. Guess there's a first time for everything. The report said it involved children, several, in fact. He saw someone pass a window headed to answer the door. He hoped this was a matter that could be easily explained and quickly solved.

"Mr. Jameson?"

"That's me. I'm the one who called, Sheriff."

"I'm a deputy; name's John Ranther." The officer removed his western hat and moved through the back kitchen. His height dwarfed Ralph Jameson, and he was every bit as wide in the shoulders and thick in the limbs. He noticed that Ralph was wearing house slippers.

Ranther ducked under the door jam as they moved through a cramped dining room into the living area. He took a seat on the front edge of a sheet-covered recliner and looked about the room, twirling his hat methodically around his fingers. Ralph grabbed his beer and a straight-back chair which he flipped around and sat in backwards.

"Get'cha something to drink?" Ralph asked. "I know you can't have no beer or nothing, but we got tea … water?" He forced a meager smile through his puffy lips.

"Some water would be fine. Could you fill me in about your children being gone … from the beginning, if you don't mind."

"Well, they're not my kids, we was just taking care of them," Ralph said. He turned and hollered toward the kitchen. "Hon, would you get the sheriff a glass of water." He rocked the chair back and forth on the wood floor and downed the last of the foam in his warm can of Busch.

"As I told your office when I called, when the misses and I got home Monday evening they were gone, all of 'em. No note or nothing. I don't know what happened."

"This is Thursday, Mr. Jameson. You waited until noon today to report a kidnapping?"

"I've been looking for 'em. Thought maybe one of the oldest one's friends from school might have driven out here to take the lot of 'em to town. Thought, too, they might show back up."

"What made you think they've been kidnapped then?" Ranther kept taking notes on a pocket pad as fast as his large hands would move. His eyes took mental notes of the room, and the home-owner as well.

"What else could it be? Would you go out in this weather, getting to be winter and all, if you didn't have to?"

"I don't know, Mr. Jameson. Like you say, maybe they had someone come pick them up, like you suggested."

"Exactly."

"Well, I wouldn't call that kidnapping." The deputy took a glass of water from Beth, and watched her step behind Ralph. He immediately felt a twang of pity for the anorexic woman with the limp hair and sad eyes who sucked on a cigarette as she stood quietly as though she were another piece of furniture. Ranther looked around. Four large ashtrays were heaped to overflowing, like pyramids, with butts and ash and toenail clippings. Several dirty plates were on the coffee table. The deputy saw a roach dart across a crusty dish. Every flat surface in the room held an empty aluminum can. The room smelled stale.

"Well, they damn sure didn't leave with any permission. Anybody who helped them run … I mean, disappear, should be prosecuted. Don't you think so, hon?" Beth didn't even move, much less contribute to the conversation.

"Is there some reason why these kids would want to take off?"

"Hell, isn't there always? You know kids these days, Sheriff." Ralph started getting all excited and threw his arms in the air.

"As I said before, I'm not the sheriff. But you said these weren't your kids. Is that right?"

Ralph nodded.

"So, whose are they?"

"We're their foster parents," Ralph replied.

John Ranther didn't know much about Nebraska's child services. His time was usually spent doing everything from moving prisoners and pulling over speeders to investigating cattle rustling and equipment theft, but the answer he'd just heard didn't ring true even before the man who'd said it paused to take another breath. This place was a dump, and he doubted if he'd ever met two people less likely to be nominated for parents of the year. He seriously questioned if child services would place minors in this environment.

"I understand. But that's not what I asked. Who are the parents?"

"The father's dead. Hon, get me another beer, will ya? The mother's in a head hospital. That's what I've been told."

"A head hospital?"

"A mental case, you know, Sheriff. A real loony tune." Ralph opened a new beer, took a swig, then belched like a fog horn for several seconds.

"Do you have the address and phone number of the hospital?"

"Sure, got it around here somewhere. But I'd be real careful talking to Mrs. Stone. She's really off the deep end, from what I hear. You should probably just touch base with the hospital staff, if you know what I mean. Don't want to make it any harder on the lady."

"I understand your concern," the deputy said as he stood. "I need a description of each child ... do you have any photographs?"

"Sure. Hon, get the sheriff those school photos. I know the oldest boy has something to do with all this. He's a regular delinquent."

"How old is he?"

" 'Bout 15, I guess. Won't take no discipline. Always a smart ass."

"I see," said Ranther. He'd seen enough during his days on the force to know a dead-beat when he met one. Once he located the children he was going to take it upon himself, personally, to find out why four children were living with these people. He got the physical descriptions and took a quick glance at each of the photographs. I'll put out an APB to all the bus and trucking companies, that sort of thing. I don't think we'll have much trouble locating them. The main thing we'll do is watch the roads." He got up from the sagging chair and began moving through the dining room toward the back door. "Oh, by the way ... did they take anything with them ... like extra clothes or food?"

"No," Ralph replied as he came around the doorway. "Nothing. Just them's gone. I hope you get them back real soon. If they'd left on their own I'm sure they would've come back by now. That's why I'm sure they were kidnapped."

"Right," Ranther said with a faint shake of his head. He let the screen door clap against the warped jam and adjusted his hat as he walked back to his squad car.

* * * * *

For the first two days Danny kept the band headed southeast by keeping the sun to his left in the morning, and headed slightly into it. They slept in ditches or under trees. Late the first night they came across an old broken-down chicken coop, but so many of the boards were split or missing that it was about the same as sleeping directly under the stars. The temperature remained in the high 30s, and they adjusted to the cold. What they couldn't adjust to were the blisters and the foot weariness caused by all the walking. Chrissy didn't complain, but Danny knew she was getting worn down as much as the Little Ones. Sam had a severe blister on his right foot, and they couldn't make any ground if Melissa was left to her own transport, so Danny had to carry both of them. Sam on his shoulders and Melissa in his arms much of the time. Chrissy would carry the shotgun and the two largest knapsacks.

Their food was still holding out. The previous evening Danny built a fire and they cooked rabbit steaks. The rabbit meat made for reasonably tender, although bland eating. The dog seemed to eat better than all of them. Kiko would get any and all scraps. And twice a day Danny would toss him a freezer-burned cut of venison, a cold slab of meat as hard as a brick and the color of tree bark. The old mutt would devour the meat as though it were a fresh T-bone steak.

This night Danny found a stand of volunteer corn amid high reeds that grew in an eroded terrace along a recently cut field. At harvest time the combine had been unable to travel over this area of unleveled ground, and the stalks were left to be. They wouldn't be able to build a fire in the high grass, but it was much warmer than an open ditch, and they still had provisions to eat besides the frozen steaks. Each shared in the last of the hard-boiled eggs, and they each had a tortilla and a slice of cheese. As they nestled together, Chrissy examined Sam's injured foot. It wasn't any worse, but she tore a piece of cloth from her yellow cotton-top dress and put it in his shoe for extra cushioning.

After tending to Sam, Chrissy retrieved her notepad and stump of a pencil from the bottom of her knapsack. Out in the country and on their own didn't deter her from her duty to her diary. In fact, it made it much easier. The writing gave her an outlet to express herself, and without consciously thinking about it, she was keeping a journal of their expedition.

Whenever they stopped for more than ten minutes, she would take out her pad and pencil. After they ate at each new campsite, she hoarded the fading light of day to write … notes of their experience in this never-ending sea of farmland, stories to friends only she knew, and letters to their mother, until the sky turned blue-black and she could see no longer. At the conclusion of each letter she'd fashion an envelope with a blank sheet of paper. Sometimes, she'd have the others sign the letters. But Chrissy never read the letters aloud. They were hers, and hers alone. A collection of private thoughts that kept her warm in the comfort of a familiar activity. She glanced at her little sister as she wrote, content in the moment. Chrissy was happiest when she had a book in her hands, or a notepad in her lap.

Melissa held her dolly close and hummed softly. She had a tiny little nose and thin lips that could jump up in a quick smile or pout with animated displeasure.

She was the baby of the family. As such she received much of the family's attention, as the others had when they were young, and she reveled in it. Where Chrissy and Sam were more reserved, Melissa was outgoing, like their mother and Danny. She shared the same thick dark brown hair as her oldest brother, and sparkling brown eyes. She was cheerful and demonstrative. Often she'd make Chrissy smile, even laugh, at things she'd say or do that her older sister wouldn't ever have done herself.

On this night she held Mrs. Leatherwood tightly and hummed to her as she might put a baby to sleep. The matronly looking doll was her constant companion, a grandmother figure with gray hair swept back in a bun. It was attired with an ankle-length gingham dress and a shawl sewn to the shoulders. Sometimes Melissa would cradle the doll like a living baby, and at other times swing it by the arm as though she were about to throw away a rag. But there wasn't a time in recent memory, with the exception of the night their dad died, that Danny could remember seeing Melissa without Mrs. Leatherwood.

Danny knelt beside his youngest sister and rubbed her tender cheeks with his bare hands. Her cheeks were warm but her nose was cold; he kissed her on the forehead. A full moon rose up and filled the night sky, and they all sat up to watch it rise.

Suddenly, a violent rustling could be heard coming toward them through the cornstalks. Danny got to his knees and grabbed the shotgun, his right trigger finger silently flicking off the safety. An instant later Kiko appeared in front of them carrying something in his mouth.

"Whatcha got there, boy?" Danny said to the dog as he reached for his muzzle. The dog had a hen pheasant in his jaws. The bird was still alive, Danny could see its eyes blinking in the moonlight. "Good boy, Kiko," he said as he turned to Chrissy. "He had to grab her right off of her nest; that's the only way he could have caught her." The bird was a mottled color of brown, gray and dull tan feathers, excellent camouflage. The hens had none of the brilliant red and green coloring of the males. Even Kiko would never have seen this pheasant sitting motionless on her nest. His sensitive nose had located the bird.

Danny petted the dog with one hand and gave him a hug as he held the bird securely in the other. With winter beginning Danny doubted that the hen would be protecting a covey of young, or even more remote, sitting on some eggs. His dad had taught him much about the land and farm crops and wildlife. Certainly the hen was by herself, just trying to keep warm as they were.

He had something else to think about at this very moment. A nice fresh pheasant, like this one, would surely make a great meal for the four of them. The food supply they had brought with them wouldn't last forever.

"Is the bird all right?" Melissa asked.

"I can't tell," Danny replied.

"What are you going to do with it?" Chrissy asked in a pensive tone.

"Let me pet it," squealed Melissa.

Danny leaned over and let his little sister pet the bird. He knew what he had to do. "Kiko did us a favor," he said, speaking directly to Melissa. "This bird can provide us with something fresh to eat, and we're running out of food."

"You're not going to kill it," Melissa exclaimed, her face suddenly an expression of horror.

"Anyway, I think its wing is broken," Danny said, knowing full well he wasn't sure of such a fact. "If we let it go now, it will just die in the cold." Melissa began to cry softly as she saw an incredulous look in Chrissy's eyes. Sam remained silent. Whatever Danny decided was fine by him. He was more reserved than his older brother, but totally devoted. His attention hung on every word Danny uttered, and whatever Danny did was the way things were supposed to be done.

Without another word Danny stood up and walked into the cornstalks beyond the campsite. There he took the pheasant by the neck and wrung it. The others could hear the rustling noise as he finished the deed, and Melissa added a moan to her sobbing loud enough for Danny to get her unhappy message. Danny field cleaned the bird and wrapped it in a sack so that the dog wouldn't make a meal of it in the night. Then he walked back to the campsite and Melissa's penetrating accusatory stare. He almost wanted to laugh, Melissa was always so melodramatic. But he could tell both the girls were unhappy with his decision to kill the bird. Their feelings seemed to run deep, and he didn't want to make light of them — he let them be. The pheasant takes care of its family, and he did what he had to do to take care of his.

# 6

BY DAYBREAK THEY were back on their journey marching across frozen cornfields. On occasion they would come to a fence, usually barbed wire, and Danny would push the strands down and climb over. For Chrissy and Sam he'd push the lower wires down with his foot and raise the upper one, letting them climb through. Melissa was short enough to scoot underneath the lowest strand of the fence altogether. The day was cold but the sun was bright. As they pushed over a shallow rise, they heard a buzzing sound floating on the crisp morning breeze.

Chrissy saw it first. Still far away, not much more than a speck in the sky, but headed directly toward them.

"It's an airplane," she cried.

Danny turned and looked, throwing Sam from his shoulders. It appeared to be a single engine plane flying fairly low. "Quick, into the ditch!" he exclaimed.

They were completely out in the open. The ditch ahead was easy to see, but at least 50 yards in front of them. The ditch had a few scrub bushes growing in it which were wind-ripped from exposure and grotesque in shape, along with some high grass and another fence. "Run!"

Chrissy had the legs of a sprinter, her lithe body leading them all. Sam shifted into an all-out run, too, and was ahead of Danny, who was loaded down with baggage. Danny turned and knelt, quickly arranging the backpacks so he could carry them better, waiting for Melissa to catch up. Already she was far behind, her five-year-old legs not up to the demands of a foot race. The harder she tried, the more her tiny steps looked like a frantic waddle of a frightened duck. She had Mrs. Leatherwood by the arm flinging the doll desperately about with each stride.

Then, in an instant, Danny's heart swelled in his throat. Off to the side, lumbering over the rise in the field, appeared a mammoth hulk headed directly toward Melissa. Danny never had a doubt as to what was now occupying the same field they had happened to cross.

He heard the buzz of the plane getting louder. He watched Melissa's pathetic struggle to cover ground. Quickly, he glanced at the ditch, the other two had made it to safety, but it was too late for him now, too. Both he and Melissa were caught in the open. The bull was pressing toward her, closing the distance between them with every millisecond.

The massive black bulk of the powerful beast cantered at a steady pace straight for defenseless Melissa. Each huge hoof drummed a deadly beat on the hard-packed earth. Its horns were held low. An enraged bellow cried forth from its lungs.

Danny didn't have the shotgun. Even if he had, it was unlikely he could bring down such a powerful animal with shells full of birdshot. Its head was down and it was charging. Steam snorted from its face with every breath. Over half a ton of sinew and muscle on the hoof. "Get down," Danny screamed.

Danny waved his arms; he threw one of the backpacks into the air, but in the brief seconds before the bull arrived at his selected target, there was nothing he could do to change its course. In what seemed to be slow motion, Danny watched in terror as the huge beast flew over the prone body of his little sister. The bull appeared to downshift even as it reached Melissa's motionless body, but her dress and hair continued to flutter, and the animal remained fixed on that target. The bull missed her prone shape with his charging head. Still, Danny's heart fell. It was so obvious that she'd been stepped on. All the pain of his father's death he had felt, but hadn't shown, overcame him instantaneously and he felt weak and helpless.

The bull turned around and returned to the prone shape. The ring in its nose touched the still form; Danny felt boiling rage rise up through his body.

"Come and get me," he screamed at the bull as he yanked his hunting knife from its sheath. The bull looked up and snorted. A spray of snot and icy steam foamed from its black glistening snout. And then it did. Like a halfback cutting behind a trap block the bull sprang at him, and from a distance of less than 20 feet. Emotion was bubbling from Danny's pores, both rage and fear, to the point he could hardly see straight. With a reflexive dodge, he sidestepped the rush as he flung a backpack into the face of his adversary. The parry was short lived as the enraged bovine lurched to a halt, whirled and again charged him.

This time Danny retreated to the fence where Chrissy and Sam lay huddled in the grass. He jumped from the bull's line of attack at the last possible instant and jumped back to his feet, making a mad dash toward safety. Before the bull could charge again, Danny was behind the barrier.

His heart was pounding, about to burst from his chest. Chrissy looked at him with concern, Sam glared at him in disbelief.

"We've got to get Melissa," said Chrissy.

"We will," he responded, struggling to get his breath. "Hopefully, the bull will go away."

The bull knew what the fence was all about. He sniffed around the backpacks, but never went back over to where Melissa lay unmoving on the ground. Within minutes the bull sauntered back from whence he came. Having once again proven he ruled this farm, he was no longer needed in this part of the field.

While the bull was still in view but heading away from them, Danny and Chrissy dashed to Melissa's location. The prostrate little girl didn't move a muscle as they dropped beside her. Danny saw the terror in Chrissy's eyes. He touched Melissa's head and gently swept his hand over her back. As he turned her over, crystal chunks of dirty snow mixed with straw remained stuck to her cheek. Her color was good and she appeared to be breathing. Then her brown eyes opened, wild with anxiety, full of doubt. "Is the bull gone?" she whispered.

"Did he hurt you? Do you hurt anywhere?" Chrissy asked as she began touching her little sister all over.

"No, but he smelled me," she said in disgust, wiping mud from her hands.

Danny couldn't believe it. He thought for sure she'd been injured. A warm feeling radiated through him, and his gap-toothed smile broke across his face. He picked her up, mud and all, and they darted for the fence.

"Don't forget Mrs. Leatherwood," she yelled as she bounced in Danny's arms. Chrissy retrieved the fallen doll and threw it jubilantly into the air with a yell. She caught Mrs. Leatherwood and wiped the mud from the doll. None of them even noticed that the airplane had flown right over their heads and kept on going.

* * * * *

That evening, their fifth night out alone and unprotected, they came to a dilapidated barn and stopped for the night. One end of the gambled roof sagged severely, now virtually resting on top of a side shed. Field mice were heard rustling through the moldy straw. Owls stirred in the rafters, flapping their wings in loud protest at the unwelcome visitors, hooting an eerie rebuke as they flew out the open door.

They cleared out a place to sleep in the cleanest corner of the structure where the walls were solid, then Danny built a fire near the 20-foot barn door. He cooked the pheasant, roasting each piece of meat on a stick over the open flame. Sam was hungry and ate readily. At first, the girls rejected the food. Chrissy acted like she couldn't possibly eat, and Melissa resumed her accusatory stare.

Danny ate two pieces of fresh meat, including half of the succulent breast, and speared a thigh, turning the stick in his hands, watching the girls from the corner of his eye. "There's only two pieces left," he said to no one in particular. "I'm stuffed. Do you want them, Sam?"

His little brother shook his head from side to side to perpetuate their pre-planned ruse. "No, I'm stuffed, too," he said. Sam couldn't help smiling and he snickered under his breath.

"Kiko's going to eat good tonight." Danny looked at Sam with a grin growing at the sides of his mouth. "Here's a drumstick and a nice piece of breast meat." Then he turned his head toward Chrissy and Melissa. "There's plenty of peanut butter left in the jar for you girls," he said.

He had their attention; they were looking toward the fire and at Sam chewing on a leg bone.

"Here, Kiko," Sam said. The dog was already near his side, and he jumped to all fours with the command. "Fetch, boy," Sam threw the bone into the mammoth empty barn. He grabbed the cooked drumstick from next to the fire and held it high in his hand. "Come and get this one, boy."

"Wait," hollered Melissa. She loved chicken drumsticks. There was no reason she wouldn't love a pheasant leg, too. In fact, she'd eaten pheasant before, birds their father had shot. She just hadn't seen them alive right before they were killed. She ran to the fire. It was obvious she was hungry, and still quite dirty from her encounter with the bull. Her appearance touched Danny. He was glad she decided to eat the bird, but it was her eyes that told a deeper story. The little girl was scared, afraid for where they were and what was going to happen tomorrow. She didn't know when she would eat again. For all her energy and effort she could do nothing but trust him and Chrissy. She was his responsibility; he had brought them out here. He promised himself he would never let her down.

"Here, Punkin," Danny said as he handed her the remaining drumstick. "We were saving this for you," he said smiling; and she nodded. "Take this over to Chrissy," he said and gave her the other piece of pheasant.

Finally, this night, they had decent shelter. Finding the fallen-down barn proved more than just convenient; it was downright fortunate. With no preamble it started to drizzle. The droplets weren't much — yet, but they were steady. It wasn't quite dark, so Chrissy dug in her knapsack for her special items at the very bottom. She pulled out a notebook and her only pencil, which was broken. She borrowed Danny's pocket knife to sharpen it. The Little Ones were already fast asleep, having nestled together only minutes ago. Sam's jacket hood was tied tightly around his head and ears, Melissa's head rested on one arm and the cloth body of Mrs. Leatherwood. They were facing each other in silent deep restful sleep. The Little Ones were exhausted; they all were.

Chrissy situated herself in the broad barn doorway next to the fire in order to have use of the final rays of light from the setting sun. She wrote in the notebook until darkness forced her to quit. Danny stacked extra firewood, old split boards and fallen tree branches inside the building as fast as he could. Hopefully, he would be able to keep the fire burning all night. Some extra warmth while they were sleeping would be a welcome change. It would also keep away any uninvited guests — the four-footed variety.

"When do you think we'll get to a road or town where we can get some help, Danny?" Chrissy asked as he joined her near the fire.

"Soon … I hope. The main thing was to get as far away from Ralph as we could."

"Don't you think we've done that?"

"Well, yeah. But you know good and well someone's looking for us, like the police, or Aunt Lois, or Ralph and his drunken buddies."

"Maybe it would be okay if the police did find us," she said.

"Not if they take us back to Ralph's. That bastard, it makes me mad just to think about him."

"Danny, you don't have to say that." Then Chrissy paused and scooted closer to the fire so he could see her face. "Danny, I'm glad we're out of there. Even if Ralph hadn't thrown us out, I was ready to do … something. You were, too, weren't you?" Danny nodded. "I'm glad you made the move as quick as you did, Danny. No one got hurt. Ralph was probably shocked to come back and really find us gone." They both gave an amused chuckle. "But, Danny … what do we do from here?"

Danny was silent. He stared into the fire, its flickering flames lapped at the saturated air, its orange glow reflected back from his eyes. Danny didn't have a ready answer. He hadn't really thought that far ahead, all he'd been concerned with was getting away from Ralph.

"Danny?" Chrissy spoke up again.

"We're going to find Mother," he finally answered. "She needs us and we need her."

"I want to do that, too, Danny, but she's all the way in Omaha. Do you know how far away that is?"

"No. Do you?" he asked.

"It's got to be a hundred miles or more. We'll have to get a ride."

"We will. I just don't want to go back to Ralph's, so we can't be caught before we get to wherever they're keeping Mom."

"But maybe the police could really help."

"No, they won't," he said. "Even if they didn't make us go back to Ralph's, they'd put us in another foster home. I'm through with that. It's a bunch of crap. I'm not living with other people ever again."

They were both quiet for awhile. Then Chrissy said, "We've got to make some real plans, Danny. We're going to need food. We can't stay out here in these pastures forever."

"We'll get there," he said with assurance. "You've been writing letters to Mom. What's her address in Omaha?"

"It's on Magnolia Street ... 1470 Magnolia, Omaha, Ne-braska," Chrissy said. She had the address memorized. "But I've never gotten a letter back," she said quite concerned. "Maybe Mom is in real bad shape. Maybe she can't write to us."

"Or maybe Ralph just never let us see the letters. I wouldn't put it past him to steal our mail."

"Or maybe Mom isn't at this address any more."

"Well," he said, "it's the only destination we got. We can't go back to the old house. They'd be waiting there for sure."

"Oh, Danny, I want to see Mom again so bad. I just know she'll get better with us around to help her. She should have stayed with us, never gone off. Aunt Lois said we wouldn't be gone from the farm more than a month or so. It's been more than four months now." Chrissy's lower lip began to    quiver, and her words became coated with apprehension. Chrissy, the introvert, the rock for all the others in the family when there was an immediate crisis. But when she thought things out and considered all the possibilities she became filled with concern, a frightened 11-year-old girl. "Oh, Danny, do you think we can make it?"

"You bet we can, sis. We'll find Mom. We're going to go to Omaha."

Danny put another board on the fire, and the two of them nestled down around the Little Ones in the pile of old hay they had scraped together for their beds. All four of them slept more soundly than hibernating bears. When the lightning cracked and the rolls of thunder crashed in the early morning hours, they just turned over in their sleep. The accompanying deluge flooded the surrounding fields. The fire went out. But the four exhausted Stone children slept as though they were back at their farm, in their own clean beds, with familiar visions of safe dreams protecting them throughout the hours of darkness.

# 7

OUTSIDE THE SKY was overcast, the weather cold and moody. Lois Devon sat at her dining room table and considered her situation. Her current options were as dismal as the weather outside, but she was about to change all that. She took a long pretentious drag on her cigarette. The way she smoked displayed an extension of her personality. When she inhaled deeply, holding it, then exhaled in a sustained cloud of noxious exhaust, it was like a therapeutic sigh. When she puffed rapidly, like a climbing freight train, she signaled her anxiety. Often, she'd sit and blow contented smoke rings, watching and studying them drift in the air. Another version of this was to let billows of smoke roll out her mouth which she inhaled in an updraft into her nostrils.

At this moment she was puffing. She had the money, but she had to keep it separated in small amounts. The unexpected windfall was, in a way, her birthright. She was going to start her life over; she deserved it. She wasn't hurting anyone. Of primary concern was how to account, distribute and conceal all this newfound money. The worry kept her up at night. But it was a good problem, and she would figure out a way to pull it off. Throughout the summer she had been discreetly funneling the funds into various channels. Soon, hopefully, it would have all vanished from any traceable paper trail — but she needed a little more time. Every day the children had remained neatly tucked away at Ralph and Beth's farm her plan had been progressing smoothly.

Now conditions had changed.

The news that her nieces and nephews had disappeared from the Jameson farm caused her considerable distress. She had not expected much from Ralph, and obviously he'd fulfilled her lack of faith in him. She never would have gone to him if other options had been available, but there weren't. Everything happened so fast, the accident, followed by her sister's nervous breakdown.

She prayed that she would get a call any minute telling her the children had been located. She didn't care for raising kids herself, but she didn't want anything bad to happen to them.

There had been a time, she thought, when a normal family life with children running around the house and clamoring for attention would have been her life's fulfillment. With Bob all things seemed possible; for Bob she would have done anything. She married him in 1979, barely 20 years old; she skipped her final year at the University of Nebraska at Omaha where she was majoring in art and interior design. He loved her, she knew, in the beginning, and she fell for him without any reservations.

He was already 30 at the time. She didn't care if he were 50. Those friendly sincere eyes, a broad genuine smile. He knew how to talk to people and get people to ease up to him. His business was people, more specifically automobiles, and he was good at it. He put more people in new cars than any other salesman at his dealership, and he did it without a lot of high pressure, phony manipulations, gratuitous flattery. He was really able to become the friend of a total stranger within minutes of meeting them. People trusted him. Even when prospects insisted they were just looking, nine times out of ten he'd have them driving away in a new car before the day was over. He'd take the pants right off the wisest and most experienced buyers, put them in a new ride, give them back their trousers, less their wallet, of course, and have them happy about the whole experience. Bob Miller was an extremely dangerous suitor for a young naïve college girl.

In the early years, their togetherness was like Cinderella's life after the charming prince fitted her with the glass slipper. Regularly, Bob and Lois took long weekend excursions to Las Vegas, Galveston and Colorado. They vacationed in the winter in Miami and took cruises through the Bahamas. He bought her everything she wanted. She had her own new car, a sky-blue Mustang with silver trim.

He gave her everything but a child. The "pill" was new then. No one worried about side effects or long-term consequences of taking the pill. It was a convenience. An insurance policy to maintain their current lifestyle. She spent many hours of pleasure in his arms, touching as they slept, resuming their love-making as soon as they awoke. But the pill was always there. Bob insisted upon it.

In 1981 he left her. She never saw it coming. He told her of his decision as though he was telling a car prospect how much a trade-in would bring. He was always in command of his words and emotions. He didn't seem to care; that was just the way it was. The revelation burned a hole in her soul. She was so devastated she couldn't even talk, much less cry. He didn't even touch her that day; they had made love just two nights before, he just told her and walked out.

They met once more after that, in court, where the judge gave her $300 a month alimony, but no more, because she didn't have minor dependents, and she had skills with which to get a job of her own. The hurt and hate boiled inside her; she wanted to pour battery acid on him and destroy that pretty boy face. She got to keep the car, and Bob paid an advance of six months on the apartment. Then the life she knew and loved was over. She spent the better part of the next six months alone in the apartment, curtains drawn, never going out, rarely dressing or bathing. She just hugged her pillow tightly and cried.

\* \* \* \* \*

Lois was going to have to go back to that godforsaken farm country. She couldn't count on Ralph calling her with updates, and she wasn't confident in his ability to track them down. A call to the police department in Madison County crossed her mind, but she decided against it for now. Lois Devon had a lot on her mind, not the least of which were four children — whereabouts unknown. But she knew better than anyone else who may be looking for them, where they might be headed, what their destination might be. She certainly knew more than Ralph, and the police knew nothing. She had that information right inside her purse.

First, the old farmhouse. Hopefully, it was still locked up tight and snug. A trip out there and then a private talk with Ralph. She would stop and see Sandra, too. She'd keep the conversation with her sister light and general. Yes, she'd have time to stop at the hospital … it wouldn't be out of the way to drive to Norfolk.

\* \* \* \* \*

In a large hall sat a frail woman in a folding chair, dressed in a flower-print housecoat, drawing pictures of farm animals with a drawing marker on a torn-off sheet of butcher paper. Her gaunt fingers were vein-streaked hands dutifully attended to the drawing project, unaware of the room full of similarly attired individuals, each working to recreate important scenes from the deep recesses of their minds. Magic markers, drawing pens of every color littered the tables. Muffled conversations between neighbors were all that broke the silence of the room until someone erupted with a boisterous cry of excitement or distress. Depending upon the seriousness of the outburst, one of the attendants would walk over and assist the individual. An atmosphere of mildew and stuffiness hung in the air, and a feeling of pathos permeated the hall.

The woman worked meticulously on her drawings, always taking them back to her room at the end of the day. Her dark brown hair was neatly combed, but her eyes were dull and lifeless. Her face had a sunken appearance.

After 140 days as a resident, Sandra Stone was still as melancholy and withdrawn as the hour she first arrived at Nebraska's state mental health branch facility in Norfolk. She roomed with an older woman who spent hours of her time neatly arranging items in her dresser drawer and her collection of jewelry boxes and hair brushes on her bureau. Whenever something was moved or looked slightly out of place, the gray-haired stooped matron had a hissy fit. This usually happened at least twice a day.

Sandra ignored the regular tirades of her roommate, minded her own business, and kept her own deep private thoughts to herself. She would respond to the staff when addressed. One particular girl she did like especially, a volunteer from the nearby college, named Nancy. But seldom did she utter a word unless spoken to. Sandra put away her new drawing, then reached in a box for her collection of photographs. There was not enough closet or shelf space in the room, so both women had many of their possessions in boxes and grocery sacks on the floor about their beds.

She looked through the thin stack of photographs. She went through them several times a day, and the corners were dog-eared, the edges covered with fingerprints. The bottom photo, the largest one, a 5 x 7, was her favorite, and she dwelt on it. It was a group picture of her four children taken several years ago under the large oak tree in the front yard of her home. In it the children were smiling, squinting their eyes against the setting sun. The littlest girl was sitting suspended in the tire swing, the others stood around her framing the scene. Their wind-swept hair attested to the spontaneity of the photograph. The bright red sweater, the emerald green baseball cap, the faded blue overalls.

When the snapshot was developed, she liked it so much she had it enlarged and kept it in a frame on her bedroom dresser. Now, she held it tight, the caring and love for her children deep within her. Only the anguish of the loss of her husband, and the resulting stay in the hospital, kept them apart. But she knew they were in good hands, for now. Her sister was taking care of that. She had promised.

The staff at the hospital removed all pictures from her collection that included her deceased husband. The doctor's entire efforts were to get her through the mourning loss, and accept it, in spite of its tragic suddenness, and get on with her life. Thus far, progress was slow. Sandra Stone's mind had not accepted the loss of the man she had kissed one routine summer morning, and who had never come back to her. She sobbed silently and rocked on her bed as she held the picture tight against her breast. She clung to the photograph as though it were her very life.

* * * * *

Two empty bottles of Mountain Dew sat on a paper-strewn desk, as empty as the leads he'd received about the Stone children in the past 24 hours. Ranther's right boot rested on the edge of his desk, and he rubbed the ache in the small of his back. Damn chair was too narrow, too flimsy, barely held his large bulk. Cussing out the chair was one of his daily rituals. He needed a pillow to support his back, and a larger chair. He never got either. He wasn't a complainer by nature, but he liked to complain about his cheap government desk chair. It was a familiar item that defined his desk space in a one-room bay flooded in florescent light that he shared with four other deputies. If anyone ever really replaced his chair, he would have undoubtedly complained more loudly about that, and certainly tracked down the culprit.

John Ranther called every bus terminal and freight yard within a 70-mile radius of the Jameson farm. No one had laid eyes on the kids. He had fared no better with the trucking companies. "Haven't seen 'em," was the standard response.

Yesterday afternoon he'd run off 3,000 fliers with the four children's photos and descriptions, along with contact phone numbers. He purposefully made the fliers look like wanted posters to catch people's attention. Then he personally delivered them to every gas station, truck stop and open business in Enola, Leigh, Clarkson, Newman Grove and Humphrey.

By this morning he expected to have his office phone ringing off the hook with information about the missing children. Even a dead-end lead was better than sitting at the station house with nothing to go on. Every time the phone rang, his boot hit the hardwood floor with a boom, and he jerked up in his cramped seat. But today, none of the calls were about the children. Not a lead of any kind.

He did get several calls asking if he had any new information. He'd beat around the bush, say the search was ongoing, and get off the line as quickly as possible. He didn't want to admit he was stumped.

Ranther reached for the phone handset and dialed a familiar but infrequently used number.

"Hey, Tommy. This is Ranther. Need your services just as soon as possible."

"Sure, John. Got Jake here, he's always ready to go. Got Mike, too. Need any more?"

"That should do it. Why don't you meet me over here at the station house and I'll take you out where we need to start. Can you be here by noon?"

"No problem. Is this about those missing kids?"

"That's it."

"Good. I'm training a new one; I'll bring him along. Besides, those kids will be easy to track. These bloodhounds just love you, John. You know how much they love to run. Better than staying all cooped up. Should be there within the hour."

"Letter writing is the only device for combining solitude with good company."

— *Lord Byron*

# 8

SHORTLY AFTER DAYBREAK Danny was awakened by an arm flung across his face. He'd been hit with the sleeve of Sam's nylon coat, crusty with bits of embedded straw, dirt fragments and ice crystals. The cold slap woke him up with a start. Kiko paced around the huddled mass of sleeping children, keeping guard, and when he was satisfied with the situation the dog settled back in his warm spot at the feet of Melissa and Sam. His tired old eyes looked back at Danny as he rested his muzzle on his paw.

The air was frigid. Light broke through the cracked boards of the sagging ancient barn as raindrops dripped from the gapping open door frame. Danny's legs were no longer sore, but his back was stiff and he had an earache. His eyes passed over the pile that was his sleeping brother and sisters. Sam's nose had been running for more than a day now, and his upper lip was all crusty from the dried mucus. The girls' hair was matted inside their stocking caps, and everyone was embedded in damp, decaying straw. Danny tried to rise. His mind was willing, but his body still pleaded for rest.

He moved slowly, rekindled the fire, stretched and relieved himself at the far end of the barn. The intense bright sun announced the new day, but provided no warmth. Danny watched his frozen breath steam out in front of him, and he rubbed his numb ears as he noticed the water puddles in the fields.

Okay, up and at 'um," he shouted. "We're burning daylight."

His dad always said that: "Quit wasting time, you're burning

71

daylight." His dad always led the way, the first up every day, the first to the table, to the barn, to the field. He led his children by example, doing and showing them the things he expected of them. Just thinking of him made Danny sad. He sure missed him. But for now, he'd do the leading, and if he was going to talk like Dad, he'd have to act like him, too.

They didn't have any water to wash up in, and they all looked like they had been asleep for a month. Sam looked the worst, his nose crusty and his eyes caked with crud. He was coughing, but not complaining. They cooked the last of the rabbit steaks. It was by no means a satisfying meal, but it blunted the keenest edges of their appetite. For practical purposes their food was gone.

Soon they were back on their journey, the sun climbing higher, shining almost directly in their eyes. The vast wet cornfields seemed to swallow them up, so barren, so empty. The band seemed adrift in a sea of plowed mud. There was hardly a tree in sight, occasionally a fence row or ditch.

Sticky mud and clods flipped free from their shoes as they walked, splattering the backs of their clothes. Melissa's walking became an ordeal as she tried to get traction; her shoes weighted down and covered with the damp goo. Danny could no longer carry either of the Little Ones as they were covered with mud on the backs of their legs. Sam coughed and wheezed as he struggled through the soft earth, then slipped in the mud and cut his hand against a rock as he fell. Danny tore a strip of material from the bottom of his undershirt and tied it around his brother's hand.

It wasn't even noon and they were already exhausted. They had to find some type of sturdy shelter. If they came across an occupied farmhouse, he would stop and knock on the door. If they saw a vehicle on a road, he would try to wave it down. Danny felt the weariness within himself. He could not force the others to press on; he would not ask. In an instant he felt sorry for himself. The effort to escape from an intolerable home, the goal to be reunited with their mother gone, vanished before he had a chance to attain it.

He looked back. In the distance, still clearly visible on the horizon, was the outline of the barn they slept in last night. Danny felt so tired. His lips were chapped; his right ear ached with a throbbing inner pain.

They had traveled ten to fifteen miles a day the first day or two, he figured. On day three, he remembered, they didn't travel as fast. The Little Ones had gotten progressively slower. Yesterday they covered maybe five or six miles. This morning they had barely gotten started. It was just too much. They would have to turn back.

The children hadn't crossed any black-topped roads in all their days of travel. They had crossed several dirt roads, however. After resting a long while, at least an hour, reclining with their backs flat in the mud, they resumed their walk. No one said a word. The sound of Sam's intermittent coughing was the only sound to break the silence.

"We'll find a road ahead and wait," Danny said to the others, his voice full of dejection.

Chrissy's mind was adrift as she plodded along holding Melissa's hand. Sam clung to Danny's coattail. They all could easily have lain back down in the open field and slept the entire day.

"My chest hurts," Sam said, "more now than last night."

"I'm still hungry," Melissa said, as if she had been holding the statement all morning waiting for someone else to speak up and break the silence.

"I'll get you all taken care of," Danny said. "I'll find some help. We'll go back if we have to, but first we'll get some food and get warm.

* * * * *

The day after the big fellow from the sheriff's department came by, Ralph Jameson had had enough of the waiting. He thought they'd be back by now, dragging their tails between their legs, kissing his ass, wanting back in. It was cold outside, and he knew they hadn't taken enough food to last very long. But they hadn't returned. Ralph was blaming himself now, mad at himself for letting them get away so easily.

Lois probably wouldn't want to pay him now, his friends would laugh at him when the word got out, and the sheriff would have a hundred more questions. More than that, there were still chores to do, rabbits to harvest, errands to run.

With winter coming on, Ralph just wanted to work a couple of days a week at the mill in town and have the kids do the work around the farm. He'd kind've gotten used to having them pick up after him. He hadn't really thought they would take off.

Ralph was motivated to get out of his warm shack he called a farmhouse and go find them. His abusive streak kept Beth in the bedroom as he seethed and plotted. He knew this countryside. Those snot-nosed kids couldn't have gotten far, and when he did find them, they'd wish they'd never run out on him, try to make him look like a fool, especially that smart-ass older boy. He'd teach that wise punk to respect his elders.

He drove into town at a little past five. Some of his friends held down day jobs, but they'd all be at the tavern by now. The Ford pickup chugged as it built up RPM, then momentum seemed to carry it down the dirt road until he shifted gears and the truck lugged down, chugged and built up speed all over again. Ralph only wanted the help of two of his closest drinking buddies, Singer and Brewster. They'd relish this kind of search and destroy mission, and anyway, they'd lived out here longer than he. They would probably know exactly where to go to find the children.

Ralph knew the kids left the farm headed south. He smiled to himself as he thought what he'd do to the two oldest when he caught them. He found his buddies, and they talked secretly in a booth in a far corner of the bar. Tomorrow was Saturday. The men made their plans as they sucked on long-necks. They would all get up at dawn and get an early start.

* * * * *

John Ranther was frustrated and confused. The hound dog search had been an exercise in futility. The whole afternoon was gone with nothing to show for it. All three hounds picked up the scent at the Jameson farm; the children had headed out the back way across the fields. But the drenching cloudburst from the night before had masked the trail. When the search party reached a wide ravine that had run with flash flood rains, the dogs became disoriented and lost and began wailing at each other, barking in circles. Tommy had steered them to the far side of the wide gully and worked them up and down the far bank. The dogs wailed louder, went this way and that. But the mud wash had carried the smell of the children down the gulch. Finally, the dog search had to be canceled. The bellowing hounds, more frustrated than the humans, would have stayed there indefinitely, barking and howling into the cold Nebraska wind.

The trip from his office to the Stone farm was only about 20 miles as the crow flies, but almost double that distance with all the turns and bends country road traveling required. John Ranther thought it best just to check out the place before contacting the mother or the aunt. The farm was in the next county over from Madison, Boone County, and was really close compared with other destinations the children might try to reach. The deputy also realized that the children were smart enough to know that their old farm was the first place people would look for them.

Ranther had called the bus line and the trucking companies. He gave out fliers to the police in Leigh and Creston to be distributed and posted in area businesses. The ALL-POINTS BULLE-TIN directed to all Nebraska law enforcement centers remained in effect. The *Madison Sentinel* ran a story about the children's disappearance. Still, the sheriff's department hadn't received any clues to their whereabouts. No one had called having seen children on the road. For now all he had was the report of four missing children. For all intents and purposes, they'd vanished.

The deputy wiggled his large body into the squad car seat, adjusting his long legs to make them more comfortable. Even with the seat all the way back he could use another inch or two for his cowboy boots. He stuck a cigar in his mouth, which he never lit, just rolled with his tongue around his mouth, and listened to one of his two cassette tapes. He had Clint Black and Alan Jackson tapes. One would stay in the audio player for about a week and he'd listen to it over and over. Then he'd switch. A week or so later he'd switch back. He'd had the same two tapes for about a year, and still sang along with the tunes as though it was the first time he'd heard them.

As with most rural addresses he had a route box number, but he would have to ask around for directions to the right farm. One question that kept poking in his mind was why did they leave *that* farm. He knew there could be many reasons, but he wanted the answer. The idea that they had been kidnapped was hogwash, and he knew it. Kidnappings are committed for money; these kids or their mother had no money, certainly no large sum of money he was aware of. If they were abducted, well, that was another thing, but the likelihood of all four of them being accessible at once, and taken at the same time … the odds against such a thing …

In Albion he stopped and talked to the postmaster. He was directed to a back road which led from town, told about the fork four miles out, and the 90-degree left turn at the Shaw's stone fence. From there he was told to keep right at the split in the road. The day was cold, overcast and gray, yet clean and invigorating in a way only the vast barren prairie can talk to a man. He found the address on a rusty mailbox — no letters, magazines or fliers of any kind were in it. He turned down the rutted drive to the white frame house.

The place was locked down tight, both front and back doors. All signs of life were gone; all evidence that the place had recently been a happy home had been blown away by the winter wind. He peered through a window at the side of the house. All the furniture seemed to be in place, but certainly no one was living there now. No fire burning in the hearth. The dented white Ford pickup with two flat tires looked as if it had found a permanent resting place.

Deputy Ranther drove away from the abandoned farm knowing that he hadn't expected to find anything. He knew why the farmhouse was empty. Still, he was perplexed. There was something about the place that wasn't right. He couldn't quite put his finger on it, but his gut told him something out there just wasn't as it should be.

He decided to talk with one or two of the neighbors. Farmers usually are a pretty close-knit group, especially with the people living around them. He drove down another long, uneven dirt drive dodging eight-inch ruts that bounced him around in his squad car. As he parked, he saw a woman standing behind the front screen door buttoning up a pink sweater. She opened the door a bit as he walked up on the porch.

"Morning, ma'am. My name is John Ranther. I'm with the sheriff's department in Madison County. I'm out here checking on a few things concerning the Stone family. Do you know those folks?"

"Oh, yes," she said. "Please come in." Her tight expression at the sight of a deputy relaxed immediately when he mentioned the Stones. She seated him in the living room and offered him coffee, which he accepted.

While she was in the kitchen he looked at the surroundings. A tapestry of *The Last Supper* covered one wall. Green glass lamps, replicas of kerosene burners stood on end tables next to thick velvet curtains. The drapes seemed somewhat oppressive, but maybe they helped keep out the winter chill. A soot black pot-bellied stove stood in a neatly arranged alcove between the two front rooms. On an upright piano in the dining room the deputy could see a dozen pictures of a boy at various ages. The woman returned with the coffee, smiled and sat down in a rocker across from him.

"I'm so glad you came by," she said. "I've been wondering if anyone would."

"Yes?" he said, sitting forward in his chair.

The woman was toying feverishly with the handle of her coffee cup. He could tell she wanted to talk; he had seen the signs before. Whether her conversation would yield valuable information, or if she just wanted to visit because she was cooped up in this house all day, remained to be determined.

"Well, what I mean is," she went on, "after the accident everyone disappeared and we haven't heard a word from them since."

"Yes, ma'am ... may I get your name?"

"Certainly. Helen Stalnaker. My husband, George, and I have lived here since we got married. Almost 18 years now ... and, of course, our boy, Freddy. That's him." She pointed to the pictures on the piano.

"Did you know the Stones well?"

"Most certainly! Sandra and I were friends. Worked together in 4-H ... went to all the boys' baseball games."

"I understand Mr. Stone was killed in a tractor accident."

"Terrible," she said taking a sip of coffee.

"Can you tell me what happened to the family after that?"

"No. Actually, I can't. I was hoping someone would tell me. One day several weeks after the funeral they all were gone. Didn't tell us anything. And my boy, Freddie, and Danny Stone were real close. He didn't tell Freddie a thing."

"So, you're not collecting their mail, or watching the house?"

"No. Like I said, nobody asked us to. Oh, I watch the place, of course, but nothing official."

"I see." Ranther finished his coffee and picked up his western hat, twirling it on his fingers.

"And it's very strange to me," Mrs. Stalnaker went on, "because Sandra was a very outgoing, energetic person. It wasn't like her to just get up and leave, especially without telling someone she knew."

"Did you know she went to a hospital for psychological treatment after the accident?"

"No, I didn't. Poor dear." The woman sounded truly sympathetic. "Will they be coming back any time soon?"

"I can't answer that. The children had been residing at a temporary foster home up near Madison. They have disappeared from that place. That's why I'm here. Just wanted to see if they'd come back this way."

"Oh, my God!" she exclaimed. She thought for just an instant. "Oh, officer, you must find them. They're such good kids."

"We're doing our very best to find them."

"That makes sense, now that I think about it," she said, peering over her cup. "Yesterday a maroon car drove into the house across the way. Maybe whoever was in it was looking for the children, like you."

"Any other cars been in there since the funeral?"

"Maybe, but yesterday was the first I saw."

"Have any idea who it might've been?"

"Not really. But it was a distinctive color car, bright red with a mix of purple washed in. You know what I mean?"

"Maybe. Any idea?"

"Well, I did see the same color car at the funeral. Talked to the woman who owned it, too. It was Sandra's sister. I don't remember her name. That would make sense, wouldn't it? Her looking for her nieces and nephews."

"Yes, that would make sense. I'd better be going. Thank you for your time, ma'am, and thank you for the coffee."

# 9

SOMETHING HAD TO change today. The four children walked over the next rise in the prairie and looked down on another dirt road. Not more than a half mile away was a stand of naked trees and farm buildings they had not been able to see until they had climbed the shallow hill. It was a large farmstead with several outbuildings surrounding the main house. Danny was suddenly nervous; had they been seen? He wanted to find help, but he didn't want to be discovered. Something about being in charge always came first in his mind. He'd accept assistance since he had to, but he wanted to do things his way.

They all knelt down in the open field. As they watched, it could be seen that there were no animals about the place, no trucks in the driveway, no smoke billowing from the chimney of the house. Everything looked quiet and abandoned.

As they walked up the back way and into the yard, Danny felt a feeling of excitement grow within him. The others, too, sensed that this place was different from all of the other farms they had avoided along their journey. Maybe it would provide them a place to stay awhile and rest, hidden and safe. The corral and chicken coops were empty. Beside the pens stood a large wooden structure with massive 15-foot high doors closed tight, secured with three steel padlocks.

From the size of the building Danny figured a tractor was in there, at least, and maybe a combine, or several farm five-ton grain trucks. They all looked through the boards to see. Sure enough, there was a tractor in there, and a pickup truck and a combine.

A milking shed back of the garage, next to a pole corral, had strands of cracked rubber tubing hanging from wall hooks. Otherwise, it was empty. A tool shack near the back of the house had a vice attached to a warped workbench. Rusty nails littered an oily floor. Piles of filthy frozen rages, useless half buckets of paint and a grease gun, which didn't appear to be in working order, lay about.

When Danny came out of the tool shed, he found the others already in the house. Melissa had her coat off with Mrs. Leatherwood firmly seated on the fireplace mantel, and she was dancing around in the living room.

"It's our new house," she exclaimed, her voice full of exuberance, her face beaming. She could do that. Full of enthusiasm and childish energy, whatever was past, was past. Her disposition always leaned toward being upbeat, optimistic, her attitude had a silver lining and her rosy cherub face infected the others.

Danny forced a smile. But the place was a dump. The front door was gone and all the windows were broken. Spray paint graffiti covered the hearth and walls. Many of the wooden steps leading upstairs were split or missing, probably used for firewood, as the house had obviously been the scene of several parties. Beer bottles and cans littered the place. Cold wind blowing straight through the old house made an eerie whistling sound.

"I don't think this would work, Punkin. With all the windows busted it would always be cold in here."

"I think it would work great, Danny," Chrissy said. "I'm tired of drafty barns and sleeping in the grass."

"It has no windows, Chrissy. We've got to have walls to stay warm."

"We can board up those holes."

"With what? Get down from there," he shouted at Sam as he

climbed up the staircase, over the missing steps, while clinging to the wobbly banister. "We'll go upstairs later."

"With boards from the chicken coop," said Chrissy.

"And let someone driving by on the road see that someone is in the house? No way! Besides, there's no hammer around here, I already checked. We'll sleep in one of the buildings out back."

"Why don't you get us some food and I'll set up a nice area where we can stay awhile," Chrissy said, not willing to let the issue die in the favor of her older brother. She knew he had good intentions, but he wasn't Dad, he didn't know everything. She felt as though the house would serve them best even though it needed a lot of work and cleaning. She looked into his eyes and saw that he wasn't convinced or persuaded. "Look," she said, "we can use the fireplace to cook in, and come here …" she walked around the stairs to the bathroom. "See, I can clean up this tub and we can use it to take a bath. I'm sure there's a well here, just like our place."

The tub and sink were full of crud, scum and beer cans. It would take a lot of work, but boiling water from the fireplace might clean it out.

"Well, you can use the fireplace and the tub, Chrissy, but we're not going to sleep up here. What if some crazy strangers come here to have another party? I don't want to be so close to the road." He looked directly in her eyes. "And that's that!"

"No way, Danny. You go sleep in the dirt. We're staying right here." Chrissy's response was immediate, her voice rising.

Danny stomped his foot and turned in a circle, gathering in what the house had to offer, getting his thoughts in order. When he came full about, Chrissy was looking straight at him. "I've got my reasons, and I say no."

"Why don't you just be the great white hunter and let me take care of the house?"

Melissa giggled. Sam just hung from the banister and watched.

"Look, I know what I'm doing." Chrissy didn't budge.

"Okay, fine." Danny began to nod his head in a semi-threatening, posturing manner. "Just remember. I *can* sleep in one of the back buildings. Let's see if you can eat old beer cans." He headed out the back door. Sam leaped from the banister and sprinted behind him.

It was obvious that this was a working spread; the plowed fields behind the house and the equipment barn were evidence of that. It was just that no one lived on the premises anymore. Danny left the others in the house and took a walk out back. He had to select a suitable building to use for shelter, then he needed to go hunting. He hadn't fired the shotgun since they left the Jameson farm, and he knew he needed to put it to work soon. He thought about devising a hook and pole, too. They had passed an irrigation backwater pit a ways back. Maybe it had some fish in it. First things first, he thought, as he surveyed the outbuildings.

Chrissy was right, the house was the best shelter, if only the windows weren't all broken, and it wasn't right near the road. But it wouldn't do. They had to make camp in the rear. The chicken coops were too flimsy; the old pig stalls too filthy. Finally, Danny decided on the milking shed between the garage and the equipment barn.

The shed had been built apparently for, at most, four cows, and it had a small corral attached to it on the east. Some cleaning would be required, but the walls were solid and tight. Danny would take some shocked corn standing in the stubble ground a quarter mile away and line the new sleeping area with fresh dry straw. He found a scoop shovel with a broken handle behind the tool shack and was hard at work cleaning out the building with Sam when the girls joined them.

"Need some help, Danny?" Chrissy asked.

"I've almost got it," he said without looking up. "You can help me carry back some fresh straw for bedding."

"Go get it then," Chrissy said to the boys, with a hint of reluctance in her voice. "I'll finish cleaning it out. You go with them, Melissa."

The three headed off to the harvested field where the shocks of corn straw stood. They walked past another crumbling wooden pen with a huge round bale of hay tucked in neatly behind it. This hay would serve their needs much better than corn straw. Danny tugged at the baling wire and loaded Sam with a mound of golden hay that covered his head.

As soon as Danny turned and pulled out more hay, Melissa began squealing and dancing about. Danny jumped back with a start. Sam dropped his load of hay. Dozens of field mice bounded pell-mell from the bale, scurrying in every direction. Kiko was delighted as he scampered after one, then another, yelping playfully at the daring mice.

Melissa loved the sight. She shrieked with excitement mixed with apprehension and danced rapidly in place on her tiptoes. Kiko could not keep track of all the bustling rodents, and he jumped a foot from the ground when several of them ran across his paws. Melissa began giggling, still running in place but going nowhere as she clapped her hands in rapid beats.

Sam began laughing, too. The dog kept barking at the numerous mice, snipping at them and snapping his jaws, but he really didn't want anything to do with the little creatures. Danny got tickled, too, listening to the Little Ones' innocent giggles, and he started laughing. Melissa fell in the hay pile behind the pen, and Sam pounded in the pile mound beside her. Danny threw several handfuls of hay on top of them. Soon the mice were gone, but the barking and laughter continued. Chrissy came running to the commotion and looked in amazement behind the pen. The three of them were enveloped in laughter, rolling about in the hay.

\* \* \* \* \*

"Look, I told you, they just ran away."

Lois lit a cigarette and studied Ralph's face. She had just arrived and they were still standing in the farmhouse kitchen. "I don't suppose you helped them along or anything."

"No."

"Kinda pushed them out the door 'cause you weren't used to them?"

"Things weren't going real good … That smartass kid always trying to tell me how to run things. But I didn't do nothing to make them run off." Ralph's words were unconvincing.

"He's 15 years old, for crying out loud. Couldn't you deal with a kid who's barely a teenager?" Lois walked past him into the living room, past Beth. The two women didn't even look at each other.

"Look! You're the one come knocking on my door," Ralph said, his voice losing its defensiveness. "I was trying to help you out." He watched her as she sat, legs crossed in a straight-backed flimsy dinette chair, puffing on her Merit. "Ya know, $400 a month for all the trouble I've been through isn't exactly a king's ransom."

"Just what exactly have you been through, Ralph?" Lois remarked sardonically.

"I'm through with them," Ralph snapped. "Damn kids. I don't want them back … ever. You find them another place."

"Why didn't you call me? I would have done something." Lois tilted her head and lowered her voice. "They're my kin, Ralph. They're just children. If things were getting so bad, you should have let me know."

Ralph was silent.

Lois regarded him, running her eyes over his odd frame, from his tree-trunk arms and thick neck, to his rubbery lips and skinny legs. She remembered quite well the time she first met him.

After Bob left her, she'd remained single for almost five years. Then she met Al, Major Al Devon. What a loser! She had never been away from Nebraska, except to visit someone. Then along came a career Army officer, sharp-pressed uniform, with promises to show her the world. He spent his entire 30-day leave with her. They went to dinner every night; afterward they went dancing or took in a movie. Just like a couple of teenagers. She had been ready for another man in her life — a permanent man. She was sure things would be different.

They continued to write after he went back to his post in Fort Riley, Kansas. She began driving to see him on weekends. He popped the question after a two-month courtship, and they were married two weeks later. Sandra and Frank, she remembered, had driven out to Junction City, Kansas for the ceremony.

All the flowers, sweet smiles and tender kisses ended almost immediately. Al, it turned out, was a practical man. At his age and rank it was in his best interests to have a wife if he expected to get an Army promotion anytime soon. When he went off to serve a hitch in South Korea with the Big Red One, she was left in a one-room officers' apartment with no one to talk to except for other lonely officers' wives, many of whom were pregnant. Daily she listened to dozens of infants crying and screaming and toddlers who created constant noise playing with their toy wagons and trucks.

Ralph was in supply, Staff Sergeant E-6, who unofficially helped newly arriving officers' families get situated on base. He saw to it they had furniture, bedding, drapes, etc. Officially, he was responsible for clothing, batteries, light bulbs, utensils … everything except food and vehicle parts that a mid-grade commissioned officer could want or need. He took a special interest in wives who husbands were on foreign tour. The women gladly accepted his helpfulness, and then giggled to themselves behind his back at his awkward advances.

Ralph was married to Beth at the time, but he ignored her. His liaisons with some of the extremely lonely women were extremely dangerous for his career. First of all, he was a non-com, his association with commissioned personnel was frowned on, except when he was serving an official function. More than that, he was playing with the wives of officers who were certain to cause him serious trouble if he were ever found out. That might well be the lucky outcome, as it wouldn't be beyond the realm of possibility for him to get shot by a jealous husband if his extracurricular activities were discovered.

What Ralph had going for him was that many of the officers weren't paying proper attention to their wives anyway. He took advantage of that fact, milking it at every opportunity.

Lois first met him when he came knocking on her door, introduced himself and asked if there was anything she needed. They were never intimate. She never saw herself in the wildest of situations ever being interested in the gorilla of a sergeant. But she enjoyed the conversation, the helping hand when she needed something done around the apartment. He seemed harmless, friendly, too. She knew what he was up to, but he didn't push the issue.

He told her about a farm he had bought in east central Nebraska, when he learned she was from Omaha, and he told her how he was going to move there as soon as his hitch in the Army was up. Come the following spring he'd have in his 20 years for Uncle Sam. He was going to take it easy, sit back and relax, raise a few chickens and rabbits. Maybe get himself a horse.

That was exactly the time that Sandra and Frank had moved their family, left Kansas City and the city way of life behind, and moved to their new farm. Ralph had given her the address of his place, his retirement farm. It was right outside of Madison, Nebraska. She wrote it down in her address book and promptly forgot about it. That was right at eight years ago.

The following summer Ralph was gone from Ft. Riley, and a year after that the Devons moved to Ft. Leonard Wood, Missouri. A more desolate, barren, godforsaken plot of worthless land Lois had never seen before. She spent most of her time in their modest quarters lamenting her situation. A year later, when Al got orders for West Germany, they divorced. She could have gone with him on this assignment, but she was sick of military housing, sick of Al, and thoroughly disgusted with the U.S. Army. All she'd seen of the world in better than four years living the Army life she could have seen from a bus. A tour from Omaha, to Ft. Riley, to Ft. Leonard Wood, and back to Omaha was a boring tour of the same old flat prairie, buffalo grass and scrawny jackrabbits. All she'd gotten to see was the dregs.

When Frank Stone was killed, it was a knee-jerk reaction on her part to look up Ralph. Sure enough, he was out there in central Nebraska. But instead of working on a constructive hobby, like whittling wildlife figures from maple boughs, he was wasting his life away guzzling Busch in his underwear.

Lois brought her attention back to the issue at hand.

"I'm going up to see my sister from here," she said. "I can't tell her about this until we know where those kids are. I don't really want to tell her about this at all. She doesn't need the pressure." Lois lit another smoke and shifted in her seat. "Do you have any idea where they might be?"

"Some friends of mine and me went out yesterday looking for them. I think they're still close by, I mean, how far can a bunch of kids walk in this weather. The news about them as been in all the newspapers and on the radio. I figure anyone who runs across them will take them into the closest town and turn them in."

"But you didn't find them yesterday," she reminded him.

"Yeah, they've gotten farther out than I thought. By the way, that sheriff guy who came by was asking about the kids' mother. I had to tell him where she was."

"Tell ya what," Lois' tone now was dead serious, "you find the kids before the sheriff, bring them back here safe and sound, and I'll give you an extra $2,000."

"They're going to fight me for sure."

"Tell them I'm coming right out to take them somewhere else. I might even take them back to their old place. Let them take care of themselves. Hell, I'll get their mother out of the hospital and they can take care of her."

"Okay, I'll find them. I don't want the sheriff hounding me

anyway. By the way, you sure are putting a lot of dough into this. Where'd you get it all?"

"That's not your concern. I'm just trying to take care of my sister's kids."

"I've got a real good idea where they're at. I'll get started first thing in the morning."

"If you want another $2,000, and no questions, you'll get started now."

\* \* \* \* \*

As dusk arrived Danny built a small fire behind the milk shed, away from the road. They ate the very last of the food, two cans of sardines. It was saved for last because Danny hated them, the tiny oily fish with their heads still on. They all hated sardines. Those were Ralph's snacks; he ate them with chips and beer. Danny was disgusted just by the thought of sardines — but it was all they had to eat. Kiko loved the little fish, but his entire meal consisted of one fish and the privilege to lick out the can.

Up to now they had been drinking pond water and managed to get by. But that was getting hard to tolerate, and they were all constantly thirsty. The Little Ones needed some juice or milk. Sam definitely needed something for his cold.

They were dirty and tired, but happy. Danny noticed a new brightness that had come to Chrissy's usually sad eyes. Despite all the miles they had covered, she had remained strong. The other night she had asked about plans — she wanted to make plans — yet she waited for him to decide — she had faith in him. Today, she made her point about sleeping in the wrecked house, but she hadn't belabored the point.

Danny knew he never could have gotten this far without her. Whenever Melissa cried, Christine would rock her. Whenever Sam had a complaint, she would give him her immediate attention and whisper to him. Danny promised himself they would make it. They would see their mother soon, no excuses or sidetracks.

Chrissy sat outside the shed in the falling rays of dusk and wrote another letter to their mother. She had lost count of how many she had written to her since she had gone to the hospital. Almost daily she had given Ralph letters to mail, hoping he would put them in the mailbox on his trips into Madison, but she really didn't know what happened to them. She didn't have any money for postage. All she could do was hope. Once she even approached Beth and asked her to mail a letter. All Chrissy received from Beth for the effort was a pained expression and a curt wave of her hand, as though it was, oh, such a bother even to be asked to do something as complicated as mail a letter.

*Dear Mama,*

*I sure do hope you are feeling better. As each new sunrise welcomes a new day it also brings you the time you need to get better. I've been taking good care of the Little Ones. Sam has a cold right now, but I'm keeping him as warm as I can. Melissa is doing fine. Danny has grown up so much in the past few weeks and months. He's more bullheaded than Daddy was, but he tries to do right. He's always around to help. He misses baseball a lot, but he knows he has to do more things now.*

*As I've written you before, I wish you hadn't let Aunt Lois send us to the Jameson's, but if it helps you get well, it will all work out. I sure do miss you, Mama. Please come home soon. I think we can take care of you if you will just let us try. I love you, Mama.*

*Chrissy*

Then, as for every letter preceding this one, she fashioned an envelope from a blank sheet of paper and nestled it with the stack that now lined the bottom of her knapsack. She lay down with the others, who were already asleep, her pack as her pillow. They were all well into dreamland, asleep in each other's arms, even before the moon had risen.

A low guttural growl snapped Danny awake. He opened his eyes to a scene that made him suck up his breath. In front of him, in the darkness of the milk shed, were two yellow eyes peering directly at him. Danny reached for his shotgun, but he couldn't feel it. He forgot where he had left it. The growl was coming from Kiko. A thick, dreadful tension filled the darkness.

Danny sat up, motionless, frozen with fear. At that very instant he prayed that the others were asleep; he hoped no one would move. He was utterly defenseless. There was nothing within his reach to use as a weapon. The transfixed glowing eyes watched him, unblinking. If only these were the eyes of a friendly neighboring farm dog just checking out the visitors. Deep inside he knew they weren't.

Beside him in the darkness he felt one of his siblings move, and a voice asked, "What's that noise?"

"Be quiet," Danny whispered, just before all hell broke loose.

Kiko tore into the animal behind the yellow eyes. His charge was vicious and swift. Danny heard ivory-fanged jaws snap in savage ripping and tearing as the shed seemed to explode. The animals crashed and tumbled around the small shed, pounding against the slats that made up the building. The entire shed shook in the melee.

All the children were now awake, crying and clutching one another as they huddled in a far corner away from the door. Moonlight illuminated the brutal fight.

Kiko was engaged in a pitched life and death battle with a mottled straw-and-gray-colored animal. The attacks and counters were ferocious. The growls from both combatants rumbled up from the bottom of hell. Danny quickly realized that his pet dog was locked in a deadly combat with a starving coyote, putting his life on the line for them without hesitation.

The girls screamed; Melissa clamped her tiny arms about Chrissy's neck. Danny searched the walls of the shed for his shotgun. He left it in the house, he remembered. In the house ... how stupid.

Blood and hair flew about the shed. The snarls increased in

volume. Only complete exhaustion or death would end this fight.

Kiko was fighting with his heart, as much as with his body. He was an old dog. His old slack muscles were stretching and tearing under the tremendous effort. Danny could see that the coyote was lame. Kiko had a large bleeding wound on the side of his head, one ear was torn in half. Each animal was attempting to clamp down on the other's neck, or slash across, with teeth or claw, their opponent's tender under-belly.

At brief moments the two animals would separate and circle, tongues lolling at full length, then smash back together. In a quick lunge the coyote's serrated teeth clamped down on Kiko's right foreleg, the crunching sound of breaking bone was unmistakable.

Because of Kiko's black hair it was impossible to see the full extent of his injuries. Yet they could all see massive amount of blood on the coyote, both his and Kiko's.

Danny was amazed at Kiko's continued fighting strength and tenacity. The dog outweighed the wild animal by a few pounds, but the old dog wasn't nearly as agile or quick. The coyote was young and used to fighting and killing as a means to survive.

Again they smashed together in a ball of flying fur. In the next split second, while the coyote was off balance, teetering on a lame hind leg, Kiko struck and clamped his canine fangs into its neck. In one mighty tearing bite he ripped open the coyote's throat. Kiko kept improving his strangle death-hold until the coyote's head hung loosely in his jaws.

Kiko had won!

Sam was the first to rush to his side as Danny carried the carcass of the bloody coyote from the milk shed and threw it behind a tree. Kiko was panting heavily, bleeding profusely from his head wound. He had another nasty tear of the flesh on his chest. As soon as the children reached him, he lay down in the whipped-up straw and his eyes began to glaze. Melissa began to sob while repeating her dog's name over and over and over. Chrissy held his head in her lap, put a cloth over his ripped ear and petted his head.

About an hour after the fight ended, Kiko closed his eyes forever. He knew he had saved his friends.

The children were not going to get any sleep that night. Under the eerie light of the moon reflecting off the barren fields Danny used the shovel with the broken handle and dug a grave for Kiko in the overgrown remnants of a garden plot behind the house. Melissa made a bed of straw for him in the hole. Sam insisted they say a prayer.

"It's all my fault," Danny said as he worked, his eyes red, his nose runny. "I should have had the gun close by."

"It's not your fault, Danny," Chrissy tried to console him. He had raised that dog from a pup. His dad had gotten it for him the first year they moved to the farm. "There's no way you could have been ready for that coyote."

"It is, too," he insisted. His voice sounded reasonably steady, but he was heartsick. Danny was crying, though he tried desperately not to let it show. It was okay to be sad, but he wasn't going to start bawling like a girl.

"I could have built the fire by the door. I should have buried those sardine cans, or taken them away from the shed." What emotions he hid from himself about crying he heaped all over his head with second-guessing and self-incrimination. "It's all my fault."

Sam tried to console his big brother, too. "It's not your fault, Danny. Don't blame yourself. Kiko is in heaven now."

Melissa made a marker, a cross with two sticks and a piece of string. They all knelt around the grave and held hands. Chrissy had to cover the grave. Danny just knelt there and stared into the hole.

"Kiko would want us to go on," Chrissy said in a somber but firm tone. "He would want us to stay together and help each other."

Danny didn't seem to hear. He didn't acknowledge the Little Ones kneeling on either side of him. He talked to the grave. "You … were … such … a good dog," his words faltered as his voice cracked. The others had to help him to his feet as dawn began to break in the east. They all walked back to the shed.

# 10

THE ORANGE HORIZON in the western sky signaled the passing of another day as Deputy Ranther pulled his squad car into his home driveway. His wife's Chevy was already inside the garage. He couldn't think of too many evenings when she didn't beat him home. Yet, she worked long hours herself as a claims representative for a crop insurance company. She practically ran the field office in Madison. Mary Ranther always tried to be home by six; home to welcome her husband, home to share time with him, just the two of them.

John was troubled tonight more than just a little bit. Other cases, he knew, sometimes took time to develop. Steadfast investigation would often turn up new leads that finally uncovered a clue that solved the crime. But with children missing, he didn't have the luxury of a long drawn-out investigation. Time was his enemy. He hated to think abut it, but the fact remained, the Stone children had been gone for 12 days, and he had no idea where they were.

An aroma of spicy deep-fried chicken greeted him as he entered the house. All without thinking, his western hat went on the hook at the left side of the mantel, his holster over on the right. He pulled off his boots without sitting and rubbed both hands deeply into his tired pliable face, giving his temples the extra benefit of a tension-relieving massage. The whereabouts of the Stone children continued to eat at him. Until he found them, until he had them back in safe surroundings, or properly buried, if that's what it came to, he wasn't going to be able to concentrate on much else. The gravity of the situation worked against his usual sunny disposition. Nothing, however, interfered with his considerable appetite, especially when it involved his wife's home cooking.

Mary heard him come in, pleased that he was home a little earlier than usual, and she received her perfunctory peck on the cheek with a smile. The kiss had meaning in its very brevity. It said "hello," "How are you," "I'm fine, how was your day?" and "I love you" all rolled together. When they ate and talked, they would expound upon the specifics of their workday.

They had been married 11 years, without children. They had a happy marriage, but Mother Nature hadn't blessed them with a child. The doctor said it probably wouldn't happen. John washed his hands and poured himself a large glass of cold fresh milk. He dug into two hot greasy pieces of chicken while Mary placed the hot bread and vegetables on the table.

"Your chicken is the greatest, honey."

She tilted her head and smiled. "You act like you're starved."

"Didn't get a chance to eat lunch," he said, reaching for a biscuit.

She sat down beside him and daintily nibbled through a salad. "Busy day?"

His brow creased and he paused in his eating. She waited for him to answer in his circumspect way. "Those kids ... can't get a handle on them. Nobody has seen hide nor hair of 'em."

"Maybe they're long gone. Maybe they got carried clear to Missouri or Kansas before you got on the case, dear," she said.

"Maybe ... but I don't really think so. No, I think they're still in the county." He filled his mouth up again with chicken and mashed potatoes.

Mary sipped her coffee, waiting for her husband to speak again. They were the same age, but to look at the two of them together one might think he was her father. His features were so weather-beaten, hers very soft and demure. They looked like the bear and the fawn. Her layered red hair contrasted greatly with his thinning top, and her petite frame was dwarfed by his sheer height and endowed belly. He was her strength and gallant knight. She polished his rough edges and mollified the stress his job put him through. Maybe because it was just the two of them their dedication to one another remained fresh and alive.

"No," he continued, "I think they ran away, and … they didn't have any help doing it. I think they're holed up someplace, freezing, hungry and without any idea of what to do next."

"What are you going to do?"

"That's what I've been racking my brain about." He showed his wife the pictures of the four.

"Oh, John, they look just adorable." She put her hand on his arm. "You've got to find them. Whatever drove them away from where they were living … these two here are nothing more than babies."

"Yes, dear, I know."

Mary Ranther walked to the kitchen window, peering out over her steaming cup of coffee into the falling veil of darkness. It had started to snow, and the wind was picking up. "I hope they are in a truck stop, or something, John. Maybe someone has found them and just hasn't reported it yet. It's going to be so cold tonight. That storm the weather bureau has been forecasting for the past two days is supposed to hit tonight." She bit her lip as she turned back toward her husband. Her face had worry written all over it. "It's supposed to be the coldest night of the year."

\* \* \* \* \*

Lois Devon drove her four-door Thunderbird past the black wrought iron gates. The ornamental ironwork was set in a prodigious stone fence made of blond prairie limestone. A leafless canopy of elm trees bordered the roadway leading up to the administration building. The buildings and grounds looked so quiet and calm, pretentious and disconcerting all at the same time. Lois checked in at the office, and then was escorted to the social room in the women's dormitory by a girl who introduced herself as Nancy.

Sandra Stone had been sleeping when her sister arrived, as her disheveled hair and tired red eyes attested. But she recognized her sister, returned a polite but unenthusiastic smile, and let Lois plant a pecking kiss on her cheek. The room looked like an oversized living room, replete with overstuffed furniture and massive table lamps. The walls were adorned with several portraits of past hospital administrators, and were illuminated with tiny lights set in the lower part of the frames.

Some people get a gold watch to remember their careers when they retire and move on, Lois thought. If you were a big shot at a major medical institution, your successors hung your portrait in the lobby, halls or waiting rooms for total strangers to get a glimpse of how these people saw themselves, and to see how hot light makes old paint peel. Having one's likeness in this gallery probably meant you were dead as well, Lois surmised.

"I'll leave you two alone," said the girl, uniformed in a pink cotton dress that designated the volunteer workers. "Let me know if you need anything," she said to Lois.

"Thank you, Nancy."

The two women sat together on a dark green couch, and Lois reached out and held her sister's hand. Lois was taken aback by the cool, damp feel of Sandra's palm, but she tried to ignore it, focusing instead on her sister's tired face.

"So, how have you been, sweetie?"

"Things are fine. I wish I had another roommate."

"What's the matter?"

"Oh … she's crazy," Sandra said as she looked about the room. Lois had the distinct feeling, however, that she was inspecting the ceiling.

"Look here, sweetie. I have some letters from the children."

"Oh, good." Sandra's eyes lit up. "I've been wanting to hear from them so bad. Are any of them with you?" Her eyes were now afire with delight and her face radiated even without makeup. The women's father was of Italian descent, and both of them had dark eyes and hair with a permanent tanned hue to their skin. But Lois envied Sandra's youthful glow. Her younger sister looked ten years younger than her actual age, and that after having four children.

"No, dear, they're in school today."

Sandra nodded.

She opened the first letter, and a genuine smile raised the corners of her lips as her eyes followed the handwriting on the page. "I don't know why that boy can't write his own letter," she said as she read thoughts from Danny, written by Chrissy. Lois had brought her two letters. When Sandra finished reading them, she folded them neatly, put them back in the envelopes, and held them tightly in her hands.

"How are they?"

"They're fine, sweetie. They're fine."

"I was wondering why Chrissy hadn't written me. She writes so much … she's such a good writer." Sandra raised the letters in her lap and gestured to them. "In all my letters I've asked her to write me."

"I know, but the doctor asked me to hold the letters in the beginning."

"Umh! I'm about tired of the good doctor. These people have been spending all of my time, and their time, to get me to let go of Frank. They act like I thought it was my fault." Even at the moment a tear began to build up in the corner of her eye. "I know it wasn't my fault … I was just so sad." She reached over and hugged her sister.

"Now, now."

"I'm going to get out of here soon, you know." Sandra's voice carried an anxiety that traveled beneath her words. "I can't stay here forever."

Lois knew that was true. But for now she was still here, and apparently satisfied about her children. "I've got to go now, sweetie. Take good care of yourself. I'll take good care of everything."

Lois stood and looked at her sister's hopeful expression. "Is everything okay with the farm, too?" Lois nodded affirmatively. "I know Danny can take care of things," Sandra said.

Lois blew her sister a kiss as she walked out the door. She still had time.

\* \* \* \* \*

For the next week the children worked feverishly to improve the livability of the abandoned farmstead they had accidentally discovered. The place was becoming a new home. Melissa kept the milk shed clean and replaced the hay bedding every other day so that they had a comfortable place to sleep. Sam cleaned the beer cans from the fireplace and made trip after trip for dead tree limbs and old boards so they had a plentiful supply of cooking firewood. Chrissy took water from the operational well and tried to clean out the filthy bathtub in the house. But her efforts were futile. The tub was rusted out and would not drain. She found a 55-gallon barrel that had been cut in half. They set it up in a back room, boarded up the window and took baths in that.

Danny improvised a hook, line and pole from makeshift materials in the musty tool shed. Over the years, so much dirt and grime had accumulated in the small building that even the walls and windows were coated in a tacky layer of oily dust. But he found what he needed to do some fishing. He bent and cleaned some rusty nails, and cut off a broom handle to use as a pole. There was plenty of old string in the shed, although black with grease, but it served his purpose as fishing line.

Every day he made the two-mile walk to the end of the barbed wire fence line and the irrigation backwater pit located there. The water was muddy, but deep, and the hungry catfish struck at anything he threw in the pit. Danny felt a strange, sad justice as he split the dead coyote through the belly and used its liver to bait his hook.

Each time he hooked a fish he had to run backward, up the shallow bank that lined the pit, because he had no way to reel in his catch. He pulled them far enough out of the water that they couldn't get back in, and let them flip around in the dirt while he baited his bent-nail hook.

The catfish made for a bland diet without any butter, salt or pepper to cook them with, but it kept them full. One day he shot down a dove, which was tasty, but hardly a meal for even one of them. Another day, while walking to the catfish pit, he startled a gorgeous cock pheasant; its dazzling golden red and green feathers cast a vivid hue against the morning sky. It flushed with a quick rustle of its wings and waffling of air that made Danny jump, but the bird was well within his range. His trained eye and steady hand brought it down with a single shot. The bird folded in mid-flight and fell back to earth. That day they ate well.

The children got through a loose slat in the locked building that housed the tractor and pickup. Sam climbed directly into the cab of the giant New Holland tractor. The massive machine sported an audio cassette player and an air conditioner. Its harvest orange paint with white trim attested to the fact that this was a new rig, modern, with the power and technology to cultivate a field in hours, not days. The Stone farm never had a machine anything close to this.

Sam daydreamed about working a machine like this one around his own farm some day. The little boy had worshipped his father, and if farming was good enough for his dad, then it was good enough for him. Unlike Danny, who was born and spent his early years growing up in the suburbs of Kansas City, Sam had never lived anywhere other than the farm. Sam had been born on a windy October afternoon, and in his early years his dad tried to hang the nickname Dusty on him. His mother objected and stifled others in the family from using the name — so it didn't stick.

Sam bounced in the tractor seat and made engine noises. At seven years old he had an intense imagination; he was rolling down the back quarter section. He was plowing the land.

Danny, on the other hand, had more practical pursuits in mind. He checked the pickup for keys. There were none around. The old Dodge Ram had traveled many ruts and furrows in its day, but Danny would have driven it if he could. He still had another year to go before he could get his driver's license, but his dad had taught him how to drive. He had driven the family pickup all around the farm, though not to town. They needed some transportation to get to Omaha. They couldn't stay here forever, and they couldn't walk all the way either. Maybe he'd be able to figure out a way to get the Dodge started. If he did get it running, he would worry about getting the truck back here later, after they were reunited with their mother.

Several days went by and they rested. The infrequent vehicles that drove by never came into the driveway, and for the time being, they were content to stay right where they were. Chrissy wrote her letters and kept them neatly in the bottom of her knapsack. Danny tried to make some plans. But he didn't really know what the next leg of their journey had in store. Even if things all went their way, he didn't know how far they had to go, or how he would handle things when they got to their mother's location. Nevertheless, he tried to come up with ideas and think ahead. He began to understand that without experience it's hard to consider everything that might come up.

On the afternoon of their seventh day at the abandoned farmhouse the weather began to change. It had been warm and pleasant just the day before. The nights were still cold, but all of the previous snowfall had melted. They had all been encouraged to hope for some extended spring-like weather, even in October in Nebraska.

The wind began to pick up, building speed that blew briskly from the north, pushing puffy white clouds quickly across the sky.

A front had come through.

An hour or so before dusk the snow began to fall. At first, the flakes came straight down, light, almost caressing the ground as they gently covered the farmstead in a fresh blanket of white. As the sun sank below the horizon, the sky turned an iron gray.

Then snowflakes descended in tumbling curtains that twisted and blew like ghost draperies as updrafts and cross winds buffeted them about.

There was no moon to be seen in the sky that night. As darkness engulfed them, the heavens grew black and the wind picked up, creating a howling cry that sounded through the trees and cracks in the buildings.

The children took refuge in the milk shed. Danny closed the door he had built onto the shed and barred it, but still the snow and wind seeped through the cracks and crevices. The shed shook in the onslaught as the storm grew in strength and force, and incessant gusts pulsated the structure.

Worst of all, the temperature continued to drop. They had no fire in the milk shed as they did their cooking in the house. They hadn't stocked wood near the shed; it was too dangerous to build a fire in it anyway. They were warm enough sleeping together in the hay, and Danny installed the door from the one in the house to keep out any roaming predators. They huddled together and listened to the roar of the blizzard.

The Little Ones usually fell asleep soon after darkness fell, but tonight sleep was impossible. The wind howled in an undulating groaning pitch; the gnawing cold forced them all to rub themselves and move their extremities. They knew the snow was drifting high around the shed. They heard loose debris flying by in the driving wind, hitting farm buildings, smashing into trees.

Little did they know that they were right in the middle of the worst winter storm to hit the High Plains in ten years. The weather bureau predicted snowfall amounts exceeding two feet to accumulate in the next 24 yours. Temperatures would sink to minus readings. The storm was coming fast and hitting hard.

Danny now wished he had boarded up the old house's windows and doors. Nobody would have seen that from the road. Why hadn't he gone along with Chrissy when they talked about it? He knew she had made a good case for using the house. They would now be in a structure that could withstand Mother Nature's violence.

He knew they were not inside a safe shelter at the moment. The shed was nothing but a bunch of boards nailed in a row, no reinforcement and no inner support. In reality, they were out in the open. Snow sifted inside the shed dusting their clothes with glittering crystals. The wind grew in intensity, forcing snow into the shed through the cracks, building up little piles of snow in the corners.

A slat broke off and flew away. Nails popped, the entire shed shuddered and shook. The roof began to go. One by one the boards were pried loose, and finally the milk shed blew apart and flew from them as it disappeared with the wind. A blast of freezing cold hit their faces. Thousands of grains of frozen ice beat on them as though they were being pelted with volley after volley of steel BBs. The wind knocked Melissa backward, rolling her several feet across the ground. The driving snow made it impossible to see.

Danny grabbed Melissa by the collar of her coat and began screaming at the top of his lungs for them to break for the house. His voice was inaudible, sucked away by the wind even as the words left his mouth. He grabbed Sam's coat collar, too, and with his back to the wind began inching toward the only shelter that could possibly save them.

It was impossible to breathe. The knife-sharp bitter cold cut through to the bone. The vicious howling wind sucked at the fragile foursome like a powerful current trying to hurl them into the barren fields. Danny felt Chrissy's grip like a vice on his upper arm. They were moving backward, she was pulling him from behind.

Danny fell on his butt, yet he kept inching backward, his hands tightly gripping his little brother and sister. The sanctuary of the old farmhouse was only a few dozen yards away, but it felt like a hundred miles.

He made it to the side of the house and an open window. He threw Melissa's body through the broken opening. Sam clung to Danny's leg for dear life. Even as they were just within the arms of safety, the mighty wind increased its roaring moans. The force of the blizzard wind threatened to pluck them from the side of the house and throw them into the freezing cornfields. Danny's eyes were squeezed shut; he was doing everything by feel. He reached down and snatched Sam up by the zipper of his coat, raised him to his chest and quickly hugged him before he threw him through the window.

Danny couldn't breathe; his fingers and ears were numb. He leaned down near the foundation to inhale. He couldn't feel Christine. He screamed out, but he couldn't hear the sound of his own voice. He pulled himself inside the house, cutting his forearm on the broken shard of glass in the window frame. From there he led the Little Ones to the center of the house where they huddled under the staircase.

"Stay right here!" Danny instructed as he looked into the eyes of his baby brother and sister. "Rub your cheeks and ears … that's the only way to get some warmth," he yelled over the fury of the violent wind.

Melissa was sobbing, a combination of fear and cold. The wailing of the wind through the empty house, void of windows and doors, sounded like a locomotive roaring down the hall.

"I've got to find Chrissy."

"I'll take care of her," Sam said in his little big man voice, and he put his arm around Melissa.

"I'll be right back!"

Danny sprinted to the back of the house, which was on the downwind side of the storm. He moved to the side where the three of them had come through the open window, and he looked down the length of the building. He could only see 15 or 20 feet at best, and there was no sign of Chrissy. He ran once around the house, then back to the staircase to see if she'd made it inside. The Little Ones were huddled together, but no Chrissy.

Danny was at a loss; a confused panic began to overtake him. She was right with us, he thought. She was holding on to me as we got near the window, wasn't she? Did something happen to her when I fell? Did she lose her grip? Is she out in the field freezing?

He ran to the bedroom window and began screaming her name, but his words were blown back into his face. Outside in the blizzard he could not see. He couldn't even see the equipment barn directly in front of him. He could run out in the snow, but where would he look? A total fear and dread engulfed him; he felt weak in his knees. If there was anything to do to rescue his sister, he would do it. But what? He couldn't risk running out into the freezing snowstorm and not be able to make it back. Someone had to protect the Little Ones. He screamed out the window again. His heart pumped adrenaline through his veins; he couldn't catch his breath, his mind spun with fear. Oh, God, maybe she got in the equipment building, he prayed. He had no choice but to go back to the stairway and huddle with the Little Ones. The direct blast of the wind did not hit them there, and together they were able to bear the bite of the cold. The Little Ones clung to him as much for support as for warmth. They waited in the darkness with wide eyes and chattering teeth. Chrissy was lost in the freezing blackness of the storm.

# 11

DEPUTY RANTHER FLIPPED to the page in his notebook with the address and phone number where Sandra Stone was a resident. It was information Ralph Jameson had given him. He didn't have a name to associate with the location he was calling, but he assumed it was part of the state's mental health network. What with psychiatric hospitals, group homes, group therapy clinics … the list of mental health centers throughout the state was a lengthy one. She could be in almost any kind of facility.

The phone was answered by a friendly voice: "Omaha Residential Center."

"Yes. My name is Deputy Ranther. I'm with the Madison County Sheriff's Department. I need to speak with someone about a Sandra Stone whom you have as a resident there."

"Let me connect you with the administrator's office."

The wait was short, and then a man with a high-pitched, squeaky voice came on the line.

"This is Duncan. How may I help you?"

Deputy Ranther repeated his name and the purpose of his call. He was put on hold for what seemed an eternity; finally the squeaky voice was back on the line.

"I'm sorry, Sheriff, but we don't have a Sandra Stone in residence here. I'm positive … checked both our inpatient and out-patient lists."

"Could she have checked out?"

"Nope. I checked on that, too. Nobody by that name has been here all year."

Ranther could hear the falsetto voice speak with a tone of self-assurance. In a way, he appreciated the administrator's effort, the fact that he checked all the records, but he was getting the wrong answers.

"Well, Mr. Duncan, it's imperative I reach this woman …"

"Last name's not Duncan," the administrator interrupted, "that's my first name. I go by it."

"Okay, Duncan," Ranther said, rubbing his tightly wrinkled forehead. He didn't need any more dead ends. An unusual gnawing in the pit of his stomach gripped him, a feeling close to panic. He felt each minute and hour as it slipped away as though the passing of time was taking a piece out of him with each vanished second.

He'd already heard reports that more than 400 cattle had frozen to death during the blizzard last night.

"As I was saying, I'm trying to reach someone who is caring for Mrs. Stone so she can be made aware, when the time is right, that her children are missing from their foster home." Ranther paused, but there was nothing but silence on the other end. "Are you positive there's no Sandra Stone at your facility?"

"You know, she might be across town," Duncan replied.

The administrator did not comment on the missing children, but began mumbling on the line like he was talking to himself.

"Is their phone number similar to yours?"

There was another long pause. "No, it's not. It's 315-6714. Maybe you've gotten the wrong number, Sheriff," Duncan said slowly and deliberately with an accusatory inflection.

Ranther quickly popped another question. "Mrs. Stone lived on a farm near the town of Albion. Could you tell me what the nearest mental health facility in that area would be?"

"I could tell you where *all* the branches are if you really need them, but you can get that information at your local library, too,"

Duncan replied, obviously perturbed now.

"No, just that one, if you would, Duncan. You've been very helpful." Ranther smiled to himself. Seemed that Duncan was more comfortable with his files, rosters and computers than with the general public. The man helped run a facility that had a purpose of assisting people come to terms with themselves and improve their relationships with others. They probably did a good job of it, too, but Ranther couldn't help thinking that Duncan himself was more a man who liked working alone, and was happiest shuffling reams of meaningless paper rather than dealing with people.

"Nearest branch clinic with inpatient services," said Duncan when he came back on the line, "is in Norfolk."

"Do you have the address handy?"

"Yes. 1700 Western Avenue. You think she's there?"

"I really don't know, but thanks for your help. A number of things have been strange about this case, and something just tells me that Norfolk might be exactly where Mrs. Stone is staying."

\* \* \* \* \*

The storm's howling wind pounded the decaying farmhouse throughout the night. Unpruned branches scraped against the house, forced by the wind, banging, scratching in a whipped fury. The noise was incessant. Danny, Sam and Melissa huddled against the hallway wall, but the sub-zero temperature still froze any exposed skin.

Danny patted and rubbed the Little Ones, and huddled them close to him.

A crashing explosion pricked up their ears. The buckling warble of corrugated metal smashing against itself, hitting the ground, tumbling, crashing into the trees, bouncing across the cornfield. The old rusty grain silo had come apart; its heavy slabs of ribbed steel being hurled into the countryside like aluminum foil. Danny wondered if the chimney would be next. It already leaned at a precarious angle atop the house. No one wanted to think what might happen if it toppled and came crashing through the roof.

The wind rushed through the open house, wailed like a freight train flying down inclined rails, its cold edge sliced at their clothes and faces, its fury rammed against them, slapping them at will, scratching their skin with burning blasts of frozen breath. Danny protected the Little Ones, prying his mind away from his own discomfort. All he could think about was what had happened to Chrissy.

Morning light began to thin the black mantel of the storm. The intensity of the wind diminished. It was still snowing, but the oppressive force of the driven flakes subsided and the temperature seemed to rise if only because the wind was not so intense.

"Come on," Danny demanded of the Little Ones. "We've got to move around … we've got to find Chrissy."

On the northern side of the house the snow was piled higher than the windows. There was no walking around that way. On the downwind side, the side where Danny had thrown the Little Ones through the broken window, the ground was void of snow. The force of the wind had carried all snow past this side of the house. The fields were clear; the only drifts were next to the farms outbuildings. Danny ran past the equipment barn, with his back to the falling wind, and forced his eyes to focus out across the barren cornfield. Ice crystals on the ground reflected back the sunlight harshly into his eyes, and he could see nothing unusual out in the fields.

He went from the chicken coops, to the barn, to the tool shed, to the equipment barn hollering Chrissy's name, but he received no response.

Danny was exhausted from the cold, sleepless night. His lips were sore and cracked, his head ached. Inside his stomach growled with a pang of emptiness. He made a snowball from the dry snow and licked. It wet his tongue, but made his stomach growl all the more.

In all the directions there was nothing unusual to be seen. The gut-wrenching anxiety that he'd felt throughout the night grew in his stomach. It was the same hollow hopelessness he'd experienced the day his dad died, and the afternoon when he thought Melissa had been trampled by the bull. The idea that Chrissy may have died in the storm was bad enough; not knowing where she was, that was even worse.

Ecstatic, excited cries turned his attention back to the house. As he ran in the direction of the voices, he heard the Little Ones calling, "Chrissy, Chrissy. She's here! It's Chrissy."

Danny's legs couldn't carry him fast enough. What had they found? Was she alive?

Sam ran into him as he ran through the back door; Danny almost knocked the little kid to the ground. Sam was pumped, his eyes wide, he was ready to spread the news to everyone around. Danny waited a split second as Sam tried to catch his breath, pointing his finger to the kitchen as he drew in air. "It's Chrissy!"

"Where?"

"In the cellar."

"What!"

The little tike turned and ran. He threw open a thin cupboard-looking door. It was nothing more than a sheet of masonite board painted white, and it tethered on a single hinge as Sam threw it open. A rusted-out water heater sat off to the side, sagging shelves that once held canned goods were on the left. Danny had opened this door before, but it looked like nothing more than an empty pantry.

"She's down there," Sam cried as Danny just stood and stared into the small room.

Danny peered into the darkness, but before he could articulate his confusion Sam jumped into the dark room, and Danny could hear him bounding down a flight of wooden steps. "Come on!"

Danny felt his way into the darkened pantry, knelt and found the steps, which didn't have a railing, and took one step at a time down into the musty cellar. The room smelled like cold, stale dirt. One narrow basement window let in a single ray of sunlight. In the beam of light danced whirls of dust and ice crystals. When he reached the bottom, Danny took tentative steps toward Sam's voice. Each step on the dirt floor felt different, one step his foot touched something soft and mushy. On another, he kicked a mound of accumulated dirt. A puff exploded on the floor and filled the basement with a cloud of dust.

"Over here," called a high-pitched voice. Melissa was down in the cellar, too. It was difficult to see. The shaft of light coming through the window was useless for seeing, but the Little Ones had found something under the window. Their voices urged him to hurry.

"We heard her groaning," Sam said as Danny neared.

Danny knelt between them and felt Chrissy's chilled, clammy skin. She was moaning, but did not answer when he called her name. "We've got to get her upstairs."

The cellar was about half the size of the kitchen itself, and directly under it. It may have served as a refrigerator of sorts; certainly canned foods had been stored there. Danny felt Chrissy's face and limbs. He put his arms under hers, lifted her torso and began shuffling toward the rickety stairs. "Pick up her legs," he instructed the Little Ones. Chrissy increased her moaning as they moved.

Danny inched up the stairs on his backside, scooting step by step toward the upper landing, with Chrissy being pulled along on his lap. Melissa and Sam went ahead to heat fresh water.

When he reached the light filtering into the pantry atop the upper landing, he paused a moment and looked over his semiconscious sister. Her hair was full of mud, but she didn't appear to be cut anywhere. He lifted her up and carried her into the kitchen.

A knot the size of a golf ball was just above her forehead. Her eyelids were bluish, as well as the tips of her ears. "We need blankets," he hollered through the drafty house, "and make an ice pack." It seemed so ironic to him that her head bump required a cold compress. Ice was the one thing they had plenty of.

Gloves were still on her hands, and Danny removed them and checked her fingers. They were okay. He checked her arms again.

Sam ran in carrying a gunnysack remnant filled with snow. "Bring in fresh straw and make a bed under the stairway," Danny said. Sam glanced at his half-frozen sister, then ran out immediately, without question or comment, to fulfill his task.

Melissa struggled in with an oversized milk bucket a third full of water. She had Mrs. Leatherwood's shawl in her hand, and she dipped it in the water and began wiping mud from Chrissy's face. When her gaze met Danny's, their fiery brown eyes looked in the other's, she said, "It was the only clean cloth around. Mrs. Leatherwood wanted to help, too." Danny nodded and tried to smile, but couldn't. He held Chrissy in his lap on the kitchen floor as Melissa talked softly and wiped her face with the wet shawl.

Danny knew they didn't have any blankets, and the Little Ones didn't waste time correcting him. When the hay bed was ready, they built the fire to a roaring hot blaze and lay Chrissy near it, covering her with another layer of hay. Danny set about nailing slats and old boards over the broken window openings. Until she woke up, if she woke up, there was no way of knowing what happened last night. She was breathing well. Until she told them where she hurt, there was little they could do. She didn't look too bad, considering she had spent a night unconscious in a freezing cellar.

The three of them spent the day watching Chrissy, washing her face, combing her hair, touching her, talking to her. During the day Danny cooked three catfish in the fireplace. The three of them ate as they maintained their vigil.

The Little Ones fell asleep in the middle of the day. The wind was calm now, the sun bright, and the temperature outside a bone-numbing, deep-freeze cold. Danny, too, finally fell asleep. It was barely three in the afternoon. By dusk the fire was nothing but glowing embers. The exhausted Stone children were deep in restful repose, huddled together, much warmer in the old house than the milk shed had ever been. A full moon rose and lit the night sky, reflecting ice crystals in the snowdrifts, the dazzling northern light of Nebraska, the starlit radiance of the frozen high plains. The Stone children slept.

# 12

BACK IN OMAHA the following Monday morning Aunt Lois was at her office desk right at 8 a.m. Hunt Building Contractors, Developers and Real Estate Brokers it read on the door. Part of her work was keeping track of costs on new commercial building projects; part was inputting data into the computer. Today, with most everyone else late arriving she was answering the telephone.

Her boss, Dan Hunt, had started out almost 20 years ago building detached garages for homeowners in the older neighborhoods of Omaha. He graduated to erecting one and two-story brick warehouses, then to large tilt-wall jobs in the new industrial parks. Nowadays, a 15-story office building was a piece of cake for the company, and the Hunt Brothers had built retail strips in every corner of the city. If the price was right, they'd build someone a tree house, and with their connections, Lois would bet money they could get it financed, too.

Lois rummaged through the classified newspaper ads between incoming phone calls and sips on her cup of steaming coffee. She never used sugar, but she doctored the beverage with enough Cof-fee-Mate to make it white. Two tablespoons in each and every cup; she'd made it that way for years. And the same stained ceramic cup, too, a light blue container lettered in gold script, which read *Bob Miller's Lexus, 1000 Main, Lincoln, Nebraska.* A friend had picked up the cup for her while on a business trip in the state capitol. Now it was the only cup she ever used. Small things can mean so much to a person. Sometimes, tiny glimmers from the past run so strong and deep that even a chasm of years cannot extinguish them.

Her eyes went down the list of estate sales advertised in the paper. She wanted to see how they were written; she was interested in how far in advance they were placed. On a pad of scratch paper she wrote a sample ad, then another. She wadded them both up, pitched them in the wastebasket, and started again. The ringing phone interrupted her several times. She nodded at Marcy and Susan when they came in, saving her tobacco-stained smile for Jack Hunt, Dan's younger brother, who was in charge of sales.

Now that other secretaries were in the office, she ignored the phone and concentrated on writing her newspaper ad. When she was satisfied, she called the paper and placed it. At 9:15 a.m. she stepped out the back door to have a smoke, and had barely lit her cigarette when Marcy opened the door and motioned. "You've got a phone call — line three."

"Yell-O."

"Is this Lois Devon?"

"Yes."

"This is Deputy Sheriff Ranther. I'm calling about your missing nieces and nephews."

Lois sat up straight in her chair. "Have you found them?" Her voice was noticeably agitated.

"No, not yet." He paused. "I was wondering why you hadn't called me or left a message at my office."

"I talked to Jameson," she said. "He told me you were on the case, and he said he'd be looking out for them, too. I didn't know what I could do. The family has lived out on the farm for seven or eight years and I ... well, I don't have any idea where the children might be."

"Well, what I've driving at, Ms. Devon, is that I've left several messages on your home answering machine. I specifically left several messages asking you to call me, and I left my phone number."

"Oh, I'm sorry about that. That machine hasn't worked right

for months. It constantly garbles and cuts off the messages."

"I see," said the deputy, and he paused again, mulling over what he had just heard. "You are responsible for the children; is that correct?"

"Well, yes. There's no one to look after them but me, with everything that's happened lately. I really hope you find them."

We're doing everything we can, but I need any help you can give me."

"I wish I could tell you something that would lead you right to them, but I don't know what it could be. Have you conducted a foot search around the Jameson farm?"

"We have now," he said. "I want you to understand, Ms. Devon, that every day that passes makes it less likely we will find them safe and sound. We got a delayed start on this case, and I'm not encouraged at this point. Not without a break. Is there anything you want to tell me?"

"No, I'm sorry, I can't think of a thing."

Lois waited again as there was a long pause on the line. She shifted uncomfortably in her office chair, rolling the casters around in a circle.

"Well, let me ask you this. I understand the children's mother is undergoing psychiatric treatment within the Nebraska mental health system. Is that correct?"

"Yes."

"What facility is she in?"

The deputy waited. There was a long pause. "In Norfolk," Lois finally said. "I had to get the phone number from my purse. It's 373-1911, and it's on Western Avenue."

"That makes sense … your sister being treated in Norfolk. That is, after all, the closest facility to her hometown of Albion."

"That's correct. That's why I took her there."

"I guess what has me puzzled is that Ralph Jameson told me Mrs. Stone was at a facility in Omaha. Can you shed some light on that discrepancy?"

"It's very simple, deputy. I told Mr. Jameson that my sister was in Omaha because I didn't want him to bother her for any reason. I'm responsible for both my sister and her children, and I wanted him to contact me if a problem came up."

"That sounds reasonable enough, Ms. Devon." John Ranther's deep mellow voice flowed smoothly through the telephone line. His line of questioning always had a purpose, a final punch line. Ask easy questions first, but questions that sound important. Something stuck in his craw about this aunt, especially since she hadn't returned his phone calls. "Did Mr. Jameson contact you as soon as the children were discovered missing?"

Again there was an unusually long pause.

"Yes, he did," finally came the response.

"The reason that I ask is he didn't contact our office about what I would consider a serious situation, for two full days," replied the deputy.

"No, I didn't know that." Lois was feeling deflated. She didn't like the endless list of questions. "But I do know we all want to find those kids," she said. "The sooner the better."

"I understand, ma'am. I guess you've been doing what you can to locate the children?"

"Well … I wish I could, but I really don't know what to do." Lois really wanted to make her words sound convincing, fill her voice with inflections of concern, but she didn't want to open a can of worms and have the deputy on the phone all morning.

Ranther picked up his line of thought without even acknowledging the woman's general statement. "When I visited with Mr. Jameson, he hardly mentioned your name. You know, he may not have mentioned you at all. I had to call him back to get your name and number, in fact, when I found out that he and his wife didn't have legal guardianship over the children." Ranther paused for a moment to let his words create a cloud of tension. "Don't you find that odd, Ms. Devon?" Silence seemed to thicken in the telephone line.

"I don't understand what you mean."

"Well, ma'am, I guess what I'm curious about is whether or not you have actually been exerting any care and supervision over your nieces and nephews since the death of your brother-in-law."

"I've been doing the best I can. I don't know what more I can say. Are you trying to blame me for the children's disappearance?"

"One last question, ma'am. You said you gave Mr. Jameson the wrong whereabouts of Mrs. Stone. Did you give the children the correct address of their mother?"

"Absolutely ... of course."

"Friendship makes prosperity more brilliant,
and lightens adversity by dividing and sharing it."
— *Cicero*

# 13

SANDRA STONE SAT on the edge of her adjustable bed listening for the third time today her roommate's anguished wails. For some reason the woman's closet hangers wouldn't all line up and remain perfectly parallel on the rod. Obviously a conspiracy to ruin all the work she had done in arranging her clothes. The woman was in the process of throwing all her shoes and slippers across the room. When she ran out of ammunition she stomped across the room and threw the shoes back at her bed, all the while swearing to God in no uncertain terms that she would never read the Good Book again.

Sandra grimaced at the irrational display and shook her head. The hollering hurt her ears. It never seemed to stop. Why couldn't the staff give the old woman something to calm her down?

But it was therapy for Sandra, enveloping her in an obscure form. The ranting of the old woman served to bring Sandra out of her hours of withdrawn self-pity. Much of what filled her thoughts was how to get away from this perfectionist lunatic. She thought of her children. She knew they needed her, missed her. She needed to get back home.

Her life with Frank was over now. Eighteen short years; it went by so fast. But there were many more laughs and smiles than tears. The sudden end hurt the most, not the terrible truth that their life together was over. She still remembered the first day they met:

She was still in high school, the pick of the class. Deep brown eyes that sparkled with mischievous fun. Almost every boy in school had asked her for a date, and she had accepted some, but she was no one's steady. Everyone in her business class had gotten part-time jobs around town to learn how companies operate and to get practical experience in the work force. Sandra got a job at Morgan's Tractor and Implement. She worked in bookkeeping for two hours every school day afternoon.

One day a scruffy, grease-covered mechanic came into the office from the back shop. He looked like a football player who had been hit in the head a few too many times: thick features, a heavy brow. She was sure he didn't own a comb. He came to her desk and introduced himself and asked for the maintenance records on three company vehicles.

When he spoke, she heard him with her heart. So polite and respectful. He spoke with a confident intelligence, not revealed by his ruddy exterior. She found out he was only several months past his 20th birthday. Yet he acted so mature. Underneath those dirty clothes was a real man. She started finding excuses to go back into the shop. He finally got the hint and asked her out to a movie. It was *Rocky*, and she loved it. That down-on-his-luck boxer was just like this man of whom she was growing increasingly fond. Her heart told her to look past the frog and go for the prince inside. She fell in love with the frog, too.

When she graduated from high school, they were married — in the same neighborhood Kansas City church she had attended since she was a small girl. Her father gave her away. She was so thankful that he was able to attend her wedding. Four months later he was dead from cancer, and she and Lois buried him next to their mother.

For ten years they lived in Kansas City, never quite able to buy a house of their own. Danny came along after three years. Frank became head mechanic at Morgan's while she worked part-time in the office. Soon Chrissy joined the family. All the time Frank wanted to be his own boss, make his own decisions, reap the rewards of his labor. They talked about buying a farm for years, saved and planned. Finally, they were ready. Frank had his eye on several farms, all the right size, all for sale at a price they could afford. It was the best decision they ever made. Getting away from the city gave them a renewal on life, and Sam and Melissa were born on the farm.

Life had been so good. Sandra Stone would make it somehow. Life had to go on. Her children would help her; she could count on them. They had been raised by the finest man she had ever known.

\* \* \* \* \*

The thin streaks of dawn had yet to break the horizon and peek into the cold crisp air of a new October day, when the deep rumbling engine of a pickup truck rolled into the driveway and approached the abandoned farmhouse. It was still dark inside the house and the Stone children were fast asleep. No one had awakened in the night to check on Chrissy. The cold and stress from the blizzard had taken its toll, and all the children had been pushed beyond endurance. Now they rested, unmoving throughout the night, senses folded in deep sleep as the truck stopped and cautious eyes surveyed the surroundings from behind the windshield.

And elderly man with a weathered face, dressed in blue denim overalls, turned off the motor. In the distance, the dawn crowing of a rooster could be heard drifting on the wind. The old man got out of the truck and studied the boards nailed over the glassless windows. He rubbed his stubbled chin and cocked his greasy green John Deere cap back on his head. He stood there for a while, listening for sounds. Only the sound of the wind whistled back at him, as the leafless trees seemed to look him over.

He could see a footpath beaten in the dirt between the barn and the back door of the house. He was well aware that teenagers came from town, at times, to party in the decrepit house. It was obvious someone had been here recently. And a question quickly entered his mind ... were they still here?

He walked to the rear of the house and examined the path. Not much to tell from that alone, except that whoever made it had been around awhile. Better to be safe than sorry, he decided, as he went back to the pickup and took his shotgun off the rack in the truck. He headed for the most obvious building on the property, the back entrance of the old broken-down house.

A scream instantly invaded Danny's sleep and he jumped to his feet, bleary-eyed, struggling to focus. The other children quickly awoke, too, and Melissa began to whimper. Tall and imposing, they stared at the figure that filled the doorway. Chrissy screamed when she heard the man approach the house. Her mouth remained open, her eyes wide with terror. She looked like she was about to wail again, but the air she needed to make the sound would not come out of her lungs.

"Settle down; settle down, young lady. I'm not going to hurt anyone," said the farmer slowly but firmly in a low, resonate voice. A bit of a smile formed on his weather-worn face, and he took the shotgun out of the crook of his arm and propped it up in the door jam. "I bet I can guess who you are."

The friendly sound of the man's voice allowed Danny to relax a tad; the setting of the gun aside let him relax even more. His head was still spinning, and his breath was short, however, because if the stranger had meant to do them harm he knew they had been caught defenseless.

"Chrissy's awake," exclaimed Melissa, the first to realize in the wake of their visitor that their prayers had been answered.

Sam was instantly at her side, staring at his sister with his astonished blue eyes like she was a newfound friend come over to play. Danny, too, forgot the man in the doorway as he rushed to her side.

"Oh, Chrissy," the words tumbled past a strange knot in his throat. "How do you feel?"

At first she was taken aback by the sudden attention. She glanced at the stranger, who was patiently watching the scene. Then she became aware of the throbbing pain in her head. Danny swept back the loose hay piled around her neck and stuck in her hair. "You took a knock on the head in the storm. Do you remember?"

"I … uh …"

Danny didn't wait for a complete report from the patient. He brushed back her matted hair and inspected her scalp.

"It's still pretty big," noted Danny. Melissa over-stressed a sympathetic moan while biting her lower lip because the bump was unsightly. "Get me another ice pack," he instructed Sam. And the kid was gone in an instant to complete his mission. Danny watched for a second as his little brother sprang to his task. Getting a ball of snow wasn't a big deal, but he saw how quick Sam did his part, how well he understood what it took to help.

"Do you hurt anywhere else besides your head?"

"Uh … no, I guess not. What happened?"

"You tell us. After the milk shed blew apart, you disappeared. That was the night before last. We waited out the storm in here. Yesterday morning we found you unconscious in the cellar."

"Oh," she paused for a moment, but her eyes were clear and they told a story. She smiled weakly. "You say a cellar?"

"Yes," said Melissa. "It was full of mud and you landed on your head. I wiped it all off of you."

"Not now, Pumpkin. Wait till she's feeling better to tell her all about it."

Chrissy was almost smiling. She was shaking her head to herself. "I thought it was a crawl space," she said meekly.

"A crawl space?" repeated Danny incredulously. He didn't know whether to laugh or be angry. "Oh, Chrissy. We thought you were stranded out in the field. You shouldn't ever leave the group." He stroked her hand. "Don't ever get separated from us."

Sam returned with fresh snow wrapped in burlap. The two boys' attention was focused on Chrissy when Melissa began to cry.

Danny turned and saw her lower lip quivering as tears ran down her cheeks.

"Oh, Punkin, I'm sorry."

She felt alone, apart from them. Danny had hurt her feelings when he cut her off speaking to Chrissy. He picked her up and sat with her on the staircase, and she sobbed and sobbed.

"I just wanted Chrissy to be all right," she choked out between sporadic breaths and more sobs.

"I know, Punkin." Danny wiped her cheeks and hugged her close. There's a way in which crying empties the soul of its burdens and replenishes it. More than sleep or food, Melissa needed to express her doubts and fears and feelings of bewilderment and insecurity that the journey forced upon her. And Danny just held her … and rocked.

"You own this place, Mister?" Danny asked, as he looked up from nuzzling Melissa's hair with his cheek.

"That's it, son. I was born in this house." He spoke with a rich voice that was pleasing to hear, and naturally made the person he was talking to want to lean to the friendly side.

"How long you been here?"

"Don't rightly know," Danny admitted. "About two weeks, give or take."

The old man began shaking his head from side to side in honest disbelief. "Whatcha been living on?"

"Catfish, mostly; some pheasant and rabbit."

"That's mighty amazing, son, what with four of you and all. You know, you probably oughta have the doc look at your sis there. A fall on the head can be real serious."

Danny just nodded and kept rocking Melissa. The giant rock feeling in his chest began to crumble as the old farmer spoke. A great burden had been lifted from him just in the fact that Chrissy was awake.

"Name's Franklin … Elbert Franklin," said the property owner as he extended a hairy-backed hand. Danny shook it and felt the calluses and strength in the old man's grip. It felt like his dad's firm, confident handshake. "I reckon you're the Stones?"

"I'm Danny, and this is Melissa …"

"I know who you are," Mr. Franklin interrupted with a smile. "Almost feel like I know you personally. I think the law in the whole state's looking for you four. Every newspaper around has written something 'bout you."

All Danny could do was shrug his shoulders and glance toward Chrissy and Sam. Melissa was now silently resting her head on his shoulder, her arms draped around his neck. He was both embarrassed and elated by such news. To him, the main objective was to always stay together. He expected to run into some difficulties along the way, although he didn't know some encounters would be so severe.

If the law had been looking and hadn't been able to find them, it must mean he was pretty good at taking care and leading the group. Whatever it meant, Danny felt a glow of strength inside him at the idea of outsmarting a bunch of adults. Didn't that go some way toward proving he knew what he was doing? Hadn't he seen them through … all the harsh living with no heat, no permanent shelter and no regular food? They were tired, but still together, healthy and strong. Except for Sam's cold, which didn't seem to be getting worse. And now Chrissy's bump on the head. If he wasn't completely sure before, he was sure now; he didn't need any adults telling him what to do. His dad was gone and his mother wasn't around. Danny sat up straighter as he addressed the farmer.

"What brought you out here today?" Danny asked.

"Wanted to check on my equipment in one of the barns out there. The one all locked up."

Danny nodded.

"You can never be too careful. Somebody might come out here and try to break into the place and steal the stuff if I wasn't to keep some sort of an eye on it."

"You sure got a big tractor in that barn, Mr. Elbert," Sam interjected. "We don't have nothing like that on our farm."

Our farm now maybe, Danny thought. Won't be for long, not after he graduated from high school. Won't be anybody around old enough to work it. He intended to pursue baseball and a college education. He looked at the Little Ones, but didn't betray his thoughts. You'll all be moving back to the city soon enough, he thought.

"You all got a good look at it, I guess?"

"We peeked in the cracks," Melissa said matter-of-factly as she brushed off her jeans with her tiny hand. She jumped from Danny's lap and retrieved Mrs. Leatherwood from the straw bed.

"I sat in the cab, Mr. Elbert. It's really neat," Sam replied.

Elbert Franklin nodded knowingly. His deep-set eyes were hard to see, but Danny saw how his bushy gray eyebrows danced every time the corners of his mouth turned up in a smile. "I've got an idea," he said, as he rubbed his chin and scratched his throat. He waited until they were all paying attention. "How'd ya like to go into town with me and let the missus whip ya up some vittles?"

"Hurray!" cried Sam, without looking to Danny for approval.

"Yes, yes," Melissa agreed.

Danny's eyes narrowed and his forehead wrinkled up. "Whereabouts in town?"

"My house. It's just on the edge of town."

Danny wanted a good meal, no doubt about that, but he didn't want to go into town, be seen by the authorities and unceremoniously shipped back to the Jamesons. The look in Chrissy's eyes told him what he really didn't want to see. She wanted to go into town regardless of the risks.

Elbert pulled a long red bandanna from his dusty blue overalls and blew his nose. "It's all settled then. Gather everything you have and put it in the truck bed. Then you all hunker down in the cab where no one can see you." The old farmer made eye contact with Danny and gave him an assuring wink.

A wave of relief passed over him and he tried to return an

acknowledging smile, but the attempt felt forced.

They didn't have much to take with them, other than the clothes on their backs. Melissa dutifully handled Mrs. Leatherwood, and Danny fetched his shotgun. The balance of their possessions consisted of the overused school knapsacks that were now filthy and worn, the makeshift fishing pole that Danny decided to keep, and a child's wicker rocking chair that Chrissy had found in the loft of the big livestock barn. Melissa enjoyed the chair immensely. Elbert recognized the wicker rocker and told them how it had once belonged to his sister. He was happy to let the little girl have it.

Elbert knew the Colfax County back roads by heart. Dry snow swirled behind them as they bumped down dirt roads. The buzz of the tires changed to a high-pitched hum each time they hit a patch of blacktop. They were headed south and east, mainly south. Elbert was headed to the outskirts of a small Nebraska town named Schuyler. He honked and waved at a passing grain truck.

The children were wide-eyed during the bouncy ride, expectant, rejuvenated at the thought of a new start, thankful that this day would be different. When they got close to town, the children hunkered down. Danny peered over the dashboard and saw a grain elevator looming high in a cloudless sky. One and two-story buildings could be seen in the distance, the outline of a small downtown. The pickup turned up a winding gravel drive toward a modern red brick ranch house that sat on a flat-topped hill. The house was trimmed in white with shutters around the windows and knee-high bushes around the foundation. A rooster-capped weather vane sat on the ridge of a cedar shake roof.

The drive ended parallel to the house where a doublewide horse trailer was parked at the back, along with another pickup and a fancy white four-door sedan.

One by one the children piled slowly from the truck, taking in the clean spacious surroundings. The grass was a dormant brown, but thick and cushy. The three older children stood together next to the truck, but Melissa ran over to an iron statue of a Negro horse groom dressed in the brilliant paint of emerald green and golden-yellow racing silks. She walked around and around the lawn figure, awestruck with discovery and childish fascination. When she determined that it was heavy and strong, she began swinging from its outstretched arm.

"This is some place you got here, Mr. Franklin," Danny said for the entire group. They had never seen any place in their entire lives quite so new and modern. Out on the farms, people just didn't have houses like this one. Certainly, none of their neighbors. Even as warm and well-built as their own home was, Danny couldn't remember a time when it didn't need a coat of paint.

The front door had a large brass knocker and was framed by a trellised porch. A large woman with sagging flesh hanging from her upper arms stepped out. She was dressed in an ankle-length white cotton dress with bright yellow flowers embroidered on a lime green apron.

"What have we here, Elbert?" she asked as her chubby pink cheeks stretched into a welcoming smile.

"We have some dinner guests, Mother," Elbert replied. "They said they're partial to some home cooking."

"Oh, you picked a perfect day," she beamed with glee as if they were expected, but didn't know just when they would arrive. "Come right on in and I'll fix you up something delicious to drink." She paused and seemed to ponder a moment. "How would you all like some creamy hot chocolate?"

"Yeah, yeah," responded Melissa, with Sam joining the chorus. Danny and Chrissy began to relax and loosen up.

"Go ahead," Elbert gestured toward the open door. "The bathroom is down the hall, first door on the right." Then he said, "Better take off your shoes out here, and pile your coats over here. We'll take care of them later."

The large friendly lady was Dorothy Franklin. She loved kids — they hadn't had any of their own — and she loved to cook. To Danny it was obvious that she loved to sample much of her own cooking, as well. Maybe that was why Elbert was so skinny. The food Mrs. Franklin prepared never reached the table. Danny smiled inside for an instant at his cynical thought, but, in truth, he was downright thankful that Elbert had found them.

Single file, the children, both tentative and anxious, walked into the house, with Danny leading the way. The sweet-smelling aroma of fresh baked pastries drifted in the air, and Melissa's feet were dancing lightly as she pushed against Sam to get him in the door. A brown-and-white Bassett hound lay on a cord rug in front of them, its big sad gentle eyes following them without its chin ever leaving the floor. All four of them piled into the bathroom and shut the door.

"Where did you find them?" Dorothy asked.

"Out at the farm. Been holed up there for weeks, from what I gathered."

"My, my."

"Can't believe the police never checked out there. It's so obvious, right on the road and all."

"Maybe they did, dear. Maybe these children started staying there after it was searched."

"Maybe, Mother. Maybe." He turned and looked at her. "All I know is that they look happy right now, but when I found them they looked half dead. That oldest girl has a bad welt across her head. Fell into the cellar." He paused and took a deep breath. "They all need proper attention. I might as well call the authorities now."

# 14

THE PULSATING BEEP of the digital clock, the flash of the green LED strobe, began another 6 a.m. ritual separating John Ranther from a vivid dream. He flung his hairy arm across the bed, squeezed together the empty pile of covers he found there, pulled them over his ears and rolled over with his eyes still shut. In darkness he reached out and shut off the alarm as he heard the faint sounds of running water in the bathroom.

Last night he'd gotten home well after midnight. He'd driven all the way to York, with the desperate hope that a report from a merchant about some kids holed up in an abandoned warehouse near the railroad tracks would turn out to be the Stone children. He mentally kicked himself for the wasted time after he checked out the supposedly hot lead. Of course, it was nothing of the kind. Still, he knew why he went. It was the only possible sighting he'd received in almost a week.

As it turned out, two 18-year-old girls, with a boy a few years younger, were headed to McCook when their Nova decided to throw a rod. They had listened to the engine tap for better than 30 miles. If they'd had any money they might have stopped at a filling station. "So, that's what motor oil's for," one of the girls said.

What pocket change they had they used for telephone calls, using the gutted warehouse as a temporary residence until relatives came to pick them up. Ranther was so disappointed he asked only a few questions. As an afterthought, he showed the photographs to the stranded teenagers. In turn, they each shook their head and handed back the pictures. He wished them well, escorted them to the bus station and gave them each an Abe Lincoln so they could get something to eat.

His stomach growled as he licked his pasty teeth. When he'd gotten home last night, his supper was in the refrigerator. He'd gazed at it, taken a couple of bites of cold chicken-fried steak, and gone to bed. The mental strain of the case left him physically drained. This morning his body was rested as his panging appetite pulled him from the bed. But his attitude was not recharged; he knew his outlook was downright poor. He was in a bad mood.

Mary exited the bathroom, followed by an ascending ball of steam. Her pink terry cloth robe was wrapped snuggly around her petite frame as she removed her shower cap and began brushing her thick copper red hair.

"Fresh pot of coffee's on, hon."

Ranther threw his feet over the bed, yawned and rubbed the bridge of his nose. He wasn't looking forward to this day. He wanted to plop right back in bed, pull a pillow over his head and hide in a goose-down estuary of denial and avoidance. He couldn't think what to do next. Maybe these kids had left on their own, and then were actually kidnapped. The possibilities were endless. It hurt to think about it.

He could always call for direct intervention of the Nebraska Bureau of Investigation, but they already had the basic information. He could call in the Feds, too, but it was probably too late for them to help in any immediate way. And no one was really pushing this case. There were well-wishers and concerned callers, but no one hounding him over the matter. To most citizens, it was just a case of runaways; they had their own problems to think about. Ranther knew that things just weren't adding up; he just knew.

"Sweetheart, I've been thinking." Mary walked to him and sat down beside him on the bed. She could already tell he'd been unsuccessful yesterday. "We should become foster parents."

"If that's what you want to do."

"Every day I've been looking at those posters you had printed of the children. It's so sad …"

"Tell me about it," he interrupted his wife, finally opening his eyes and looking directly at her. "I'd rather face a hundred bank robbers than have to search for missing children."

She hugged him. "John, I just realized how many children are out there that need care and attention and warmth from a stable family. We can provide that. We can give back some of what we have been blessed with … I can't imagine who could benefit more than children."

"You've been thinking about this quite a bit, haven't you?" Ranther said.

Mary nodded. "John, I know you're going to find those kids. Considering all that they've been through, I think we should take them in until their mother is released from the hospital."

"What? Hon, I don't know about that. Foster parents don't get to select the children assigned to them. We'd have to go through a training program too."

"But you work for the county; you can get the Human Services or Child Protective Agency to assign those kids to us."

John was awake now. He stood up and began rubbing his temples. "Are these specific kids what this foster parents thing is all about? Mary, do you know what you're asking? I can't just waltz into child welfare and tell them what to do."

"Why not? They going to need help after they are found … and I want to help." Mary's voice wavered. "I want some children around here," she said, emotion building in her words. "I want to take care of someone besides you … I can do it and I need to … oh, John, I never realized how precious a group of children could be."

Standing toe to toe he held her close as she cried into his chest, soaking the white T-shirt he wore as a pajama top.

"Now, Mary, now. It'll be all right. I'm sorry I didn't see how much an empty house was wearing on you. Becoming foster parents sounds like a great idea."

* * * * *

Dorothy grabbed Elbert's arm, horrified at her husband's suggestion that they turn in these vulnerable children. "Wait a minute, Elbert." Her voice was stern, but her eyes remained the clear, loving, same compassionate pale blue she had shown to the children. "Do you think, right this minute, all dirty with nothing decent to eat for weeks that they need to be spending the day in a police station?" She waited until her words had a moment to soak in. "Let me feed them and clean them up before you make any phone calls. Okay?"

He nodded.

"I want to hear their story, too, dear. After all I've read about them in the paper, I'm curious. These kids need some time to adjust. I'm sure they've been through a lot. A few extra hours isn't going to hurt anything."

He nodded again. "You'll have plenty to do after they leave, Mother. Did you see how dirty they were? There's bound to be mud all over that bathroom after they wash up."

Now it was her turn to nod, and they smiled at each other.

In the bathroom the children stood in front of a four-foot-long counter with two sinks. A mirror covered the entire wall over to the toilet. They stared at their blackened faces, blinking, looking at the strange reflections. They turned on the water and let the sinks fill. Danny helped Melissa roll up her sweater sleeves.

They were a sight. Rings of soot covered their nostrils, their hair was filthy and matted, the ridges of their ears caked with dirt. They all had red chapped lips. Sam's runny nose was most unsightly. Their sleep-filled eyes glared back at them.

Melissa started up with her exaggerated moans.

"It's only dirt," said Sam.

"Help her wash her hands and feet," said Danny. Then he looked at Chrissy's head. "How do you feel?"

"It hurts, but otherwise I feel okay," she said.

"Why don't you take a bath first, and I'll have Melissa bring you back some hot chocolate." Danny helped the Little Ones wash their faces and hands, and then the three of them went into the kitchen.

Everything in the kitchen was made from or covered with wood — the floor, the walls, the cabinets, the counter tops. It was all heavily varnished, revealing the knots and the grain of the wood. Every cooking utensil ever invented hung from a metal rack above a butcher block island. Most of them were made of wood, too — mixing spoons, ladles and spatulas. And a giant rolling pin. Wooden mixing bowls of every size imaginable sat about the counters. Mrs. Franklin's metal pots and pans all had shiny copper bottoms. Never in their lives had any of the children seen a kitchen like this.

Dorothy Franklin handed each of them a giant oatmeal cookie before anyone spoke.

"Where's your sister?" she asked.

"Taking a bath. Her head hurts and her hair is so dirty I thought it would be a good idea for her to clean up first … so we can tell how bad her bump is. Is that okay?"

"Sure, sure. Tell you what," continued the woman, who looked as if she were the mother of the Pillsbury Dough Boy, "why don't I make a real breakfast?" She gazed at the three very agreeable faces. "And while I'm doing that, why don't you clean yourselves up? Leave your clothes on the bathroom floor. We'll get those washed up later. I'm sure I have some things around here that you can wear for now."

Danny felt safe. The Franklins seemed so genuine and friendly. The house felt so warm. All of the cautiousness and the last of his reservations fell away. He looked to Dorothy for directions.

"You boys go this way," she pointed through the kitchen. "There's a guest room through that door with a full bathroom.

You, little lady, can go back to the bathroom down the hall where your sister is."

"Thank you," replied Melissa. "And, ma'am …"

"Yes?"

"May I have some hot chocolate now?"

"Why, sure, sweetie. I have some right here. Would you like to take some to your sister, too?"

"Yes, ma'am."

The boys had disappeared, so the heavyset farmer's wife poured a cup of cocoa in a large ceramic mug and watched the little girl drink it up. She hardly blew on it to cool the beverage. Melissa's pigtails looked like two strands of muddy rope, and Dorothy felt a twinge of sadness as she sat across the table from the little girl, who ignored her until her mug was empty. Then Dorothy refilled it.

The childish mustache the cocoa created only served to wet the dirt on the little girl's upper lip.

"That sure is good," she finally said.

"Do you want some more, sweetie?"

"Some people call me Punkin, but my name's Melissa," she corrected politely.

"What would you like for me to call you?" Dorothy asked.

"Melissa, I think. Really, only Danny and Momma call me Punkin … and Daddy did; but now he's dead."

Dorothy just sat in silence. Melissa puckered her lips and rubbed her hands around the warm mug. "I wish Daddy wasn't dead," she said, then she began sobbing. Elbert was watching from the doorway, and he went to the child, picked her up and carried her around the table to his wife. Dorothy rocked the girl until the episode was over. Her white dress was covered with dirt, but she rocked until Melissa was ready to head off to the bathroom. As Elbert led her down the hall, he looked back and saw the well of tears that swelled in Dorothy's eyes.

When they came out from their baths, Danny was wearing a T-shirt and a pair of blue overalls rolled up several notches to his ankles. Sam had on a blue Turkish towel robe pulled tightly around him and tied in the middle. The boys could hear the washing machine sloshing away as they walked into the kitchen. The girls each had white robes around them, their hair wrapped up in towels.

The four of them sat down at the table, and Danny led a prayer. Then they feasted on a mouth-watering breakfast of sausage patties, scratch biscuits smothered with thick crème gravy, mountains of scrambled eggs, melon slices, crisp slabs of hickory-smoked bacon, and washed it down with glass after glass of delicious cold milk and orange juice. Dorothy kept bringing more food to the table until the troop was satisfied. Elbert just watched. When they were finally full, they sat back from the table, wiped their mouths, and smiled.

"That was great," said Danny. "Thank you."

"Don't mention it, son." A brief silence passed among them as they all looked at each other. Dorothy wiped her hands in her apron while Elbert took several puffs on his pipe.

"So … tell me how all of you made it to the farm," the farmer asked, as though the question had just crossed his mind.

Danny looked at Chrissy, who was touching her head around the edges of the bruise.

"Walked," she said matter-of-factly. Danny sat up straight and looked closely at her.

"All the way from Madison?" Elbert asked.

"I guess," she replied. "We didn't exactly live in Madison."

"Still …" Elbert had a hard time believing that information. "I figured someone dropped you off there."

The children shook their collective heads.

"Mother, that's better than 50 miles. In weather like this, that's unbelievable."

"Elbert, stop your prying. You don't need to be asking a whole bunch of questions," Dorothy said.

"You're probably right, Mother. I don't need to know everything. Guess what I'm really curious about is *why* you went to all the effort to walk all the way to that old farm house," His squinted eyes peered through the haze of pipe smoke, and he looked directly at Danny and Chrissy. "Could you tell me that?"

Danny stared down at his lap, unwilling to answer. Chrissy's lips likewise became sealed and her eyes got that faraway look she was able to present whenever she was uninterested or inattentive.

"We had to," said Melissa. "We just had to."

"I see," said Elbert. Then he added as he pointed, "Better tend to that head and that nose, Mother. Looks like this bunch needs some doctoring."

Dorothy gave Sam some children's aspirin and cough medicine and rubbed Vicks on his chest. She applied a compress dressed with ointment on Chrissy's head, and gave them a bottle of lotion to use on their badly chapped faces and rough, dry hands. As she bandaged Danny's cut from the broken glass in the windowsill, he looked at her with pleading eyes and whispered under his breath.

"We really appreciate what you and Mr. Franklin have done for us. You don't know how thankful we were when he came by — cold and all out there. But we really have to keep going. You see, we got a place to go; we just got to get there. Please don't turn us in. We'll leave whenever you want, just please don't turn us in."

At first Dorothy Franklin listened with just a sympathetic ear, but as Danny's pleading touched her heart, she felt an ache of compassion swell inside her. "Isn't any reason to turn you in, is there?" she said in a soothing motherly tone. "You haven't committed any crimes, have you?"

Danny shook his head. "No, ma'am," he said, drawing out the two short words. "We haven't done anything wrong, matter of fact. We just got to find our mo…" He caught himself short. "What I mean, ma'am, is … you don't need to fret none about us. We'll be all right. We just can't go back where we were. And if you turn us in, then all we've been working for will be wasted."

Ten minutes later she found the boys in the back bedroom seated on a double bed, and she handed them a pile of clean clothes, soft and warm. She talked to them for a while and suggested they take a nap. "We'll work something out later," she assured them. "Go ahead and get some rest now." With another armload of clean clothes, she found the girls in the hall bedroom. Melissa was already asleep.

"Mrs. Franklin," Chrissy said, as the woman set the clean clothes on the dresser.

"Yes, Chrissy?"

"Can I ask you one big favor?"

"Sure, honey. What is it?"

"Would you please mail these letters for me? I don't have any postage — would you, please?"

"Of course, dear."

Chrissy had the stack of letters clutched tightly in her hands. "I may need to tape up some of these envelopes."

"I'll help you, dear. How many do you have?"

"Twenty-one, ma'am. I just counted. They're to our mother. I wrote one each day. That's how I was keeping track of how long we'd been out." She tried to smile, proud of her simple method of keeping track, somewhat surprised they had been in the countryside that long.

Dorothy put her hand on the girl's thin shoulder. "You might even have missed a day or two with your accident."

Chrissy's eyes got big. "Oh, yeah."

"That's very sweet of you to be thinking of your mother. I'm sure she is thinking of you. It will be an honor for me to get these in the mail for you."

"Thank you. I've been wanting to get these mailed before something happened to them."

"Why don't you try and sleep now? I'll wake you all up for supper."

An hour later Dorothy brought Elbert back to the hall bedroom door, opened it slightly, and they looked in on the sleeping girls. "They're so beautiful, the poor things," Dorothy whispered.

"They'll probably sleep all day and all through the night."

"You're probably right, Mother. That'll give them plenty of rest before the sheriff comes to pick them up and take them back to Madison."

"What?" Dorothy cried. "Did you call him already?"

"Not yet. I wanted to let them rest. But they have to go back. Children those ages can't be running around the county on their own."

"Elbert Franklin, what are you thinking?" Her voice began to rise in volume as she followed him back to the living room.

"What do you mean, what am I thinking? They've got to go back. I can't believe you thought we could do anything else."

"After all they've gone through." Her face was growing red and her eyes moist. "They've obviously come from an intolerable situation."

"I don't know that, Mother. They wouldn't talk, remember?"

"Elbert Franklin, I can't believe you'd send them back. Children don't usually run away from warm, caring homes. Certainly not the whole lot of them. Why couldn't you help them get to their destination?"

"I don't think we should do that. Besides, they haven't told us what that is, and I doubt if they would."

"They told me," she said. "They're headed to Omaha ... to find their mother." She showed him the stack of letters.

Elbert began shaking his head. "I knew you'd want to see them, Mother, feed them and all, but I didn't think you'd pull this on me. There are laws, Mother. Laws about who's supposed to be taking care of certain kids and where they're supposed to be."

"Just wait until tomorrow morning before you do anything. Somebody has let these kids down, and I want time to see if I can think up something better than just sending these children back to the place they came from."

As the two adults talked, they weren't aware of a bedroom door slowly closing. Although all the children slept soundly throughout the day, right through the supper hour, when the sun went down one of them lay fitfully in bed waiting for the night hours to pass. Then early in the morning, when the moon was shining brightly in the night sky, the other children were awakened. On tiptoes, past a silent Bassett hound, they exited out the back kitchen door. Dorothy's supply of newly baked cookies was significantly depleted in their parting.

In the wee hours of the morning, as the glow of dawn was about to break in the east, the four renewed children headed for the little Nebraska town of Schuyler, a mile and a half up the road.

"Speak when you are angry and you will make the best speech you will ever regret."

— *Bierce*

# 15

By DUCKING INTO the roadside ditches whenever headlights approached, the clan was able to make the walk into Schuyler in a little over an hour. The children walked hand in hand, silent in the morning cold, each playing audience to individual thoughts.

Just past a darkened lumber company entrance with the gate locked and chained was a service station. The sign read SCHUYLER TRUCK STOP. It looked more like a run-down all-night convenience store with a diesel pump on the side. Trash barrels were heaped to overflowing. The windows were completely covered with sale notices, merchandise promos, direction arrows, announcements and multi-colored flyers.

Danny huddled his siblings in the ditch to the side of the store and spelled out the sketchy plan he had conceived. They remained out of sight while he headed for the pumps. He pulled his collar tight around his neck and shivered as the touch of cold denim sent a chill down his spine.

A blue beat-up Ford half-ton pulled away from the pumps headed in the opposite direction as he walked up. He noticed how it looked just like his dad's truck. Everything except the color. As far as he knew, that old truck was still sitting back at the farm, idle and unused. He sure wished he had it now.

Then he saw a poster in the window that caught him short. MISSING, the flyer proclaimed in high block type. Underneath the word were photos of himself and his brother and sisters. He crept closer to read the small print at the bottom. It mentioned the day they disappeared, their ages and heights, and gave a number to reach the Madison County Sheriff's Department should someone have any information. He quickly memorized the phone number and then glanced about, nervous that someone might be watching him.

He moved around the building, keeping away from the door. Through the window posters he spotted the attendant behind the register, a fat gal in a platinum wig who was sucking on Cheetos while her eyes were glued to a six-inch portable TV. Danny couldn't tell what she was watching; he didn't care. What he wanted was a ride, or go inside. Just for a minute or two, just to get a little warmth soaked into his clothes. But he didn't want to chance being recognized. He patted his pockets out of habit, but he knew they were empty. When the four of them were guests at the Franklins, he knew they'd be needing money, that they wouldn't be staying long. But he hadn't looked for money lying around. He wasn't going to do that. He hadn't been brought up to take other people's money. Even when he learned that they planned to turn them in, he didn't intend to resort to being a thief to make their immediate future easier. Now Danny thought about it, and he knew he'd made the right decision. They would accept the food and the baths, but he wasn't going to steal.

Even in the freezing cold, his mind thought of ice cream. The thought of being right outside a convenience store loaded with ice cream treats made him lick his lips. But he couldn't do anything about it. Besides, he had others to think about. He struggled to think of something else as he blew moist breath into his hands and swung his arms back and forth.

A bobcat delivery truck pulled into the pumps. On the side was painted in black letters — PACKAGE EXPRESS — ON TIME DELIVERIES. Yet the lettering was almost obscure from the dust and road dirt that covered the white truck like a black veil at a funeral. Finger-painted figures were written in the grime, a happy face, and an admonition — WASH ME.

Danny watched with great interest as the driver got out of the truck and turned on the pump. He was an older man with a beer gut who moved about with a slight limp. A red stocking cap was pulled down tightly over his head and ears, but he wore only a light jacket. A cigarette dangled from the corner of his mouth.

Light was now streaking the eastern sky. Soon it would be daylight. It seemed like now or never. Danny decided to approach this man. He walked to the back of the truck, then stepped out by the line of pumps where he could be seen by the driver, but where the truck blocked the view of anyone inside the store.

"Mister," he said, "gotta cigarette?"

"Don't smoke."

Danny flashed him a wide friendly grin. "Ah, c'mon. I just saw you smoking one. Just one?" He shrugged his shoulders. "It's cold out here."

"So?"

"It sure would take my mind off it."

With one hand on the pump, the man reached for the cigarette pack in his jacket pocket and shook them until one popped up. Danny took it quickly and stuck it in his blue denim jacket. "Thanks, mister. I'll wash your windshield for you, too. No charge. It sure could use it."

Slowly he washed the windshield as the driver went into the store to pay for the gas. Now was the moment of truth. He prayed the driver and the clerk wouldn't get into a conversation about him. Hopefully he'd just pay for his gas and come right back out. But surely they knew each other a little bit if she worked the night shift every day and he drove the same route. Danny moved between the truck and the pumps and watched him at the counter. With just a nod to each other, she took his payment and turned back to her TV program. Danny breathed a deep sigh of relief.

"Hey, mister. Where you heading?"

"Council Bluffs," he said as he looked Danny over, seemingly noticing him for the first time.

"Is that east of here — toward Omaha?"

"Yea, it's toward Omaha," the man said with a smirk.

"Bet you could use a little company?" Danny cocked his head. "Huh, whadaya say?"

Danny's heart held still as the man appeared to mull over the idea. The two of them stood in the cold as the driver bit his lower lip, and then flipped a Winston into his mouth. Danny rocked on his tiptoes, his hands stuck deep into his pockets as he tried to stay warm. The man seemed in no hurry to make a decision. He turned his back to the wind, lit his smoke, then turned back to the boy.

"Okay, kid. Hop in."

Danny jumped in the cab and stuck his hands under the dash, rubbing them over and over in the hot air stream from the heater. The driver plopped his overweight frame behind the wheel and reached for the gear shift.

"Oh, one more thing," Danny said in a matter-of-fact tone. "Got some others over there by the side of the road need a lift, too."

The man gave Danny a crossways glance, but didn't seem surprised. "Where?"

Danny pointed. "There. On the side there, huddled in that ditch."

"Who are they?" the man asked.

"My brother and two sisters."

Brows tightened down over the fat man's eyes. "Hey, what the hell is this, kid? This ain't no damn bus line, ya' know."

"Listen, mister. We're the best darn company you're ever gonna have on this cold lonely stretch of Nebraska nothing road. Besides, I like you. And I'm a good listener — or a talker, if you like. I said I'd keep you company. Anyway, we don't weigh much nohow. You'd barely made a dollar if you charged us by the pound."

The man listened to Danny's crap for another moment, then let out with a sarcastic "haw." "Okay, kid. Have it your way." He slammed on the brakes, and the truck slid to a stop on the thin coating of frozen crystals that covered the concrete parking lot. "Your friends are going to have to ride in the box though," he said. "Ain't enough room for everyone up here."

"Is it heated back there?" Danny asked.

"No, but I got an extra blanket behind the seat."

As the driver stopped and opened up the cargo box, Danny fought with the notion he should go to the back, let the Little Ones in the warm cab, or Chrissy because of her fall and head injury during the snowstorm. But what if the driver changed his mind and decided to let them off at the next town? He stayed, sat tight and waited for the driver to return, and rubbed his hands under the heater vent.

"My name's Danny," he said when they were a few miles down the road. "What's yours?"

"Look, kid. You asked for a ride, I'm given it to you. You don't really need to make a lot of small talk."

"Sure, mister. Whatever you say. I was just …"

"Going to tell me who you are," he interjected. "Right? Well, save your breath. I knew who you were from the moment I first laid eyes on you. Do you think everyone around here's a damn fool or idiot or worse? Jeez, boy, your face has been plastered all over these parts for weeks. Only thing would have surprised me would have been if you hadn't taken me to the others."

"Oh, no," Danny exclaimed. "You're not the police, are you?"

"No, I'm not."

Danny's relief was obvious, and he sat up straight in the seat. "I really appreciate your help, mister. We'll be out of your hair soon."

"Tell me, kid. What's your game? What are you really up to?" He dragged long and hard on his cigarette and handed it over to Danny's side of the cab. "Here, have a smoke."

"No thanks. I don't really smoke."

"Didn't think so, kid. What else is it you don't really do, besides tell the truth, that is?"

"Well, I didn't mean to be lying to you, mister, it's just that we needed a ride. Can't stay out in that cold forever. We were just passing through that town back there. We're headed to Omaha, Okay? We got reasons for heading that way, that's all." Danny sat back deep into the dusty truck seat. His feet were nestled in a pool of old papers and crushed beverage cans. The truck engine droned in a labored whine as the sun cracked the horizon in front of them, and mixed with dry snow that flew back from the tires and danced off the windshield.

"All I heard about you was that you were all a bunch of runaways," the driver finally said. "Don't seem to me you got much sense running away from a nice warm home in the middle of winter."

"No, no!" Danny exclaimed. He felt a lump borne of misunderstanding forming in his throat. "We didn't run away. We were kicked out. I would never put my brother and sisters through this if it wasn't necessary."

"Whatever … all I know, kid, if you were mine I'd bust your butt when I got you back home." He blew smoke in Danny's face. "My old man didn't put up with no crap from kids. Would have beat my ass good if I'd pulled a stunt like what you're doing … causing a commotion in town … getting the family name plastered all over the papers."

Danny couldn't believe his ears. His face grew hot. Words he might speak in his defense stuck in his throat. This stranger was siding against him, and he didn't have a clue as to the real facts.

They traveled in silence mile after mile. At one point they rolled across an open expanse, water on either side, traversed by a narrow ribbon of a bridge. "What's that," Danny asked? "That's the Platte River," the driver said. "Don't you know nothing?" In every town the driver dropped off a box or two on the loading docks of various businesses. At one stop Danny quickly went around to the back and checked on Chrissy and the Little Ones. Danny couldn't believe his eyes. The blanket the driver had given them had a dozen holes in it. It looked like little more than a flannel sheet. Danny felt the indignant anger boiling inside him again.

Chrissy said they were all right. They couldn't sleep much because of the cold and the bouncy ride, but they were managing. Danny kissed Sam and Melissa on the foreheads and pulled the flimsy blanket up around their necks.

Soon Danny no longer needed the sun visor down to keep the glare out of his eyes. Traffic alongside of them had picked up, most of it headed their way. Through the morning mist Danny could see the outline of tall buildings in the distance.

The truck pulled into a run-down warehouse district on the outskirts of the urban sprawl, and backed up to a narrow loading dock.

"C'mon, kid. Make yourself useful," the driver demanded. Danny followed him around to the back of the truck. The driver had another cigarette dangling from the corner of his mouth as he rousted the other three children out of the box. Then he retrieved an appliance dolly from the front of the cargo hold and motioned Danny to follow him.

"This here's brand new irrigation pump engine," he said pointing to a wooden crate. "Push the edge of it up while I slip this here dolly underneath."

Danny leaned against the top of the crate and pushed with all his might. The crate didn't budge. "Gee, mister, how much does this thing weigh?"

"Plenty. That's why I brought you along. Come here, kid," he said, motioning to Sam. "We'll push it up. You stick this here base plate underneath. Got it?"

Sam nodded.

Danny and the driver threw their weight into the crate, and it lifted just enough to get the dolly underneath. They tightened the straps around the crate, and together pulled it aboard the delivery truck. The driver wheezed for a full minute afterward as he tried to regain his breath and feverishly wiped a soiled bandana over his face. Then he got back to his feet, shut the overhead door and fastened the latch.

"What's up, mister? Why did you shut the door?" Danny asked. "We ain't in town yet."

"No … well, this is as far as the lot of you go."

"Why? We ain't given you no trouble."

"Got all the weight I can carry now," the driver retorted. "Besides, you were telling me how good you were at taking care of your brood. You're quite a resourceful person from what I gathered."

Danny felt his blood drain from his skin and felt like it was pooling in his feet. Loss and a sense of hopelessness enveloped him as he pulled Sam close to his side. "But where are we, mister?"

"Nebraska," he said followed by a raucous belly laugh as he opened the cab door. "Besides," he hollered back, "you're a lot closer to Omaha than you were a few hours ago."

"He's just like Ralph," Chrissy said, shaking her head.

Danny picked up a chipped piece of brick and started to throw it at the departing truck, but held back and let the chunk drop from his hand. Melissa picked up a rock and threw it, all of ten feet, then another, and another until the dirty white delivery truck rounded a sharp corner, flickered between several buildings, and disappeared.

# 16

IN THE THREE days since Ranther had called, Lois Devon's time had been spent in non-stop planning. Not only did the children need to be found, but they needed to be found by the right people. Time was running out, and she hadn't heard from Ralph in more than three days.

Once the children were found, however, she had taken care of one pressing issue. A retired couple in La Vista on the outskirts of Omaha had agreed to take them into their home. Her employer had built the couple's retirement home a few years back, and Lois had gotten to know them well. They had "the room for four young'uns," as the homeowner had put it. It was an arrangement for one month at a time, and for $1,000 a month. All she had to do was get them there. She had plans to be long gone from Nebraska before the first thirty days were up.

She'd placed a classified ad in the newspaper for a garage sale this Saturday and Sunday ... an estate sale of every stick of furniture in her house, along with every piece of junk she didn't want or wouldn't fit in her car. She was discarding the excess baggage of her life. Lois was dead-set on moving ahead, and starting anew. Now, if she could just locate those damn kids. What began as the tragic death of her brother-in-law became an opportunity. But first, the children must be found. All the tedious planning would become nothing unless they were safe and sound. She could leave after that, and not look back. If something happened to her only nephews and nieces, she would have a hard time forgiving herself.

She knew where they were headed. It only required that she wait. She would call Ralph and have him drive to Omaha. If they weren't caught or killed along the way, they might just make it. If only there was enough time.

Lois caught a glimpse of Sandra's picture she kept on her hutch, and she went over and picked it up. It was her favorite photo of her little sister, long before the children, even before Frank. Back when the photo was taken, almost 30 years ago, Lois would never have suspected that someday she would lie to her little sister, take advantage of a tragic situation, and betray a sacred promise just to make life better for herself. She didn't want to think about it. Even after five months of putting her plan into action, the thought of it pricked her conscience. Yet, as each new day passed the guilt slowly faded.

Back when they were little girls, after their mother died, Lois was the consummate big sister for Sandra. She spent hours helping Sandra learn to read. In Brownies and Girl Scouts Lois helped Sandra sell her cookies. Whatever Sandra wanted to try, or whenever she had any difficulties, Lois was there to help. Lois cooked and cleaned. Many days their father worked late, so it was up to Lois to keep up the house. And she did, and cared for Sandra as well, a big sister with so much to share.

Lois wished many nights while lying in her bed that her mother was still around to take care of her ... to take her places and show her things that other girls got to do. In a way, Sandra owed her. She wasn't hurting anyone now, just taking what she rightly deserved. It wasn't pleasant, but it had to be done. Lois realized she was almost 50 years old. Life had denied her until now. She wasn't going to let this opportunity slip by.

\* \* \* \* \*

It was obvious they'd been dropped near the heart of a good-size city, probably Omaha, but neither Danny nor Chrissy was sure. Danny could see the outline of modern skyscrapers through the cold misty fog that hung overhead. But most of the buildings immediately around them were old-looking and empty, all the same dark red brick with spalling mortar. Many second-story window screens flapped loosely in the winter breeze, barely held in place by warped and splintered sashes. Telephone poles ran right down the alleys. Vehicles streamed along a section of freeway in the unseen distance, and the children could hear the accompanying low-octave buzz of hundreds of automobile engines.

They walked the streets for several hours. Soon they would need to find something to eat, and Danny had no idea where they could safely bed down for the night. The week-old snow and ice made for treacherous footing as they walked down empty streets, curbs heaped to overflowing with crushed cigarette packs, decaying newspapers and broken bottles of Thunderbird. Danny had visions of them trying to sleep on rock-hard filthy concrete or in a drafty warehouse full of rats.

A stooped man, his face full of whiskers, passed by them. He moved slowly, measuring each step, bundled in an assortment of OD Army surplus, his hands thrust deep into the coat pockets. Danny held Melissa's hand to assist her footing as they passed by ancient businesses — Broderick's Office Supply where stacks of yellowing 8-1/2 x 11 paper and boxes of curling file folders stood behind grimy window glass. Verna's Flower Shop was all boarded up; only the faded letters of a sign above the door could be read. A wig store looked much the same. The children could see dozens of wigs on cracked and broken mannequin heads and in open boxes, but it didn't look like the place really did any business. They were walking down vacant streets of an obsolete and discarded part of the city. It was all a glimpse into the past, a sad testament of some people and their means of livelihood long gone, and no one else much cared one way or the other.

They criss-crossed the streets and alleys. Twice their path was blocked by sewer repair barriers, and they doubled back, retraced their steps. This section of town was an island unto itself, cut off by an elevated freeway, a railroad and a river.

Between two structures they found their way inside an abandoned warehouse. Chrissy found loose bricks in the alley wall next to a gas meter attached to the building. They all pitched in and removed enough bricks to create an entrance. Chrissy was pleased with herself and smiled at the others with a seldom seen glow in her eyes.

"Nice job, Chrissy," Sam said as he held out his hand. "Gim'me five."

Chrissy just patted him on the head.

"Come on," said Melissa.

"Yeah," said Danny. "Let's see if we like this motel."

Chrissy was already inside.

"Yeah, let's see if we like it," Sam repeated.

"What's a motel?" asked Melissa.

Inside, the place was perfect. All around were discarded boxes and folding cartons that would make excellent beds. Spools of yarn and twine lay about. Mildewing upholstery fabric stood in the corners, but otherwise the place was clean. It was much better than the vehicle maintenance building they gained access to earlier, but rejected because the place had nothing but a dirt floor covered in motor oil and globs of frozen grease.

"I'm going to go round up some food," Danny said as they sat on crushed boxes.

"Got any money?" Chrissy asked,

"No."

"So how are you going to get any food?"

"I'll think of something."

"Do we get to see mother today?" Melissa questioned.

Danny just looked at her. Their clothes were just cleaned yesterday at the Franklin home, so that wasn't a concern at the mo-

ment.  Now they had a place to bed down.  Food was the next
order of business, so his thoughts were on their next meal.  If the
others weren't hungry, Danny knew they'd be getting that way soon
enough.  But mother?  He hadn't even thought about his mother
all day.  That's why they were out here, at an unknown location,
freezing one day, starving the next.  He could hardly believe that it
took Melissa's innocent question to make him think of his mother
for the first time all day.

"Not just yet, Punkin.  Soon though … soon."

"Find out where we are, Danny, while you're at it," Chrissy
said in a monotone.

Danny left his siblings to find a convenience store.  He thrust
a chapped hand into each pocket.  They were still just as empty as
the last time he'd checked.  His destination was a food store of
some sort, and the thought of ice cream again drifted in his mind.
He shook his head to dispel the image.  But the thought lingered
and he licked his lips.  He could do nothing more than snatch a
handful of ice crystals from the ground to suck on which did little
to relieve his craving.

Just beyond the old warehouse district of empty red brick buildings Danny passed what had one been a playground.  Two wooden
bleachers and a wire backstop stood barely visible above a ball dia-
mond now thickly overgrown with dead weeds.  Down at the end
of the next block he could see the lights of a gas station.  A liquor
store was across from it.  The closer he got, the more the flickering
red-and-blue beer sign above the door held his attention as the
light buzzed and quivered as though it was surely about to pop
and go out forever.

A wide ribbon of railroad right-of-way lay far in front of him.
The street he was on came to a dead end just past the gas station
and liquor store.  The end of the line was clearly marked by the
piles of mildewed mattresses and rusting appliances on the far
side of the intersection.  No other open businesses were in sight.

Stooped winos congregated around the liquor store, old woolen overcoats pulled tight around their collars. The latest in Goodwill winter apparel was on display. Smoke billowed from the circle of huddled men as they passed around a bottle of Ripple.

Danny's pace slowed. He focused his attention around the My-T-Fine convenience store and its two dented gas pumps. A white sedan was parked in front. A man came out pounding a pack of cigarettes against the back of his hand and began walking in the opposite direction. Danny rubbed his ears and stopped walking. He thrust his hands into his jeans and surveyed the scene.

Three white boys, several years older than he, were standing together near a trash dumpster. They had spotted him. They rocked in unison, back and forth, shifting from one foot to the other to keep warm. They were talking amongst themselves, alternately looking his direction, their hands thrust deeply into their pockets except to handle their smokes.

Danny made his way around to the front of the store. At least he could go inside for awhile to get warm. Maybe bum a quarter to make a phone call. He should have asked Chrissy for the name of the hospital where their mother was staying.

Inside he walked through shelves of chips, peanuts and donuts. An old-timer with sunken cheeks on a long face dotted with white stubble watched him closely as he milled along the isles. No one else was in the store, and Danny finally made his way to the register.

"Mister, I need to make a phone call real bad," he said.

The old boy's eyes narrowed, but otherwise his expression remained the same. He looked Danny up and down.

"Think you could spare a quarter?"

After a few more seconds the clerk reached along the counter and flipped him a coin. He never said a word.

"Where's a phone?" Danny asked looking around.

The old man pointed outside where it was beginning to snow.

* * * * *

The implications of the deputy sheriff's telephone call pestered Duncan Riley for an entire weekend.  First thing Monday morning he arrived early at the hospital, just past 7 a.m.  He was always early to work, the glow from his computer held a connecting bond for him, a tonic for his basic insecurity.

The policeman's insinuation that he didn't know how to do his job caused his neck to bulge and his temples to throb just thinking of the conversation.  That name, Sandra Stone, was etched in his brain.  If she were anywhere in the Nebraska mental health system, he would find her.

The psychiatric in-patient facilities existed in Omaha, two in Lincoln, with satellite clinics in Hastings, North Platte and Norfolk.  The sheriff had mentioned the town of Albion.  Duncan looked it up on the map again.  Norfolk was the closest treatment center all right.  He typed several keystrokes on his IBM, accessed the modem, and dialed the Norfolk facility, then entered the password to connect with its computer.  Within minutes his printer was spewing paper, and a quick check of the "S's" revealed that the sheriff's hunch had been correct.

*SANDRA STONE, admitted June 10, Depression, Dr. Rowe*

Additional information listed her home address as Rural Route 4, Albion, Nebraska.  He thought of calling that deputy sheriff; Ranther was his name, wasn't it?  His phone number was around here somewhere.  Then he thought better of it.  Duncan dialed the phone number for the Norfolk facility.

When the phone was answered, he asked to speak with Dr. Rowe.

"I'm sorry, sir.  Dr. Rowe is in Chicago this week attending the Midwest Conference.  Could someone else help you?"

"I'm with the Omaha Hospital.  I'm calling in regard to a patient you have there, Sandra Stone. Connect me with the charge nurse in Mrs. Stone's ward or someone who works directly with Dr. Rowe."

"One minute, sir."

A brusque voice came on the line, informed Duncan that he was talking to the morning charge nurse of Building C, and implied he could have sent a memo rather than taking up her valuable time just as the shift was beginning.

"Do you have a Sandra Stone there in your care?" he asked.

"Yes, yes. What it is you need?"

"Well, I'm calling about a matter of great importance concerning Mrs. Stone." Duncan could visualize a thick-boned nurse who stretched the fabric of her white uniform at every seam growing perturbed with his call, while staring at the telephone receiver as if it were an insect to be squashed under her thumb. He was both intimidated and angry at her inhospitable tone.

"Are you a member of the family?"

"No, I'm calling from the central hospital in Omaha. You may well have a deputy sheriff calling on you concerning Mrs. Stone. I'm calling to let you know in advance about the situation."

The nurse responded with an indifferent "yes," and paused. The line seemed to go dead except for the sound of breathing.

"Could you write this down, and make sure Dr. Rowe is aware of this information when he returns? Maybe it should be added to her chart."

"I'll take care of all that," she replied impatiently. "What's the message?"

"Mrs. Stone's four children are missing … gone from their foster home as I understand it, and they haven't been seen or heard from in almost a month."

"Oh, my," said the nurse as she scribbled in pencil on a half sheet of yellow ruled paper the note:

*Sandra Stone Room 9C: Stone children missing from foster home, almost a month, sheriff department looking for them.*

"Do you have a phone number the doctor can call when he gets back?" Duncan looked up the number Ranther had given him and he passed it along. The nurse added it to her message.

When the phone conversation was over, the nurse was immediately brought back to her duties at hand. She taped the yellow paper with the message inside Sandra Stone's chart in the rack at the nurse's station, and promptly forgot about it.

Unless a patient was being seen by a doctor or receiving medicine, the charts remained in the central rack, updated once or twice a week with a brief paragraph on the patient's daily activities and progress. But Nancy Shira, who came at 3 p.m. on weekdays, always like to take a peek at the charts. There were no restrictions against it. She was, after all, a volunteer, giving freely of her time after getting out of her college classes, and she had a special bond with the patients she helped. She had a deep interest in their progress. She had every intention of becoming a nurse some day.

When she opened Sandra Stone's chart, the message on the yellow note caught her attention immediately. She wanted to ask someone about it, but all the nurses on second shift were dispensing meds, and everyone on the first shift had left. One thing was for sure, this note was of extreme importance, and it was directed to Mrs. Stone. Maybe it had already been passed along. If not, Mrs. Stone must be informed. Nancy removed the note from the chart and walked to room 9C.

Sandra Stone was watching TV, an episode of *I Love Lucy*, when Nancy came in the room. Sandra smiled at her volunteer friend and turned down the TV sound when Nancy approached the bed.

"Have you heard about your children?" Nancy asked, looking for a sign that Sandra was familiar with the situation.

Sandra's head tilted. Her eyebrows wrinkled as her mind recycled the question. A blank look came over her face, and Nancy knew that she had no knowledge of the information in the note.

"What do you mean?" Sandra said.

Nancy handed her the note. A second later Sandra popped up from the bed and held the note under a table lamp, reading it several more times.

"Where did you get this?"

"It was at the nurse's station. I was hoping you'd already been told."

Sandra Stone didn't say another word. She tore open the closet and began throwing aside hangers. "I've got to get out of here," she said without looking at Nancy. "I don't need to be here anymore. I should have left weeks ago."

"But you can't just walk out, Mrs. Stone. You have to check out officially." Sandra turned to the college freshman. "You'll have to help me, Nancy. Tonight, after your shift." Sandra now closely watched the girl. She saw her confused expression change to one of understanding and cooperation. "They're my children. I have to find them."

Nancy's eyes were wide. Suddenly she was scared, but she understood. She would do what she could for this patient, really her friend, Sandra Stone. Nancy nodded in agreement.

# 17

"THOSE WERE THE nicest bunch of kids you'd ever want to meet, deputy," Elbert Franklin said as he lit his pipe and gestured the officer into the living room.

"I'm glad you called," Ranther replied. "You're the first folks to have actually seen them since they disappeared."

"Oh, you will find them, won't you?" Dorothy Franklin asked as she joined them carrying a small tray of freshly baked oatmeal cookies. Ranther quit twirling his cowboy hat between his fingers and took a cookie when the tray was offered.

"Believe me, we are doing the very best we can. I'm the only one assigned full-time to this case. We just don't have the manpower in our department. Up to now I was at a loss as to what direction they headed, and their condition. The fact that you've seen them helps a lot." He flipped through his note pad. "We were even told that they might have been kidnapped, but there was never any evidence to that effect."

Elbert put his feet up and pushed back in his easy chair. "I'd rather say they ran away from wherever they were living as a group, you know." He gestured to the officer. "They wanted to stay together as a family. They looked pretty weather-beaten, but certainly not defeated."

Dorothy nodded. "Oh, they weren't kidnapped. I'm sure of that. They're a very determined bunch of kids," she said as she got up and left the room.

"Did they say where they were headed?" Ranther asked, unable to postpone his eagerness to ask the question.

Elbert shook his head slowly as he thought. "They didn't talk much at all really. I can tell you one thing though. They're determined not to go back where ever they came from. It must have been bad where they were at."

Dorothy returned with another tray. This one was filled with cinnamon rolls. The warm, fresh-baked aroma of cinnamon and brown sugar caused Ranther's mouth to water. He put his hat down and helped himself.

Dorothy moved next to Elbert and sat beside him.

"I knew exactly who they were the minute Elbert brought them in from the old farmstead," she announced. "They were such darlings. Been reading about them in the paper almost every day. Elbert and I had even been talking about them just the night before he went out to the farm."

"Guess we should have called you as soon as we brought them to town," Elbert said, as he puffed hard on his pipe.

"That's water under the bridge now. Don't worry about it. Really, it's good just to know that they are alive and well."

The pipe smoke mixed with the aroma of the fresh pastries giving a charred smell to the air. It bothered Ranther's enjoyment of his cinnamon roll, and he put in down half-eaten. He turned in his seat toward Dorothy and directed the main question on his mind to her.

"Did they say anything at all about where they were headed?"

"They were pretty closed-mouthed about their plans," she said. "They were sure scared bejebbers that we were going to turn them in. I'm sure that's why they snuck away in the middle of the night."

Dorothy paused, and then continued. "I don't know exactly what their plan is, but the oldest boy kind of let it slip … they want to find their mother. That makes sense, doesn't it?"

Ranther let the words sink in, and began nodding. "Sure. It sure does. She's the only one they have left in this world." He stood and began pacing the room, "Why didn't I realize that before?"

He gave the Franklins a brief rundown of their mother's status after their father's death. He didn't mention a lot of details. Primarily he was rehashing the information in his own mind.

"Can I get you some milk, officer?"

"That would be much appreciated, Mrs. Franklin. But one thing doesn't add up. Their mother is a resident up in Norfolk, north of where they were staying. Your farm is south of that place." All Elbert could do was shrug his shoulders when Ranther looked his way. "Since they're headed south, what could be their destination?" the deputy said almost to himself.

"They sure were tired and dirty," Dorothy said as she returned with three tall glasses of milk, "but they certainly aren't stupid."

"What do you mean?"

"Like I said, the oldest boy said they were out to be reunited with their mother. If that's their goal, then they must believe she's somewhere other than Norfolk."

Ranther nodded, his eyes focused in the far corner of the room, lost deep in thought.

Dorothy set down the drink tray and retrieved a stack of envelopes next to the telephone. "After looking at the address on these letters, it's quite clear where they are headed."

"Let me see those."

"The oldest girl gave them to me and asked me to mail them. They're all for their mother."

"1470 Magnolia, Omaha," Ranther muttered under his breath as he ran his fingers over the soft flowery handwriting on the envelopes. "I know who lives there, and it's not an address of a psychiatric hospital." He paused as he flipped through the entire stack. As Dorothy had said, they were all addressed the same. "Now tell me exactly. When was it you first found them, and when did you know they were gone?"

"I found them yesterday morning at 6:30 out at my farm. We discovered they were gone this morning about the same time. We started calling around to the authorities immediately."

"You should be able to find their trail now, don't you think?" Dorothy said hopefully.

"It should give the search a big boost."

"I sure hope you can," Elbert added. "I think they're getting to the end of their rope."

"How's that?"

"Exhausted, spent, just plain tuckered out. The oldest boy's their leader, of course, and I think he's at his wit's end as to what to do and where to turn next."

"And that little boy has a bad cold. Getting worse, too," Dorothy said, worry written all over her face. "You must find them real soon."

"I understand. I'll do my very best."

Ranther took a scrap of paper from this shirt pocket and scratched some notes. "Thank you for your help. Call me at this office number if you hear anything. They may even come back here because you were of such help to them. I'm going down to the police station right after I leave here and ask the chief if he will help me search all of Schuyler. I'll find them before it's too late," he promised as he gulped down the last of the cold sweet milk.

Ranther grabbed his hat and headed for the door. "Let me give you my home number, too," he said as an afterthought. "If you hear anything about the children, the sooner I know about it, the better."

\* \* \* \* \*

Danny squeezed the quarter tightly in his fist and huddled against the phone stand in a feeble attempt to block the blowing snow. He had one phone number on him, a number he had scrawled on a scrap of paper months ago, and stuck in his billfold – the number of Aunt Lois. Calling her was the best way to go. They hadn't seen eye to eye on everything, but surely she would understand, once he explained how bad their situation had been at the Jameson's farm. Besides, he had to think of the best for Chrissy and the Little Ones. They had been through enough. It was time to ask for help. The three boys near the trash dumpster got into the beat-up white sedan, but kept their attention on Danny.

Someone had burned cigarette craters into the phone receiver. The metal conduit cord was bent, twisted and frayed, the directory long gone. The line buzzed as Danny kissed the quarter, dropped it in the slot, and prayed for a dial tone.

After six rings a voice answered, "Yell-o."

"Aunt Lois, is that you?"

The voice on the other end of the line perked up, "Who's this?"

"It's Danny. I sure am glad you're at home."

"Good God, boy. Where in the hell'r you at?"

"We're in the city."

"Omaha?"

"Yes, ma'am."

"Good God. Do you know a whole damn army is out there looking for you?"

"Yeah, I guess. We just wanted to find Mother. Since she's here in Omaha, you can take us to her. We had to get away from Ralph ... we just had to."

"Where are you at? Gimme me your address right now."

Danny looked above the door of the store, but the numbers were faded out. At the street corner a sign leaned back from the curb. He squinted to read the words.

"I'm at a convenience store at the corner of Basser and Dove," he said. "Please hurry and come and get us."

"Now just wait a minute. I can't go out right now. The WHEEL just came on the tube, and besides it's snowing something terrible."

"Well, give me your address, and we'll get ourselves over to your place so you don't have to bother."

"Just hold your horses, young man. I'll send someone for you.

You've done enough to upset everyone as it is. Just sit tight. I'll have someone there within hours."

Danny listened, but he could hardly believe his ears. "Can't you send a taxi? We're completely out of money." He could hear the begging tone in his own voice.

"Daniel, now listen to what I'm saying. You did the right thing calling me. I've made new arrangements for all of you. I know about the trouble between you and Mr. Jameson, and I would never make you go back there."

"But ... we want to see mom. We all really need to see her. That's why we headed this way in the first place. And she needs us." Danny listened for a comforting response from his aunt. All he heard was silence. "Don't you know she does?"

"Jeez, Daniel, that's very sweet. But to tell you the truth, last time I heard, your mother wasn't seeing any visitors."

"Whadda you mean?"

"I mean, Daniel, she's very sick, and your running around the countryside isn't helping anyone. Just a minute."

Danny's mind raced with a barrage of thoughts as he held the lifeless receiver. His knees began shaking, but it wasn't from the cold.

"Listen, Daniel," Lois said when she got back on the line. "It's all going to work out, you'll see." There was a long pause as she took a deep drag on her cigarette. "I'll have someone on their way to pick you up in a jiffy. You'll all be eating as much as you want tonight, and sleeping in a warm, clean motel. How does that sound?"

Silence. Danny couldn't say a word. He wanted to scream. He wanted to rip the phone receiver from the booth until the wires squealed and snapped. She didn't give a hoot about what they wanted. She had hardly heard a word he'd said. The telephone seemed to be growing in size, the receiver encircling his head, Lois' words crushing his brain. A voice came back seemingly through a tunnel now, a million miles away. "I wish I didn't have plans tonight. But I'll see you all tomorrow. Take good care of that darling little sister of yours. Got to go now, Daniel." Click.

Danny stared in utter amazement and stark disbelief at the silent phone in his hand. He started walking in a daze back toward the warehouse where the others were waiting. He didn't notice the white sedan slowly following down the street behind him.

\* \* \* \* \*

The ringing telephone woke Ralph from his late afternoon nap.

"They're in Omaha," said the voice on the other end of the line. "Pick them up and take them to the address in La Vista and the $2,000 is yours. No funny stuff, no retribution. Got it?"

"When did you find out?"

"Five minutes ago."

"What's the address?"

"The corner of Basser and Dove. And you better be quick. The kids are expecting someone tonight."

"Why don't you do it?"

"I thought you wanted to make some money? Besides, I've got other plans for tonight. They're okay, no one's been hurt. Now pick them up."

# 18

THEY WERE 30 miles down the road before Nancy caught her breath. Once Sandra Stone learned the news about her children, she had awakened from her depressive state like a starving tiger craving fresh meat. It had been more difficult than pulling someone's teeth without pain killer for Nancy to keep Sandra in her room until her shift was over at 11 p.m.

Now that they were on the road, Sandra gave the orders. She put on what clothes she had and took all the loose money in the room, including that of her roommate.

Straight south they drove on Highway 81. Twenty-two miles later they turned west at Humphrey on state Highway 91 for Albion, and the farm she knew as home. Nancy wanted to help. She knew something was dreadfully wrong, that Sandra Stone had been withheld important information. And yet, her future as a registered nurse had vanished in those very moments. No one would ever hire a health care worker who aided the escape of a patient. She felt a little sorry for herself as her Dodge bounced over the uneven blacktop. Even more, she felt scared as Sandra kept the needle pegged at 70 miles per hour.

"Mrs. Stone, where are we going?"

"It's not far. We're almost there," Sandra said, her eyes glued to the outer reaches of the headlight beams.

"But where? Please tell me. I want to help."

Sandra pointed to a gas station ahead. "I need to make a quick call." She was back in the car in less than 20 seconds. "The phone's dead."

"What phone?" Nancy pleaded.

"At my home. No one's there. Why aren't they there?"

Sandra's talk answered some of Nancy's questions, but in a very real sense Sandra was talking to herself. She hardly acknowledged Nancy at all. "It won't take long … just to make sure. If my kids aren't where they're supposed to be, I know where to find the person responsible."

The Dodge careened onto a dirt road. Streams of ice and dust jettisoned from behind the tires. The accelerator was flat on the floorboard. Nancy fastened her seat belt and pulled it snug around her waist even as the car barreled down both sides of the road, and she choked off a muffled cry.

A full moon lit the night sky as they wheeled down the drive to the farmhouse. Sandra slammed on the brakes and threw open the car door. The pitch darkness of the house threw her into frenzy. "Danny!" she cried. "Where are you all? It's Mother. Chrissy, Chrissy where are you? Melissa! Punkin, it's Mommy. Sammie! Can you hear me?" The doors were locked. She tore off a window screen with her bare hands and forced open the window. Only a faint, familiar smell of home, and total darkness greeted her. "Where are my children? They should be HERE."

Nancy watched as Sandra Stone slowly seated herself in the ice and snow under the window. The silvery shine of the full moon cast a stage light glow on the women. Sandra wrung her face in her hands for a minute, then popped to her feet.

"Nancy, you've been so good to help. You'll never know how much it means for someone who hardly knows me to be so helpful." She brushed ice crystals from her flimsy housecoat. "But my kids should be here. This is their home." She walked to the garage and opened the door. "I hope this old truck will start, because I have one more place I must go."

The key was in the ignition, but the engine didn't turn over even once. The battery was completely dead.

Nancy pointed out the flat tires. "Don't worry about that old thing, Mrs. Stone. I couldn't leave you anyway until we find your kids. Where is it you need to go?"

\* \* \* \* \*

The off-again, on-again snowfall was oppressive. The cold was bone-numbing driven by the relentless prairie wind. Deputy John Ranther felt a hopeless emptiness in his stomach that acted as a constant reminder for his thoughts: You haven't got forever to find these kids. You better turn up something soon. Why hadn't that old couple, the Franklins, called as soon as they picked up the kids? Because they failed to act, the children were now adrift again in the hostile world. Anything could happen to them.

The search of Schuyler had been fruitless. The children were long gone. All of the empty buildings had been searched. The bus ticket agent hadn't sold a youngster a ticket in the past 48 hours. In fact, he hadn't sold anyone a ticket in the past three days.

Ranther had come across two weak possibilities. The night the Stone children ran from the Franklin home the clerk at the town's truck stop sold two gas purchases on credit. One was to a man listed as a Denver resident. The other was with a trucking company. Ranther would check them both out, see if maybe they gave a ride to the children or, if not, possibly saw them. But he wasn't very optimistic. The clerk's records indicated she also tallied eight cash gasoline purchases last night, and there was no way to track those.

He had stayed around Schuyler for the entire day, but drove home late last night and crawled into bed with his sleeping wife.

Today, back in his Madison County office, with his boots cocked on the edge of his desk, he reflected on what he now knew and didn't know about the case. With all the hours, all the work, chasing all the leads and returning all the phone calls, he knew he was really back at square one.

"Ranther, call on line three," came the voice of the switch-board operator through the phone system intercom.

"This is Deputy Ranther."

"Yes, officer, my name is Bradford Morgan. I hope I'm not bothering you."

"No, not at all. How can I help you?"

"What I mean is, I hope the information I have can help you. You're working on finding those missing kids, right."

"Yes."

That's why I called. I just ran across some paperwork that seems rather odd to me."

"What do you mean?" The police officer's feet were now on the floor.

"I work at Midwest Farmer's Life. That's where I'm calling from. I work in the processing department."

"Yesssss!" Ranther was anxious that he get to the point of the call.

"Well, back in June we issued a check on the death of Mr. Frank Stone. It was cashed five days later."

"That sounds right. Mr. Stone died in a farming accident in late May."

"Yes sir, deputy. I can understand how a tragedy like that could tear apart any family. Anyway, the check was made out to Mr. Stone's wife, Sandra."

"Nothing unusual about that, is there?"

"Oh, no, sir. But on large sums we look them over, double-check the cause of death, make a second review of the paper-work ... that sort of thing. It's an internal follow-up we do. You understand?"

"Uh huh ... and?"

"Well, we have on record that the family banked at the First National Bank in Albion. They'd been customers there for better than eight years. And well ... the bank has several original signa-tures of Mrs. Stone on file."

"Yessss," Ranther interjected.

"Well ... there's no way the endorsement signature on the insurance check is Mrs. Stone's. Her name is on the check, but the handwriting is completely different."

"Is it a woman's handwriting?"

"Appears to be."

"Any idea whose it is?"

"No, but that's why I called you," answered Morgan. "It definitely looks fishy."

"Okay, I appreciate the information." Ranther began rubbing his forehead. He had a good idea who this 'fishy other someone' might be.

"By the way, you didn't tell me the amount. What was the face amount of the life insurance check?"

"This guy, Frank Stone, was prepared. Maybe it was because he realized that farming was so hazardous. He sure had those children's future in mind. Whatever his reason, he sure paid a pretty penny each month for the coverage."

"How much?" Ranther almost shouted, unable to contain his curiosity.

"The death benefit on Mr. Stone's life was eight hundred thousand dollars."

"There is no revenge so complete as forgiveness."
— *Billings*

# 19

SNOWFLAKES SIFTED INSIDE his collar as he headed back to the warehouse. The quarter he spent on the call to Lois was wasted, and he didn't have another dime to his name. He hated to think about it, but they'd all have to go hungry tonight.

"Hey, where you headed?" Danny was startled by a voice coming from over his shoulder. "Not much up that way."

The voice sounded quizzical, not demanding. Nevertheless, Danny was unsure whether to respond or not. He decided to acknowledge the comment and keep moving, which he did with a quick nod of his head. All he could see was half of a face talking out of a white sedan that cruised slowly down the street. He pulled his collar a little tighter around his neck.

"Hey, pal," the voice lilted with a chuckle. "Don't run off. Ain't nobody going to bite you." Danny could hear the voice getting closer. "Got something might interest you."

Danny stopped and turned. A thin guy got out of the sedan. He was young, no older than early 20s, and he looked Danny up and down as he approached.

"You're new around here, ain't you?"

Danny just nodded. Two missing teeth in the middle of the other man's plastic smile caught his attention, and he just stood there and waited.

"Name's Eddie. I'm known as Reddy Eddie 'round here. What's yours?"

"Danny."

"I'll bet you could use some help. Am I right?"

"What kind of help?" Danny wanted the words back as soon as he said them. There was something about the guy that was easy-going, but Danny would rather be left alone. Besides, he didn't know who all was in the car. But he did need some help; he had no other place to turn.

"Money help, kid, that's what," he said as he combed snow-flakes out of his greasy black hair. "This is my turf, so to speak. You're new around here ... so it's my business to make your acquaintance. Where you staying?"

Danny pointed up the street. A queasy uncomfortable feeling about this guy getting too familiar descended upon him. He didn't like all the questions. Danny knew a simple NO wasn't going to be good enough.

He looked Eddie over, too. He had half a dozen gold chains draped around his neck with gaudy pewter rings on every finger. His eyes were cloudy with deep black pupils, gaunt cheeks, and nose of smashed cartilage that lay wide across his face. Although tall, his frame was all skin and bones. Even inside a full-length woolen trench coat Danny could tell that Eddie's limbs were as skinny as pencils.

"Look, kid. Let me give it to you straight. I want to help you. I don't like seeing nobody sleeping on the streets. I got a place I can put you up ... if you want. And I can get you some work." He watched Danny closely, attentive to any response.

Danny looked at the car, then back to Eddie. "I'm not alone," he finally confided. "I have others with me back up the street."

"Like who?"

"My two sisters and a brother."

The easy-going expression on Eddie's face changed as he faced Danny, and he looked him over as if he were a horse he was planning to buy. A cigarette appeared from under the wool coat.

Eddie pursed his lips. The inside of his mouth rolled like he was licking the last of sticky peanut butter from his gums. Then he opened his mouth and struck a match on a tooth.

"Tell you what, kid. Let's go meet the family. I'll buy you all a meal, and we can discuss business. How's that sound?"

Danny stood and listened. He wasn't physically afraid of the slender stranger. But he couldn't really refuse. He didn't want to create new problems for himself by offending Eddie. "What then?" Danny asked as he adjusted his collar again.

"Make some money, what else?" Reddy Eddie sent the cigarette butt flying across the pavement with a flick of his wrist. "Hop in the car. I'll give you a ride and we'll pick up your family."

The two other guys in the car sat quietly in the back. Eddie didn't even introduce them. Danny directed him to the warehouse where the others were holed up, the car stopped, and he and Eddie got out. One of the other guys got behind the wheel, and the white sedan drove away.

"So this is the family … is she still in diapers?" Eddie pointed to Melissa.

"What's that supposed to mean?" Danny asked, caution in his voice. He still didn't have a good reading on Eddie, and the obvious wisecrack kept him wondering.

"I mean," Eddie emphasized his words, she's kind of young to be dragged around the countryside, don't you think?"

"I don't wear diapers," Melissa retorted. Her eyes flashed their accusatory stare, and her mouth puckered in a comical pout.

"We have our reasons."

"Yes. Don't we all? Where did you say you were all from?"

"I didn't."

"I guess I've seen worse," Eddie said, and left it at that. "Okay, if you want to eat, now's the time. I don't do this every day."

It was now dark. A silver-dollar moon shone high in the sky. They headed on foot through shadowy alleys, across foul-smelling gutters, toward the freeway. The children trotted at an unsteady gait behind Danny, who in turn was trying to keep up with the long strides and hurried pace of his new acquaintance. Along the service road stretched a row of lighted signs, each pulsating with bright pinks and blues, yellows and reds. The electricity in them crackled. The artificial light reflected off the asphalt created a surreal, midnight glow around them. Sam was enthralled by the hum and bright colors of the signs, and slowed to a shuffle to look at them. Chrissy had to pull him bodily by the arm to get him to keep up.

Eddie knocked on the back door of the Waffle Barn. He spoke briefly to a cigar-chomping man with an acne-scarred face he addressed as Benny, then ushered the tiny band into the building, and an isolated corner booth.

"Okay." Eddie stuck his face out into the middle of the table and peered around. "You all look like you could use something to eat. I'm buying. Try not to make a mess."

Chrissy took a menu from behind the sugar dispenser and opened it so that Sam and Melissa could see it, too. The place was deserted except for a wino at the counter and a couple of black leather-clad love birds with pastel-colored hair seated at the other end of the diner.

"Coffee, Eddie?"

"Coffee, you got it, sweetheart. I'll add the cream if you'll add the sugar."

"Yeah sure, Eddie." The waitress was a big girl, smacking her gum, leaning to one side, balanced on one hip. "Whatcha doing? Babysitting tonight?"

"Got a new business partner." He winked.

"Yeah sure, Eddie. Coffee, hash browns and toast. Ya want any eggs?" She waited a moment while Eddie dug his face deep into the menu. "Benny said you can have some eggs."

Eddie's eyes dropped down to his coffee cup. "I think I will … and a side of bacon, too."

"And what for the brood?" she said sarcastically as she made a circling motion around the table with her order pad.

"Give 'em bacon, eggs and toast."

"Just a second… I may want something different," Danny said without looking up, his face stuck in the menu.

"Whatcha want — a burger?" the waitress half-shouted. "I know good and well that's what you're going to order."

Waylon Jennings began blaring on the juke box two notches above loud. A toothpick-framed gal, the spitting image of Olive Oil, walked in with an old geezer. They slid into a booth, and without looking about began making out next to the wall. The bald-headed dude immediately had his hands all over the anorexic with her hair tied up in a bun.

"Come on, kid. I look like I want to stand here for my health?" The waitress paused for a moment, eyes aflame with impatience. "I know what you're going to order … so order it." Danny kept reading the menu, so she finally walked away from the table acting pissed, mumbling to herself. She didn't really care for Eddie. He was always sponging off Benny or selling him drugs, or both. She didn't like the people he brought around. She didn't feel any obligation to dose out a measure of hospitality to those kids neither … especially if one of them was going to take all night to order.

"Here's your coffee." She sat a cup in front of each of the Little Ones. Sam and Melissa looked at the cups, then at each other, and shrugged their shoulders. The waitress glared at Danny and made a face as though she detected a foul odor. "We're all waiting. What's it going to be, hot shot?"

Danny folded the menu and looked up into the overly made-up, fleshy eyes of a woman who'd long ago thrown in the towel on life, and was now just going through the motions. Too old to go back and start over, but young enough to kick up a fuss and bow her back like a stubborn mule. She had a mindset that liked to blame other people for her problems.

"Ma'am," he said. "I'd like a hamburger with everything if you don't mind."

"You little son-of-a-bitch," she screamed. "Whadda ya think this is, the gawd damn Hilton?" She held the pot of coffee high over his head like she was going to pour it on him. "I knew what you were going to order. You had to be a prima donna, and make me wait. Well, you can just wait on your food now, you prick. You ain't getting no food until I feel like it." With that she stormed back to the kitchen.

"She'll get over it," Eddie said without enthusiasm.

The Little Ones looked at each other and held each other's hand under the table where they were seated next to Chrissy on the inside of the booth. Danny sat across from Chrissy who looked back at him with her large, expressionless, non-judgmental eyes. She knew Danny hadn't done anything wrong. All they could do was wait and hope the fat gal would bring them out some food.

Eddie puffed on a smoke. Seated across from the Little Ones, he poured a stream of sugar into his coffee and gulped it down. "Go ahead. Drink your java," he said.

Sam had a glint in his eye and a cup of hot black beverage in front of him. He looked at Chrissy with an excited expression on his face. He always liked to experience anything new or different. He was impulsive in many ways, but in these strange surroundings he waited a moment for permission from either Chrissy or Danny.

"No, you aren't drinking any coffee," Chrissy replied as she caught him spying the cup. "Drink the water. That's it."

While the others ate, Danny sipped on coffee and listened to Eddie mumble in his ear.

"I've got the perfect set-up for you," Eddie said. "Tomorrow morning I'll take you down to the block. Just do it how I tell you."

"Do what?"

Eddie just put his index finger up to his lips, but didn't answer the question. "Jasper and Ricky both got nice little set-ups. They'll give you some good tips."

"Who's Jasper and Ricky?"

"The other guys in the car."

"What is it you do?"

"Listen, don't talk," Eddie admonished. "By tomorrow night …" he shrugged his shoulders, "do what I tell you, and you'll have at least a hundred-dollar bill keeping your pocket warm."

Danny didn't like the sound of any of it. The mention of a hundred dollars only made it more mysterious, not more attractive. He was for sure now, he didn't like Eddie, and he didn't like to look at him or listen to him.

When Eddie finished his meal, he motioned that he wanted out of the booth. "Wait at your warehouse place. I'll pick you up." With that he left them.

With Eddie gone, they quickly finished their food and then walked in silence back to the warehouse. Chrissy, Sam and Melissa were enjoying full stomachs. Danny felt only the hollow slosh of six cups of coffee, and he was hungrier than ever.

\* \* \* \* \*

"Here it is, Basser and Dove," Ralph squinted through the windshield as he checked over the words on the street sign. "There's a store and a phone," he pointed. "That's probably where the little asshole called from."

His friend Singer pulled the brown-and-silver Ford King Cab into the parking lot. Charlie Brewster raised his head from his reclined position in the jump seat and rubbed his eyes. "We there yet?"

"Yes, we're here," retorted Ralph. As friends went, Brewster wasn't tops on his list. Too slow in the head. After a few beers he'd start drooling at the corner of the mouth. It wasn't that he was drunk after a beer or two. Yet it always happened. Even Ralph got nauseous looking at it. Spit dripping off his chin, and Brewster was oblivious to it. But Ralph brought him along because he was willing to make the two-hour trip on short notice.

Singer, on the other hand, was his best buddy, and he'd do whatever Ralph asked, even at the drop of a hat. In their tiny clique of beer-drinking, pool-playing red-neck buddies, intellectual prowess wasn't high on the list of priorities. Loyalty was, along with being able to fart on cue, and sport a beer belly that would put a pregnant woman two weeks past her due date to shame.

"So where do we go from here?" asked Singer, as he rolled a home-made cigarette with one hand.

The temperature was frigid, the air still. The convenience and liquor stores were dark and batten down tight. "They're close by," said Ralph, nodding his head in confidence. "Can't expect them to be sitting out in the open in this cold just waiting on a ride. But they're close."

"Let's get some coffee," said Brewster as he sat up.

"Yeah, some coffee," echoed Singer.

"Drive up and down a few of these streets first," instructed Ralph. "It's the Army in me," he chuckled. "Do some reconnaissance while everyone's asleep."

They drove slowly past boarded-up brick buildings, faded signs and trash-filled store fronts. A huddled body lay in one entryway on a pile of leaves and flapping newspaper without even one blanket.

"They could be huddled up in almost any of these abandoned warehouses," said Singer.

"Right. It may not be too comfortable, but there are plenty of places to get inside," agreed Ralph. Ralph looked in all directions. "I bet they're within a few blocks of that store."

"Definitely around this old section of town."

Ralph nodded. A big rubbery grin came to his face. Let's go get some coffee," he laughed. "Finally, I'm going to see that little prick again. Finally … I'm going to teach that little shit some manners."

# 20

WELL PAST NOON a pounding began on the back door of the warehouse. A heavy hammer clinked against the rusty lock while missed blows thudded against the warped wooden door. When the pounding stopped, a burst of daylight shot into their sleeping quarters as the door flew open. The children waited, their breathing halted, muscles coiled, ready to flee or fight according to Danny's lead.

"Morning, family," came the familiar voice. Eddie stepped through the doorway. "Now you don't have to crawl through those bricks any more."

Danny stood up. He really thought Eddie was going to show up hours ago. Had he known, he would have tried harder to get some sleep. But the gnawing emptiness in his gut kept him on the edge of consciousness throughout the night and morning. He felt as though an angry cat with bared claws was doing flips in his stomach.

"Where'd ja get those?" Eddie asked, rather impressed as he pointed at the cloth each had wound around them.

"It was all in here. There are rolls of vinyl over there. Gunny sack material and cotton, I think there's leather there, too."

"Neat," replied Eddie. "Keep you warm?"

"Yeah, that's why we used it. Some of it's dirty and all cut up, but it's dry," said Danny.

"I wonder if it's worth anything?"

"Maybe. It's yours as far as I'm concerned just as long as we have enough to use for bedding."

"Sure, sure. Say, we better be going." He addressed the other three. "Better stay close to here today. I'll make sure big brother here brings you back some grub."

"When will you be back?" asked Chrissy.

"Don't worry," said Eddie with a tooth-missing grin. "I'll have him back here by sundown. Now it's off to work we go."

The office was a street corner. The merchandise — hard rock cocaine. Crack. Thirty-cent bags. Eddie fronted each accomplice ten plastic-twisted bags. But the bags were all different sizes, and they sold them for what they could get. Competition was plentiful. Free enterprise at its finest.

The marketplace was wherever the dealers said it was. The customers always managed to get the word. Eddie had his favorite corners. Best of all, he had his regular customers. Moving around a bit didn't hurt business. In fact, the customers preferred it. They didn't like going to the same addresses, neighborhoods and corners all the time … too easy to get caught in a police dragnet.

All parties to the game, the dealers, the customers and the police all knew this was the drug-dealing section of town. The biggest vocational hazard was avoiding the gun battles when turf wars flared. Downright rip-offs of drugs and money were often attempted by those bold enough to try to change the rules. But in this game, all sides were cautiously prepared. Often as not, a rules violator got an all-expense-paid audience with a funeral director.

Eddie slipped Jasper ten heat-sealed plastic baggies no bigger than the tip of his pinkie finger. He pulled the white sedan under a large tree near the corner of Clarmont and Boles.

"Hang loose over by the bus stop. Move around, let the cruisers see you. They'll stop, so just be cool," Eddie said to Danny. Jasper and Ricky knew the routine and were waiting for the signal to go.

When Eddie's customers made referrals to friends, co-work-ers, whoever … they asked for Reddy. Like a password. Like grease on a set of ball-bearings, it made things easier and facilitated the sale. For one, it reduced the chance that the customer was a cop, and second, it slowed down the competition from horning in on the business. Sure, any runner would try to make the sale, but if they didn't know the customer it kept them off balance.

Back in the car Eddie continued Danny's formal training.

"You and Ricky are going to work Master's Park. You'll be moving around most of the time. Now, just do what I tell you. People will stop you. You don't have to do a thing, just fill their order." He grinned and pointed at Ricky. "He'll be watching you."

"Why?" asked Danny. "I don't use this crap. I ain't going to steal it."

"Didn't think you were," replied Eddie. "If I did, you wouldn't be here now."

"I'm going to keep an eye on you in case somebody tries to dis on you," said Ricky. His black baseball cap was on backwards over a hooded sweatshirt. A black leather jacket was buckled up tight. His face sported a sparse sprinkle of whiskers and ear lobes with two silver rings in each. He chain-smoked like Eddie.

The ten-shot nine millimeter gun in his hands was the object of Ricky's affection. "Nobody will give us any shit," he said, talk-ing to the easily concealed weapon.

Danny had been around Ricky for all of ten minutes. In that short time Danny could tell he was a clone of Eddie, although he looked somewhat better, had a straighter nose, and carried a little more body weight. When all was said and done, he was a druggie with vacant hollow eyes and a one-track mind. Make some money in order to buy more drugs, then mainline the profit.

"Here's ten bags," announced Eddie. He dropped each one in Danny's palm, counting each one, making a ceremony of the pro-cess. "Keep them in your drawers, down low. One in your palm, one in the lining of your cap. Cop comes down on you; throw and go! Don't take no shit. Don't admit nothing. I'll take care of you if something happens. It probably won't. Those chicken shit cops don't like the cold. But if they do come around, the main thing to remember is, get caught with as little as possible. Got it?"

Danny nodded, but inside he felt hopelessly trapped in the situation. More than the cops, he was afraid he'd get shot. If not, this was still not the way he wanted to be making some money. But he needed it. He had to play along for now. Maybe tomorrow he could bow out or turn it down, or just not be available. Today, however, he'd have to play the game. He should have known. He probably did. One part of him wanted to see what was up; the other wanted to do the right thing. Curiosity got the cat this morning. Ricky put the gun deep inside his belt and pulled his jacket down over the exposed butt. They got out of the car and walked across the street to the park.

Shortly after 5 p.m. the cars of the after-work crowd began driving down the streets along the perimeter of the park. Runners would dart from the trees and bushes to the BMWs and Lexuses, as well as the pickups and Chevrolets, completing narcotic transactions in the blink of an eye. The business was terrific. Never a congregation of vehicles or people, but never a let-down either. It was like passing out jars of honey at a bear convention.

By sundown Danny had exchanged better than forty bags. He was thankful the customers usually kept the talk short and sweet. He'd nod that he had what they were looking for, they'd say the amount they wanted to pay, he'd take the money and give them the rocks.

He took three one-hundred dollar bills from somebody's grandmother in a gray Dynasty. She wore a platinum wig with false eyelashes that fluttered near the end of her nose. But her face was loose and wrinkled. The back of her hands were blotched with liver spots and tight stretched veins.

Later, he traded one small rock to a teenage in a blue Trans Am. The front seat of the car seemed to swallow her up. She had only 18 dollars and became anxious when Danny was about to tell her to head on down the line. When tears came to her eyes, he gave in. She paid him in ones. Danny felt sorry for her, and himself, as the Trans Am drove away.

Eddie showed up again when the last of the sunlight faded and they headed back to the warehouse district. Eddie had a half-case of cold Coors in the car. Ricky and Jasper popped a top immediately and drank like they were dying of thirst. Danny passed. He was thirsty, but a lot hungrier. The one pattie burger Eddie had gotten him earlier in the day his stomach had long since forgotten.

Eddie collected the money as he doled out the baggies throughout the afternoon. Then he took up the remaining baggies and wads of bills from Ricky and Jasper. They stopped near the pool hall Danny remembered from the night before. Eddie gave the boys their cut of the proceeds, and they got out.

"Manana," said Ricky as he slammed the back door.

Eddie took a gulp on a beer, then quickly rolled down the car window and hollered into the cold. "Hey, come back here!"

The wind threw his words into the darkness. Eddie jumped out of the car and ran into the pool hall. When he returned, he was adjusting his belt and mumbling under his breath.

"Son-of-a-bitch was trying to run off with my gun. Last time I let him use it. You can carry it tomorrow, Danny my man."

"No! No! I ain't carrying no guns, Eddie. No guns."

"Have it your way." He glanced back at the pool hall. "I just know that chump was trying to sneak off with my piece."

"Well, you got it back now," Danny said. "Hey, can we stop at the store. I'm real hungry and I need to get some groceries for the others."

"Sure, but first I got a place I want to show you."

Most of the street lights were out as Eddie drove in the direction of the convenience store where Danny had made his phone call to Aunt Lois. Only one headlight was operational on the white sedan, and it appeared as if it were in the super low position. Eddie popped the top on another beer, gulping down half of it in one swig. A lone street light cast its yellow circular halo across the hood and into the windshield as they passed under it. Then darkness. The green dial of the radio emitted the only light in the car in a vast sea of black.

"I was watching you today," said Eddie. "You did good."

The car stopped behind an ancient art deco gas station. All the windows were broken out, and Danny could see half the roof lying inside the station floor. Next to it was another brick building identical to the one he and his siblings were holed up in. Eddie used a key on a back door lock, and they went inside.

It was warm. It was his first contact with a heated environment since the restaurant last night. Eddie flipped a switch. A bank of fluorescent lights came on.

Couches lined the walls. Two formica inlaid coffee tables on wobbly legs bracketed an electric pot-bellied stove in the middle of the shag-carpeted floor. Each was heaped with overflowing ash trays, pot-smoking paraphernalia, syringes and trash. Piles of empty beer cans decorated the corners of the room.

"This is my home away from home," Eddie announced with a tone of accomplishment. "It's our official party headquarters."

The place was a dump. Danny liked the warmth. That was about it. The stagnant odors made him gag. He didn't want to know what matter of fungus grew within the fibers of the orange shag.

"Very nice," Danny said. He hoped it was enough.

"You'll be our guest of honor this weekend. Bring the whole brood."

"Whatever ... we're not exactly into the lifestyle."

"No sweat, Dan-my-man. I got some real smooth, easy-going shit for you ... soft as a baby butt and as relaxing as an enema."

"Look, man, I'm tired. Just get me back to my place."

"Sure, Dan-my-man. Here's your split." He handed Danny a wad of bills.

"This is fifty bucks. I thought you said a hundred?"

"Hey, I'll make it up to you. Fifty is fifty. It was a little slow today. I said you looked good, but you need to be the first to more cars. Tomorrow will be much better. Let me have the rocks you got left over."

Danny knew he'd handled over a thousand dollars. He was getting mad. He was also very tired and very hungry. Fifty bucks was more than he'd had to spend on the needs of the four of them since they ran from the farm. For now, it would do.

The white sedan outside attracted some attention. The light that sifted under the door into the dark night focused even more. Neither Danny nor Eddie heard the door open. The gathering in the "party room" got considerably cozier.

"Can we join you?"

The voice made Eddie jump, as neither of them were facing the door. The voice sent a shiver through Danny. His recollection traced the voice immediately. Without looking, he had no doubt. Ralph had found him.

"Hey, bunny lover. You're a waze from home, tain't ya?"

Danny turned and faced the object of his disgust. This pathetic excuse for a man and a husband personified everything Danny distrusted in adults. The rage boiled up within him just looking at the fat rubber-lipped slob who tried to pass for a foster parent.

"Yeah. So? You're here. What good do you think that's going to do you?"

"It means, you little prick, that you can call your travel agent for a refund. There's only one place you're going."

"Who is he?" Eddie asked in a whisper while his eyes darted about in an excited dance.

"He's a nightmare," replied Danny, his eyes locked in a threatening stare with Ralph. "He's a pervert, and those two are a couple of mental defectives he runs with because no one else will have him."

Now Singer's demeanor changed from one of an adventure to one of wanting to beat the shit out of him, too. His face contorted and he bared his teeth, green and orange decay quite evident. Danny could swear he saw holes right through the man's remaining teeth.

"Why you in the big city, little boy? Could it be you're looking for momma?"

"What about her? What have you heard?" screamed Danny. The subject had caught him off guard. Ralph's words hit him like a kick in the solar plexus. He lost all sense of how to deal with this enemy. The mention of his mother combined with the fact that he, of all people, had found him caused his knees to shake. "Is she out?"

"You stupid kid. She's in Norfolk. She's always been there. That's about 30 miles north of your farm." He slapped Singer and Brewster on the back. In unison they laughed and mocked him. "Who's the mental defective now?"

Danny was shocked. He dropped his gaze at Ralph. He couldn't believe what he'd just heard. None of the men paid any mind to Eddie. Ralph was only interested in Danny and his siblings. He knew how to engage in verbal warfare; certainly with a tired, beleaguered, inexperienced teenager. Ralph brought the mother into the fray right from the start, hitting below the belt right out of the gate. When Danny's eyes dropped to the floor, Ralph rushed the youngster. His buddies were right behind him.

A split second later the room erupted in a searing flash of light. An accompanying boom dropped everyone in their tracks.

# 21

THE GUN SHOT exploded. The sound reverberated off the walls with the boom of a head-on collision. Danny was stunned by the ringing in his ears, but his eyes told him all he needed to know. Ralph was writhing on the carpet, gut shot, bleeding like a stuck pig. He hit the floor with the spastic wobbles of a Jell-O mold, and continued to wail and moan in agony.

Both Singer and Bender were oblivious to his screams as they crouched wide-eyed, reading Eddie's every move, hands high in the air.

Eddie toyed with the gun. A blank expression painted on his face. He didn't act like he was going to shoot again or like he was afraid. He just looked stupid, like he was trying to figure out what he'd just done, and what it meant. He'd probably never shot someone before, Danny figured.

Danny's mind, however, was racing. During pressure-packed moments like this it clicked with practical thoughts like the workings of a precision watch. He didn't always come up with the best decisions, but he didn't just freeze or panic.

"Cover 'em for me," he yelled.

Ralph's two lily-hearted buddies didn't move a muscle. Danny whisked through their pockets, throwing their wallets on the floor toward Eddie. He grabbed Singer's keys tight in his fist, the one and only item he was really after.

"Run, Eddie," he cried, "get rid of that gun."

Reddy Eddie's eyes broke from the visual fixation of his writhing victim, and he scooped up the wallets and fled the building. With that, Danny also sprinted out the door.

There it was: a vehicle. The one item Danny had thought of most in the past two days. A rich deep brown Ford King Cab pickup just about as sleek and bright as the day it rolled off the showroom floor with shiny chrome bumpers and dual rear tires. Danny had never driven a vehicle this big. The bench seat was deep and thick. He scooted it forward in one instant, slamming the keys in the ignition the next. The beast roared to life, belching a frosty cloud of white exhaust.

Ten blocks later he screeched to a halt behind the warehouse the four of them called home. He threw open the warped back door with such a yank that it broke loose from the upper hinge and fell against the door frame. The three of them were there. Chrissy was writing. All of them now stared at the door, afraid at the sudden noise. Danny's wild, startled face did nothing to calm them.

A brief sense of relief swept over him, but the rising tension engulfing his body quickly displaced it.

"We've got to go. NOW!" He ignored their perplexed looks and hurried them into the truck.

Danny's eyes focused directly on the road beyond the windshield. The Little Ones climbed into the jump seat as Chrissy fastened their seat belts and accidentally swallowed the paper wad in her mouth she had substituted for gum. She knew when to speak up and when to remain quiet. But she had never seen her brother so terrified. Her usual ability to remain calm and put things into perspective was destroyed as he raced through the old warehouse district, found the freeway headed west and climbed the on-ramp.

The cold winter wind whistled through a crack in the passenger window that would not close completely. Danny braked behind a slow-moving RV, and slid on the thin layer of ice that covered the road. He blasted the horn, swerved around the silver Air

Stream, and then stomped the accelerator back to the floor.

"Where are we going?" Melissa spoke up and asked the question they all wanted to know.

"Norfolk. It's up north, north of the farm. Mom's not in Omaha. She never was."

"Slow down, Danny," Chrissy pleaded.

"How do you know?" asked Sam as he pulled himself over the seat and stuck his head between his older siblings in front.

"Ralph told me. He found me along with Eddie. This is one of his buddies' trucks. They were going to beat me up and take us back to the farm."

"Wow, Danny. Cool. You got away," exclaimed Sam.

"Yeah," said Danny, keeping his eyes glued ahead, " 'cause Eddie shot him."

"Oh, no, Danny, that's terrible," said Chrissy.

"I couldn't do nothing about it. It happened so fast."

"Is Ralph dead?" Sam asked with anticipation.

"I don't know. Sit back, will ya?" Danny pushed his younger brother into the back. "I want you all to listen now, and listen good. I took this truck 'cause we're going to Norfolk to find Mom, and ain't nobody stopping us." He glanced at Chrissy.

"The address you have to write to Mom is in Omaha, right?"

"Yes," Chrissy said, "on Magnolia."

"And it's always been the same address, right?"

"Yes."

"Have you ever, even once, in all this time gotten a letter from Mom?"

"No."

"I'm pretty sure Aunt Lois has been lying to us. As far as I know, she's the only person who knew for sure we were here ... because of my phone call. She has to be the person who got Ralph back on our trail. He isn't smart enough to track us all the way here by himself. It seems to me that for some reason Aunt Lois doesn't want us to be reunited with Mom."

The truck cab became silent as they mulled over Danny's words. The miles streaked by. The hum of the tires sang to them; the illuminating beams of head lights guided their way. Danny sat as high in the seat as he could when driving through towns. He made sure the others were ducked down out of sight.

Danny's eyes were getting heavy with all the driving. That, combined with his general lack of sleep and the trauma of the fight with Ralph, left him virtually asleep at the wheel. As they passed through the town of North Bend, the snow began to fall again.

They sped through the night. Snowflakes licked at the windshield wipers and danced in the headlight beams. The monotonous flash of the highway center stripe beat like a nocturnal metronome in Danny's exhausted brain. The other three were already fast asleep when Danny's chin fell to his chest, and the massive king cab drifted off the road.

The pick-up truck left the highway and bounced across a shallow ditch; it tore through a barbed wire fence, catching the twisted wire and thrashing it about like a monstrous tail. It crashed into a wooden windmill on its way down a steep grade. Dried timbers splintered across the grill. The derrick tumbled like a drunk stepping off a curb with the massive metal blade smashing to the ground, and spinning deadly cartwheels across the earth. The wide truck's double wishbone suspension took every jolt in stride even as the engine screamed with increasing RPM.

Within seconds they were all awake, but the severe bouncing threw them about the cab like popcorn kernels in a popper. Chrissy's head hit the roof and she bit through her lip. Melissa cried out.

Danny clung to the steering wheel with all his might. All he could do was hold on; his feet kept bouncing off the pedals. The headlights jumped about like darting fireflies. At the bottom of their descent was a pond of sorts that filled up with water in springtime. In the fall and winter it was dry. A sharp drop-off surrounded the walls of the pond. If they drove off into the pit, the stop would be sudden and instant.

The truck pitched and tilted as it plummeted over uneven terrain, the tires crunching through packed ice and snow, their descent unabated as they barreled down the hill. The Little Ones, though buckled in, were tossed about in the jump seat like rag dolls in a hurricane. In the front seat, Danny and Chrissy fared no better. Chrissy was thrown repeatedly against her shoulder harness, bruising her neck and ribs. Danny's face repeatedly hit the steering column as he forced himself under the wheel and jammed his foot against the brake.

A violent lurch of the vehicle strained every pop rivet and weld in the truck. It groaned and shook. The few seconds of the wild ride seemed like an eternity. Then they flew off the ten-foot embankment into the mud pit.

The Ford engine squealed. It felt like they hung in the air forever. But the landing was hard. The shock absorbers and springs hit bottom. The truck recoiled in metal-tearing shudders. Glass shattered. The radiator burst and spewed boiling steam. The engine died with a final harsh clunk, and silence descended upon the wreck and its battered occupants.

Melissa was knocked out. Sam pulled her up and over the seat into Chrissy's arms, who checked her breathing, then held her tight, even as she worked to stop the flow of blood from her own mouth. Danny's knee hurt bad; so did his head. He could feel a knot growing on his forehead. Sam was knocked about, but otherwise unhurt. He climbed silently into Danny's arms. Their labored breathing filled the cab with sounds of terrified panting. Slowly, reality set in, but they didn't leave the truck. There was no place else to go.

For the rest of the night the four Stone children sat in the darkness listening to each other's breathing. The shiny new Ford King Cab was totaled, but the radio still worked, and it continued to play.

Danny offered up a silent prayer as he held his little brother. He knew he asked so much of his brother and his two sisters. They never really questioned him though. They all wanted to be back with their mother. They would all do whatever it took to accomplish that goal. He squeezed Sam and planted a tiny kiss on his cheek. None of them could sleep after that harrowing ride. So they all just rested, and dealt with their private individual thoughts. They would assess their situation at first light and begin their journey again. This time the destination was Norfolk.

At morning light Danny watched his breath cloud into frozen vapor as he exhaled. The sun crested the hill behind them, but the light was unaccompanied by any warmth. They were sitting in a wrecked truck out in the open. Shattered window glass littered the cab. The faint moo of a cow carried in the dense cold air.

They were all hurting, sore and bruised. Melissa was asleep in Chrissy's arms, Sam in his. It was time to move on. They had to if for no other reason than they would never find help out here unless a passing motorist just happened to notice the downed fence out by the highway and stopped to investigate.

He checked the glove box. It contained a pouch of roll-your-own cigarette tobacco, which he threw out, and a five-dollar bill, a pocket knife, and a state map of Nebraska, which he kept.

Their best bet was to keep heading west, parallel to the road. Certainly they would come to a town eventually. Plus they could keep to the river. On the south side of the highway was the Platte River. It was over there somewhere; they had seen glimpses of it ever since they passed through the town of Valley. And down by the river it was less likely they would be detected.

He looked at his little brother in his arms, so content and peaceful. At this moment he was safe in his dreams, possibly conjuring up simple visions of little boy fantasies. Danny hated to wake him. He waited a while longer and stroked his cheek. Sam's breathing was strong and steady, but a large amount of mucus had gathered around his nose. The mess was semi-frozen on his upper lip. "I've got to get you to a doctor, little fellow," Danny thought.

"Time to get up," Danny whispered. "Let's get out." His driver side door opened easily at first, then stuck. He forced his feet against it, leaving Sam on the seat.

He stretched and tested his legs. His face and head were sore, his knees ached. But he could walk; nothing was broken.

Chrissy watched him as he moved about. "What are we going to do now?" she asked. There wasn't even a hint of throwing in the towel in her voice. They had long ago made their unspoken pact to see this to the very end. Nevertheless, Chrissy wasn't asking for the time of day. If anything, her tone let him know she expected an immediate implementation of Plan B. And he had better have a Plan B.

The truck had been a windfall. Now it was nothing but a pile of twisted metal sitting on four blown tires. If he'd had a concrete plan of action yesterday afternoon, the gun fight and truck wreck had hanged all that. If anything, Chrissy was practical. She wanted to know what they were going to do today.

"Is Ralph dead?" Sam asked, rubbing his eyes.

"How am I supposed to know? I didn't stick around to find out. Quit asking me that."

"I'm hungry, Danny," said Melissa.

"I know you are, Punkin. We'll eat soon. How is she?"

"A knot on the head. That's all, I think," replied Chrissy.

"Well, I got a big one, too," he said, rubbing his temple. He tried to smile for the girls, but even his face hurt.

"It's not funny, Danny. You could have killed us all. Not to mention, we're back on foot."

"I'm sorry, Chrissy. I'm as thankful as I can be that we're all Okay. It just happened. I'm sorry. Too much truck, I guess. I wish I had it to do over. I'd be much more careful."

"Well, we don't always get a second chance, Danny."

He walked around and opened the door for the girls. For a minute they stretched and yawned. The oppressive cold enveloped all of them like they were standing naked in a walk-in freezer. But none of them mentioned it. They had learned to deal with whatever Mother Nature dished out. Complaining, even for a short time, wasn't going to change anything. The elements were included in the equation; Mother Nature was along for the trip. Something about living outdoors made them stronger, even with all their youthful weaknesses.

It was time to move on.

\* \* \* \* \*

Pay dirt … maybe. John Ranther felt light-headed from the news. He knew this was a real lead. "Rewards Come to Those Who Persist," was how the cliché went? … or something like it. He didn't care. He knew what he meant. And for the first time in days he felt good.

The driver of the delivery truck who stopped at the Schuyler Truck Stop the night before last had picked up the children. He was reluctant to 'fess up at first, but Ranther had his ways. Whether on the phone or in person, he could be quite persuasive. In this case a personal visit didn't become necessary.

As soon as he felt the truck driver knew something he wasn't offering up, Ranther sat back deep into his office chair and threw his boots up on the corner of the desk. His voice would slow, get rich and mellow, and he would begin talking of subpoenas, obstruction of an ongoing investigation, and calling one's superiors and customers. It was amazing how much he could learn with his slow-building pressure approach.

The truck driver told him everything, even as to why he picked them up in the first place. Ranther just wanted to know where he dropped them off. The driver gave him an exact address.

As soon as he got off the phone, he called Lois Devon's number again. No answer. Since the call from the employee at the life insurance company yesterday, he had tried to reach her at least ten times. The only voice that ever answered the line was the same six-word message on her answering machine: "Call back or leave a message." The line was never busy. In all likelihood she probably didn't answer her home phone herself. All through the afternoon, the evening, and this morning all calls to Lois Devon in Omaha received the same tired message. Ranther left a few messages of his own, and then he began hanging up after the fourth ring. He was ready to drive down to Omaha himself.

"Ranther, call on line two," came a voice through the telephone speaker.

"You the person looking for those missing kids?" The voice was anxious, bordering on desperate.

"Yes." Ranther sat straight up, concentrating completely on the telephone receiver.

"Oh, I'm so glad I caught you. I can't believe what's happened the last day and a half. You've got to help, or something really bad is going to happen."

"What's going to happen?"

"I don't know, but Sandra is beside herself."

"Sandra who?... Mrs. Stone?"

"Yes. Oh, I know now I shouldn't have done it, but I helped her leave the hospital. I really couldn't stop her once she found out her kids were missing. All the time she was in the hospital she thought they were at their own farm, not living with other people."

"That doesn't surprise me."

"She dumped me off several hours ago when we stopped to get gas."

"Where are you at now?"

"At a Phillips 66 in Blair."

"And what is your name?"

"Nancy Shira, I just knew I had to do something. Everything has been going so fast. All I had was your number on a note from the hospital. I hope I haven't waited too long."

"Now don't worry. Sit down and relax. You did the right thing. What kind of car is Mrs. Stone in?"

"My car, it's a white Dodge Spirit, like an Acclaim."

"Do you know the tag number?"

"Oh, yes. BR-2413."

"Thank you for your call, Nancy. I'll have someone come and lend you assistance."

"Don't you want to know where she's headed?"

"Did she say specifically?"

"No. Just the town; she's headed to…"

"Omaha," interrupted Ranther.

"Yes, Omaha."

Ranther's boots hit the floor without a good-bye. It was time to have the rubber on his patrol car tires kissing some asphalt highway. He called the Douglas County Sheriff's Department on the car radio. He updated what information they had on the children and requested an APB be issued. Then he filled them in on their mother and the car she was driving.

"Be on the lookout for all of them," he cautioned. "The sooner all are located and reunited, the better. The longer they are all unaccounted for, the greater chance exists that tragedy in some form will be the final outcome."

Soon police cruiser computer boards in and around the city of Omaha, Nebraska, flashed the following message:

**Escaped: Norfolk Facility Mental Patient. White Dodge Spirit BR-2413 Nebraska. Erratic behavior. Approach cautiously. Known to be headed into the Omaha area.**

# 22

THE WALK BACK to the road was a struggle. Their immediate destination was, once again, unknown. How long it would take to reach help, food and shelter was anyone's guess.

Melissa hummed to Mrs. Leatherwood. Uneven steps on frozen terrain bounced her tune in the crisp air, but she continued on, singing the words in the chorus to a sweet melody their mother loved to sing, *You Were Always on My Mind.* At this moment Melissa was carrying their spirits, singing and humming to her one faithful companion who never let her down, her soiled, rag-tag, grandmotherly doll, Mrs. Leatherwood.

Danny's knees ached something terrible. He felt like his limbs had been bent backward. Chrissy was deep in her own thoughts. Her determined steps were steady, yet her shoulders were dipped, her face locked on the ground in front of her. One step at a time. Were she to contemplate much more she might falter.

Sam, however, was running ahead.

"Did you kill him? Gee, Danny, you got him good. I knew you'd get him. I just knew you would."

They crossed the highway without being seen. Danny grimaced at his little brother's misplaced enthusiasm and said nothing.

Along the shoulder of the road they walked, then down a shallow ravine.

There was the river — the Platte River. It moved as a silent wide serpent, slow and steady. A glistening reflection like a changing mirage attested to its constant movement downstream. It looked so gentle and serene.

But Danny noticed the lapping slaps of water at the shoreline and the muddy surges of rushing water as it barreled between partially submerged boulders. The icy pinpricks of the wind made him shiver, thinking about how cold the water was in the river. The shoreline offered little shelter from the elements. Walking was difficult, too; inclines, rubble and soft earth all made the going difficult. But they would not be seen walking here. He said nothing as they struggled through patches of high grass, wet ground and shards of loose rock.

Eventually, they could not continue walking along the bank. A precipice broke in front of them, straight down to the water. They climbed back along the shoulder of the roadway, still headed west; the faint outline of distant buildings broke through the misty overcast. It was the town of Rogers, Nebraska.

Danny kicked himself mentally for wrecking the pick-up. He knew that he never quite took full advantage of opportunities that came his way. He knew his dad would have done things better.

Deep in thought, Danny didn't hear the siren that wailed in the distance. It was Chrissy who motioned for them all to stop and listen. She had to cover Melissa's mouth as the youngest among them continued her singing, and she drew her doll into her chest as Chrissy pulled her close.

Yes … a siren. Coming from the east. Danny knelt down and concentrated. Maybe it was an ambulance. The wail grew louder. They watched the road behind them and listened. Soon a red and blue rainbow of lights appeared in the haze of an overcast sky. Within seconds, the pulsating strobes broke through the misty fog, the high decibel horn blaring. A police cruiser was bearing down on them at better than 90 miles per hour.

Without a word, the four of them broke into an all-out sprint along the road. They dropped down a slick grassy embankment, sliding on their rear ends, shuffled through a concrete culvert, through a gap in a chain link fence, and huddled behind a boarded-up wooden building on the outskirts of town.

"Think they're looking for us?" Chrissy asked.

Danny shrugged. "Don't know. Wouldn't be surprised though."

"Maybe they found the truck," said Melissa.

"That would sure put them close if they did, Punkin."

The police cruiser flew into Rogers. They lost track of the lights, but heard the siren until it stopped suddenly somewhere in the middle of town.

Sam was really excited. "They must have found Ralph's body. "They're searching everywhere to find his killer."

"Good grief," replied Danny. "Would you put a sock in it? I don't know if Ralph is dead, and I didn't shoot him."

"But you should have."

"Sam, don't say things like that," Chrissy was shocked. "You don't really mean that."

The little boy stared right into her eyes, his face was determined, his eyes like lanterns of fire. "Oh, yes, I do. Everything he did to us. And ... he killed my rabbit." He maintained his determined vengeful expression; his eye contact didn't waver. Chrissy saw her father's hard-nosed set-jaw visage, at the times he meant business and was not to be swayed, in her little brother's face. She found a new dimension of respect for this typically sweet boy even though she didn't like the implication of what he said. She wanted to kiss him; she wanted to spank him.

She turned her eyes away. "We'll talk about it later."

"Going to be hard to get out of this town during daylight," said Danny to no one in particular.

"Where are we at?" asked Chrissy.

"Let's see if we can get inside. I got a map we can go over. I know the last town we passed through was North Bend."

The side door to the building was fastened with only a hook. Inside were stacks of 50-lb. sacks of hog feed arranged in neat rows on a sawdust floor. Overhead, such a collection of dust-laden cobwebs hung that it looked like a thousand brown icicles draped from the rafters. Exhaled air from the breathless youngsters formed semi-white clouds that tumbled the suspended dust in the frigid building. Danny spread the map out under a window. The girls gathered around him.

Sam remained by the door to keep watch.

\* \* \* \* \*

"MC-12, this is base, over."

Ranther was headed east on U.S. highway 91 just east of Clarkson. He displayed no pretence about running at or near the speed limit. His squad car could do 100 MPH without getting its second wind, and on the open road it hadn't seen 80 since he left Madison.

"This is 12," he replied into the handset.

"Douglas Sheriff Department reports a shooting last night involving a one Ralph Jameson." The dispatcher's voice droned through the two-way speaker without the least bit of enthusiasm as though she were reciting the ingredients to a familiar recipe. A brown and silver Ford King Cab pick-up was stolen. License number PF D-7254."

"Where?" Ranther broke in.

"Omaha," came the reply.

"The victim is in stable condition after surgery. One of the men with him said one of the children you're looking for was the shooter — a Danny Stone."

Ranther's heart sank. The whole complexion of this case had now changed. He would be getting a lot more help in locating the children, but by law enforcement officers who would be looking for an attempted killer. Service revolvers would be drawn. Questioning was the last priority, after the handcuffs were on, after the suspect was behind bars. The way these kids ran and slipped away tormented his thinking. There may never be a time for questions. The boy may be dropped by a law man's bullet and die in front of his siblings.

"Do you have a location?"

"We just received another call less than 30 minutes ago. The truck has been located in Dodge County, four miles west of North Bend. It was wrecked, a total. No one in it or around it."

"Roger," answered the deputy. He skidded to a stop on the gravel shoulder, tires kicking up snow and spitting ice chunks across the roadway. He flipped on the emergency lights. He grabbed at the state map in the clutter-filled seat beside him, and cranked to full volume Alan Jackson on the cassette player. He knew he was close to Rogers, and there it was. No more than 20 miles as the crow flies, but the back roads might be snow-covered and closed.

He spun the cruiser in a fierce U-turn back to state highway 15, and flew south. He would be in Schuyler within minutes. Then east on highway 30, just eight miles to Rogers.

If only he could get there first — if only. He knew this was it, he knew he was close. He had to be. The siren wailed its cry into the vast open plains, while country music blared into his ears. Ranther's eyes were locked on the road, his foot pressed to the floor. There wasn't a second to lose.

Only half a dozen brick buildings comprised the downtown area of Rogers, Nebraska. The rest were tin sheds and dried broken-down wooden warehouses with a definite lean. Even at that, Ranther almost drove by the police station. It nestled between the bank and hardware store. Faded black letters outlined in gold script read: LAW ENFORCEMENT, but it was barely visible on the grimy plate glass window even when he got to the door.

He shut down the cruiser's lights; the siren's loud wail fizzled to silence as the squad car slid to a halt at the curb.

Deputy Ranther rushed up the station's steps. His eyes were searching every corner of the front room even as he bolted through the door. A sweet-natured gal squinted past her chubby cheeks as he came in. Her smile was genuine, and she waited on him imme-diately across a thick counter where time and elbows had worn through the vinyl top down to bare wood.

"Hi, I'm Vicki," she said with a lilt in her voice. "May I help you?"

Ranther caught his breath. "Is the Chief in?"

The young woman's cherry face fell as she sensed his anxiety. "Yes, I'll get him for you." Ranther watched her scurry to the back. She entered an office next to the water fountain. Within seconds she was back in the doorway with a lean uniformed young man. He said something to Vicki and began walking to the front. He adjusted his belt buckle as he walked, patting his shirt pockets. His gray uniform was clean and pressed, heavy starch. Royal blue trim ran along the crease of his shirt and slacks. In every detail he looked as the head of the department except in the face. He couldn't have been a day over 25. With a hairless chin void of any trace of stubble and skin as smooth as a baby's behind, Ranther had to take a second look at his badge. He was the Chief all right: Jason Cole — Chief of Police.

"Name's Ranther, Deputy John Ranther, Madison County Sheriff's Department," he said, extending his hand.

"Yes … well how can I help you?"

"Have you heard of the Stone children, four kids that have been missing for a month now?"

"Oh sure. Two boys and two girls."

"Well, I think they're in your town right now."

The youthful policeman's eyes widened. The job in this one-light town usually consisted of writing traffic tickets, and nothing else. This visitor had brought some excitement with him. Chief Cole was ready to do something besides flip through wanted posters and watch Vicki buff her nails.

"Have any idea where?"

"The truck they were riding in wrecked just east of here is the last report I received," Ranther replied.

"That truck," said the Chief. "My deputy Luke is at that scene now. Let's take two cars. Follow me. I know exactly where it is."

\* \* \* \* \*

Nothing — absolutely nothing.

Her phone had been ringing off the wall, but none of the calls was the one she desperately wanted to receive. Where were those children? Lois hadn't been to work for three days. She complained of a cold, then the flu. When her boss called this latest time, she said it was doctor's orders she stay in bed and rest. And the incessant messages from that pesky deputy sheriff were just plain irritating. She both despised and feared him. She wouldn't call him back; she didn't care how many times he called.

Yet Lois continued to watch the phone as though any minute it might get up and run away. She circled it. Sat next to it reading *Cosmopolitan,* but her mind wasn't on the magazine articles. The nerve endings in her ear pricked at the slightest sound. Within her brain a telephone was constantly ringing. But not a real one. The one she prayed would ring, the telephone that would speak to her, the news she had to hear, and before it was all too late.

Why hadn't Ralph called? Good grief, she thought. That fat slob couldn't do anything right. Her energy had been drained by the whole ordeal. If only those damn kids had done what they were supposed to do, this delay would not be eating on her so.

In spite of all the stress, the fact that her endurance was pressed near exhaustion, her determination to see this through had not faltered. And it wouldn't. It wasn't every day a person got the chance to lay hands on $800,000. She could change her life handsomely with that kind of money. Lois Devon had no intention of letting it slip through her fingers.

The television kept her company with the volume on mute. It was time for the noon news, and she turned up the sound and sat back in her chair. As she watched and listened, her blood pressure dropped to zero and her face turned ashen white.

An on-camera news reporter stood in front of a hospital emergency room entrance while photos of her nieces and nephews flashed in the corner of the screen. All of her senses were glued to the television set. Hairs prickled to attention on her forearms. Her shoulders felt cold. The details of her evil plan shattered around her feet even as her emotional strength faded and left her feeling hollow and weak.

"Early this morning near the old warehouses along Metropolitan Avenue," said the reporter, "a gun battle left a Madison man critically wounded. Police have identified the man as Ralph Jameson, who we just learned was the foster parent of the four Stone children who have been missing. Initial police reports list the eldest, Danny Stone, as the shooter.

"Mr. Jameson was brought here to Our Lady of Mercy around eight last night. He is out of surgery at this time, but still listed as critical. We don't know what exactly led to the confrontation, but it has certainly put a sad twist on a story many of us had been following very closely. Back to you in the studio, Chris."

"In light of this tragedy, Rita, have the police located the children?" the news anchor asked.

"Not yet. We were told less than an hour ago that all available manpower from the sheriff's department and police from both here in the city and outlying municipalities are joining in an all-points search. A brown Ford pick-up truck driven by a man with Mr. Jameson was also stolen last night. Police believe the children may be the ones to have taken the vehicle, so they are looking for it as well."

"In any event, the authorities are now looking for a group of children, the oldest of whom is believed to have committed an assault with a deadly weapon. Of course, if Mr. Jameson dies, the charge will be murder. This is Rita Rhome reporting from Our Lady of Mercy."

Lois couldn't move. She felt the clamminess in her hands, the beads of sweat rising along her hairline. A catatonic hypnotic cloud descended over her. She thought she was going to throw up.

Yet her mind was racing. Too much time had been lost. She

had to think of herself. If she waited another minute, she would never escape. Lois jumped to her feet.

She ran through the house tossing odds and ends in her purse. Within minutes she was warmly dressed, a conservative business outfit, and her pearl necklace. She had one last business item to attend to before she left town, and now she was dressed for it. She could have left town weeks ago, but she wanted to disguise and launder the paper trail connecting the insurance money to her. Now she had to move. The curtain was rising on her final act in Omaha, and she didn't have a second to spare.

"Think of your faults the first part of the night when you are awake, and the faults of others the latter part of the night when you are asleep."
— *Chinese Proverb*

# 23

SAFELY INSIDE THE feed warehouse, Chrissy took charge scanning the state map. It occurred to her that she didn't really know where they were in relation to other towns and places. That was unacceptable. Actually, she had never known where they were or where they were headed, even though they all talked so much about Omaha. But a map… a map would give her that knowledge.

She wanted to know where home was, the farm, and their little town of Albion within the state of Nebraska. And, Kansas City, too.

The map and its criss-cross lines of red, black and blue was confusing until she located Omaha on the right side of the paper. She had no experience using one. Sure, the world maps in school had taught her directions, but she'd never read a highway map before. Along red highway lines her fingers moved out from the big city, and she saw the names of familiar towns, like Fremont, and she saw Norfolk and Schuyler.

"There's the river, Danny," she showed him, "and there's North Bend. We're right along this highway."

Danny eyes scanned the sheet. He noticed the roads and distances from North Bend to Norfolk. Town names and the distances between them opened a new horizon in the children's minds. Chrissy was enthralled with everything within the state outline. Danny ran his finger back and forth under the word Albion.

"We can't wait 'til nightfall to get out of town," Danny said to the others.

"Can we eat now?" asked Melissa. They had made it to a town and found a safe place to hide out for awhile. To Melissa it seemed to be the perfectly appropriate time to bring up the question. Now it was time to eat.

"I'll go this time," announced Chrissy. She gave a faint smile and a sparkle darted from her eye as she held out her hand to Danny for some money.

"We'll eat," he insisted, "but we have to keep moving. Let's head back to the river. We'll find something to buy before we get too far away."

"Let's stay here for awhile, Danny," Melissa pleaded.

"I'll carry you, Punkin. It's warmer walking during daylight anyway. We'll find someplace warm to sleep tonight."

"But my head hurts, Danny. I want to stay here awhile."

Sam walked up and shook his finger in his little sister's face. "We can't stop! Didn't you hear that siren come into town? Danny knows what he's doing. Now get up."

"Sam, stop!" Chrissy cried as she pulled him away.

"We ought to make a raft and ride down the river to get away," Sam said.

Danny grimaced at the logical, yet totally impractical suggestion of his brother. "We can't do that, Sam. It's winter. We'd get wet and freeze. Maybe drown. That's a very powerful river."

"Okay, but … let's go. I don't want to stay here anyway. The sooner we get going, the sooner we see Momma."

Danny was stunned at Sam's behavior, although he had noticed the growing changes in his attitude. Sam had his own opinions and was now expressing them. Sam had heard the Franklins planning to call the cops and had stayed up half the night in order to warn the others. Because of Sam they had escaped. He was no longer a sleepy little boy willing to follow. He had his own concerns, his own ideas and opinions. And now, he had no hesitation in speaking his mind.

Back out into the frozen winter cold they went. If they had to move on, they would. Triumphs and setbacks for the group were temporary and inconsequential. The final goal was the only thing that counted. For them the trials of last week were only a faded memory, the numb ears and chapped lips of today only a brief discomfort. Their minds dealt with reality. Their short memories protected them. Who else but children would endure such bone-aching cold, hunger and pain while drifting about in a busy, indifferent world, and maintain such steadfast optimism? They might fail, but they would not give up. The most important person in their world had been snatched from them. It was only natural that they do everything within their power to be reunited.

They shuffled across an open field behind the wooden warehouse and through a thicket of dead tangled vines and high grass. The churning gurgle of the river could be heard before they reached it. Erosion had cut sheer dirt cliffs along sections of the river where the power of the water sliced the banks with the precision of a backhoe. Yet where the water slowed, the shores were wide, the surface of the water calm. The mighty Platte had a personality. Danny noticed the majestic strength and beauty of the river as it flowed through the winter landscape. So did Chrissy. Along its shores they could move westward and be unseen.

When they reached the high bank of the Platte, they were confronted by a chain link fence. It prevented access to the river within the city limits. Across the water's expanse, a horse fed on a bale of hay within a pole corral behind a small white frame house. Otherwise, they were far enough from any roads or buildings to be seen. Bent and jagged wind blown trees grew on the upper banks, and they moved west in a choked belt of dead plant growth.

"Stop right there!" thundered a baritone voice through the icy breeze.

And they did. Danny felt as though his guts had hit the ground. They were caught in the open. Had they been detected by a shot-gun-toting, red-necked landowner? Melissa began her infant-sound-ing whimper. Chrissy quickly knelt beside her and squeezed her tight. Chrissy held her close; she needed her little sister now as much as Melissa needed holding. Chrissy could figure things out for herself. She was as smart as Danny, if not smarter. But it was times like these when Chrissy needed him in the worse way, and she would let him handle this in any manner he decided.

Sam hesitated for an instant when the voice echoed, but his overall attitude was defiance. The seven-year-old drew on the anger steadily growing within him. He was still dedicated to the group, but increasingly he was dissatisfied with their progress. He had learned to hate Ralph. He knew the truck driver had given them the shaft. He despised Eddie, too. Anyone who got in their way was the enemy in his mind, and he had no intention of cooperating with some unknown voice yelling through the weeds.

"Just relax, kids. I'm here to help. Your mother is looking for you. She's very worried, and I can take you to her," John Ranther lied. Whatever came into his mouth, he said without thinking. He had been so relieved when he spotted them moving through the underbrush.

Still Danny could not see who was speaking. Who was this person? He certainly knew who they were, but could he be trusted?

Ranther was alone. Police Chief Cole and his deputy were north of the highway, and certainly out of earshot. He knew the children were tired and afraid. Talking a suicide jumper off of a ten-story ledge would be easier than getting these frightened kids to trust him and come in peacefully. He thought of Mary and he wished his wife were here. She could talk them in; she would touch them and love them and make everything all right. But it was in his hands. He had done the easy part. He had finally found them. He didn't want to treat them as criminals, rough them up and bully them around. He wanted to talk them in. Somehow he just wanted to do it that way. He wanted to let them know someone cared.

"Stay where you are," shouted Danny. He wanted an easy way out, a quick reunion with his mother without the struggle of additional days or weeks in the frigid countryside. But he was afraid, upset that they had been discovered, distrusting that they would be thrown into another "foster home." He had to know for sure the intentions of this unseen voice before he willingly surrendered.

Sam crawled next to him. "Let's run, Danny, let's run," he said.

Danny turned his head and gazed into his brother's eyes. The little boy's snotty nose and cherry cheeks looked so familiar, but his eyes blazed newly found determination and defiance. The confusing experience of the past summer and the life and death struggles of the last four weeks had added wisdom and courage borne of practical experience. He was growing in a sort of universal maturity, and Danny was not sure he liked it.

"I'm here to help you," boomed the voice again. A crackling rustle through the high grass and twisted underbrush testified that the voice was getting closer. "My name is Deputy Ranther. I'm from Madison County … where you're from. Let me help you. You don't have to stay out here. No one is going to make you do anything you don't want to."

The boys scooted near the huddled girls. Danny brushed Chrissy's collar and whispered in her ear, "It's only one guy. We can slip away; we've done it before. If he wanted to help us so much, why didn't he come by the farm after Dad died?"

Chrissy's eyes were wide with excitement. She sucked in a high gulp of air and searched Danny's face. His anxiousness reflected back to her. She squeezed Melissa and glanced at her, then back toward Danny. "Point the way."

Danny led them away from the oncoming voice. They ran in a shuffling crouch, their shoulders below the tops of the high grass. The only sound they made was the crunch of their footsteps in the iced-over snow. Within seconds the boys were far out in front of the girls. Melissa couldn't keep up.

And behind them came the lumbering footfalls of their pursuer. "Stop! I'm here to help you." Ranther sprinted after them.

He could see them darting ahead, his holster slapped at his thigh with every stride, his chest was already hurting as freezing air bellowed in and out of his lungs.

Melissa's short strides betrayed her. The towering policeman was gaining, cutting the distance between them with every passing second. A shriveled vine caught her toe, and she fell with a splat on the ground. Terror flooded her senses. "Chrissy," she cried. Before the sound of her voice faded, Ranther was upon her, and he stood above the prone Melissa panting to catch his breath. "Chrissy," she cried out again.

Chrissy heard, she knew. She dropped to her knees and looked in the direction of Melissa's cries. She didn't want to go back. Surely the cop wouldn't hurt Melissa. Her eyes shot back in the direction of the boys. She saw nothing, but she knew she could follow the trail. Conflicting thoughts flooded her mind. She didn't want to give up ... give in.

Up ahead the boys stopped; they waiting and listened. Chrissy remained on her knees and looked up at the overcast sky. She took a deep breath and rubbed her eyes. She knew what she had to do. It wasn't a matter of what she wanted. She wasn't responsible for just herself. "Go on, Danny," she stood and screamed into the air. "Don't let them catch you. I've got to go back. We'll be all right."

As soon as the boys heard that, they gave a knowing glance to each other, and then they were gone, slinking through the undergrowth along the north bank of the river. They zigzagged around scraggly trees, through a ravine, and sprinted across an open stubble field.

Chrissy found the sheriff's deputy helping Melissa up off the ground. The man looked at her with a sympathetic face, but said nothing. Neither did Chrissy as she took her little sister's hand and followed the policeman back toward the road.

As he and Sam ran along the river bank, Danny knew this was no longer just a matter of being reunited with their mother. It never had been, really. A simple hitched ride into town and a complaint to the authorities after he and Ralph fought at the farmhouse would have produced an investigation. The children, in all likelihood, would have been removed from the Jameson's control, then and there.

No ... it was all more than that. This entire episode involved complicated issues of a 15-year-old boy struggling to understand why his father had been yanked from his life. He wanted to get off the farm. The result of the tragedy was that he needed a whole new direction in his life. In the process he became acutely aware of adults and what they really are ... regular people with frailties and weaknesses just like kids. Some were honest, caring and helpful. Others were not.

In just a few short weeks the Stone Children had grown and matured far beyond their youthful years. Even Melissa and Sam were no longer "Little Ones."

Now, the boys were on their own, making one last effort to maintain control of their personal circumstances. No one was directly responsible for them; they were responsible for their own well-being. Sam was on the same wave length as Danny. There was absolutely no hesitation in either one of them as they darted along the river bank away from town and anyone who intended to bring them in.

\* \* \* \* \*

Lois cranked the defroster to high as she frantically scraped thick layers of rime ice from the windshield. Why had she called Ralph? Mentally she kicked herself. As much as she hated him now, she knew why she had called. She figured he could get the four kids out to the new location, whatever force it took. She did not think she could talk them into going there. She should have forgotten about them; she knew she had wasted entirely too much time.

Ralph had gotten himself shot. Now everyone would be looking for her kin. The whole story would come out.

Ever since she'd made the initial deposit of the insurance check,
she'd been making regular withdrawals using Sandra's checkbook,
forging her sister's name. Some of the checks she deposited in a
checking account she had set up in Kansas City under an assumed
name. With that money she purchased thousands of shares in several mutual funds. She bought shares in more funds, then sold
them, and deposited the proceeds in third and fourth bank accounts. She set up simple, low-interest-bearing savings accounts,
and funded with cash a $150,000 life insurance annuity that she
could begin receiving monthly income checks after just five years.

Lois didn't know if such tactics would actually insulate her
from a financial paper trail. She could only hope. The main thing
was to separate herself as much as possible from her original bank
account in her neighborhood held under her correct name.

Today she had only one more withdrawal to make. Twenty-six
thousand nine hundred and eighteen dollars remained in her bank
account. The officers at the financial institution had bought her
story hook, line and sinker of how expensive it was to care for four
minors while paying for the professional care of their mother. She
had shown them a newspaper clipping about the farm accident.
After the second visit they didn't ask any more questions as to why
she deposited and withdrew such large sums. She just needed to
make one more withdrawal, keep it simple, and remain calm and
collected. One more withdrawal and she'd be long gone.

Lois' attention was focused on her ice-scraping chore as the
sound of an automobile engine pulled up to the curb. It braked
quickly, sloshing in well-traveled snow-slush pushed over from the
middle of the street. The mighty slam of a car door broke her self-
submerged thoughts, and she looked up just as powerful fingers
clamped down a handful of her hair.

She cried out. Her head was slammed against the hood of the
car. Another hand slapped her full in the face. Her hair was yanked

and twisted. When Lois righted herself from the assault ... she stood ... facing Sandra.

Sandra's eyes were red and moist, pupils pinpointed in a fierce penetrating stare. A flimsy trench coat turned up and buttoned at the collar appeared to be the bulk of her winter protection. Her hair was uncombed and frayed under a scarf. She was wearing house slippers, gripping a huge clump of brown hair.

"What is the matter with you?" Lois screamed. She tried to move, put some space between Sandra and herself, but the knuckle punched between her breasts held her against the car.

"Where are my children?" Sandra said with the snarl of a rabid pit bull.

Already Lois' head felt as though her scalp had been dragged across rough concrete. Any thought of lying to her sister faded just as quickly as the thought entered her mind. The jig was up. She had to help Sandra find the kids, and she would if she had to. In the back of her mind she still hoped no one knew about the money.

"I don't know. I don't know. I've been praying for weeks the police would find them." She covered her face with her hands and held her head as her back slid down the car door, and she fell to her knees in the snow.

"Get up! Get up! You're not getting off that easy. You're going to help me find them. Then you're going to do some explaining ... a lot of explaining."

Lois quickly related what she had seen on the television earlier that day. Sandra uttered an "Oh, my God" under her breath, but listened to it all.

"We're going to keep looking until we find them," Sandra finally said, the tip of her nose within a millimeter of her sister's. "They weren't supposed to be living at someone else's farm; they were supposed to be living in their OWN HOME! That's what you promised me. Now, get in!" She pushed Lois into Nancy's Dodge sedan that was idling at the curb. "You drive." And with that, they headed in the direction of the highway.

"He who loses wealth loses much;
he who loses a friend loses more;
but he who loses courage loses all."

— *Cervantes*

# 24

"STOP AND DON'T move!"

The crisp command cracked in the frosty air as though the boys were wearing audio earphones with the gain cranked off the dial. Their steps halted in mid-air, each dropping to the ground in a heap of panting chests and darting eyes.

"Stand up," came the order. A lean young man in a starched gray uniform stood less than 20 feet in front of them, a walkie-talkie in one hand, a revolver in the other. "Luke, come in. I'm behind Dresser's lumber yard along the river bank. I've got the two boys. Find Deputy Ranther and get over here."

"Don't shoot," hollered Danny, shocked to see a gun pointed in his direction. He rose to his feet and took a step forward; his boot crackled the dried grass and frozen vines encased in ice crystal sleeves.

"Get your hands up, boy." Chief Cole waved his revolver up and down. "Your little escapade is over." He glanced at Sam standing several feet behind and to the side of Danny, but quickly focused his attention back to the older boy. "Luke, hurry up. Get your butt down here," he said into the handset.

Sam walked up beside his brother. "Should I raise my hands, too?"

Chief Cole didn't reply. His tight lips accentuated his penetrating stare; it was all directed completely toward Danny. "Turn around," he ordered. "Put your hands against that tree behind you and spread your legs."

Sam looked the policeman over one time, from head to toe. His gaze shot to his big brother, then back to the cop who ignored him completely. Sam couldn't believe his eyes. He tried to speak, yet all that came forth was blather of rattled "buts" in series like a toy machine gun with weak batteries, sounds caught in his throat, a muffled protest surrounded in confusion and that grew into white hot rage. "Leave my brother alone," he screamed.

"Back, boy," was all the cop said as he pushed him aside. "You're next."

"Don't do it, Danny. You didn't do nuthin'," Sam said with wide, disbelieving eyes. The cold wind stung his exposed skin, and yet his face felt warm. Salty tears ran down chapped cheeks, icy sweat dripped in his eyes. The cop had one hand in the small of Danny's back as he patted him down, searching for weapons. Sam slowly backed away, his fist clenched, unable to accept the scene before him.

In those frightening seconds, Sammy Stone saw his last and final emotional rock being taken from him. Barely six months before his father had been torn from his life forever; shortly thereafter, his mother. As far as he knew, she too was dead. Today, he had left his sisters behind to an uncertain fate. Despair overwhelmed him. He felt short of breath and sick in his stomach, even as the policeman reached to his belt for the cuffs to shackle his brother.

Emotions gushed through his small body, but he wasn't about to accept the situation. He had heard the Franklins planning to turn them in. He had waited up half the night to warn the others and get them all out before the sheriff came. If he took off now, maybe this cop would be distracted; maybe Danny could break free. The girls were gone now, but not necessarily for good. If he and Danny could stay free, maybe they could get back together with them. First, he must help Danny right this moment. He had to do something. He couldn't allow Danny to be handcuffed and led away like a criminal.

"You'll never get me. Never!" With that Sam turned and

sprinted for the fence that lined the river; the crunch of refrozen snow pack under his footsteps signaled his sprint for freedom. One steel cuff was already clamped around Danny's wrist, but when Sam shouted both Danny and the police chief glanced toward the fleeing boy.

Less than 30 yards down the high river bank stood a single concrete block building that served the town as a slaughter house. Painted in red were the words ROGERS MEAT COMPANY. The business slaughtered and butchered cows, pigs and goats for anyone in the county who wanted to bring an animal from the farm and return home with wrapped steaks for the freezer. The average kill was one or two head a day, except during hunting season when they did a land office business processing deer.

A three-foot-wide trough ran from the kill floor through the concrete block wall out the back of the building, through a cut-out in the chain link fence down to the rushing river. When an animal was being butchered, the channel ran with water carrying discarded parts and unwanted trim into the hungry mouths of waiting fish. When Sam jumped into the chute, it was dry, yet freckled with snowflakes and coated with ice.

As Sam climbed into the open culvert, Danny broke and ran up the shallow rise toward the slaughter house, the free end of the handcuffs slapping his forearm with every stride.

Chief Cole cried, "Stop!" His hand reached for his revolver. The gun barrel rose to his shoulder, he cocked the hammer, the crack of a shot split the air. But the sound didn't slow Danny down, and Cole didn't want to shoot into the air again. He holstered the revolver and brought the handset to his mouth. His attention was strangely concentrated on the younger boy. Maybe it was because of the desperate tone in young Sam's voice. Again he keyed the mike on his two-way. "Luke, we're behind the meat company. Get your butt over here … and call North Bend for an EMS ambulance, too. We may need it."

Danny paused once to cry out, "Come back, Sam, come back."

But he knew he wasn't heard. He dashed ahead, sprinting toward the trough on muscular legs as fast as they would carry him.

Sam scooted and slipped along the trough to a point several feet out beyond the river bank where the flume descended at a steeper angle. He braced his hands against the sides to maintain his position and looked into the gurgling water below. It would carry him away; he would make his escape. It was the only thought that stuck in his terrified mind.

Tears still stung his eyes; he didn't look back. He didn't understand why the policeman had arrested his brother. He was the only one left, the only one left to find their mother. He would do it. He would complete the mission they had all set out to accomplish. One way or the other, he would finish what they had all started.

He could swim. He could float on his back until the water reached a calm stretch. He buttoned the top snap on his coat, sucked in a deep breath and pushed himself forward.

Danny reached the top of the flume just as Sam's bundled frame disappeared below the end of the chute.

"No o o o o," he wailed. A faint splash echoed back at him. Danny scrambled into the open trough and pushed himself to the precipice. Without wasting a single millisecond, he dropped into the icy drink below.

It was a good 20-foot plunge into the freezing water; the impact slammed his body like a linebacker meeting a fullback head on at full speed. The swift current rolled him, disoriented him, sucked at his sodden clothes and slapped him in the face. He struggled for air in the freezing river spray that bit his face with pin-prick stings. He legs thrashed wildly, fighting to keep him up. The taste of muddy water filled his mouth, and he almost sucked his belly full as he gasped for breath.

His brain pulsated at full throttle. With every muscle fiber he battled to stay afloat and scan the surface of the relentless rushing river for a glimpse of his little brother. He prayed that his larger and heavier body would move more swiftly, that he might catch up to Sam before it was too late. Already his shoulders were aching, tightening, failing to respond to his mental commands to stroke. Numbness crept through his body in spite of his concentrated labor to keep his arms and legs moving.

Just ahead, entering a bend in the river bed, Danny spotted Sam's frantic thrashing body. Only several dozen feet separated them. The current hurled them through a vortex between two large rocks, the undertow pulled them down, then spit them up, and they were swished about like soap bubbles spinning down a bath tub drain.

He was getting closer. Danny kicked with the tenacity of a doomed man sinking in quicksand. He could no longer feel his fingers or toes. If it weren't for the steady flow of the water, he would certainly have sunk to the bottom, but the surging volume drove him ahead, like an insignificant splinter of driftwood, pell-mell through a flash flood roaring river bed, and nothing would slow him down until the river spent its power.

Danny fought to look ahead. Every time he opened his eyes the river slapped him in the eyeball with muddy foam. The pain caused him to wince even as he forced himself to open them again. He breathed at the top of the crests. He tasted the slimy grit in his mouth, his chest was on fire.

His right hand touched soggy fabric, smooth and silky, the feel of nylon. Danny forced his head high out of the river to see. A drop in the water's course knocked him down, but he held on. He had a grip on the lower edge of Sam's 4-H jacket. His fingers tightened in a vice-like clamp.

Danny was unable to bring his left arm forward, to move under or beside his brother. The sheer speed of the current kept them riding high in the water. He didn't need to get his body under Sam. At least he had reached him. There was no way he would let go now. But he was already scared, a second fear talked to him, a menace now much more threatening than the rushing Platte River.

The kid was not thrashing about, screaming, choking, twisting. He wasn't doing any of that. He was just riding the swells like a cork, washing in the counter forcing eddies, bobbing in the rapids, all with Danny hanging onto his coat.

They pummeled through another narrow opening between a rock outcropping and a boulder. Danny grabbed for the water-carved rock with his free hand. He impregnated his fingerprints in the stone even as Sam dangled in the surf on the end of his other arm. The unconscious boy's dead weight strained Danny's elbow, stretched his shoulder ligaments to the breaking point. The weight of a ship's anchor on the end of a kite string. But there was no way Danny would let go. He would lose his arm first.

Danny squeezed his knees around the submerged boulder, fighting to secure a toe hold. Struggling against the powerful current he pressed against the rock … hugging … squeezing. Every filament of muscle fiber in his body sucked him closer to the limestone while at the same moment he willed his mind and body to reel in his limp, unconscious brother. The relentless water pounded him, beating him like an unleashed fire hose, open throttle, peeling the bark off a tree. Within seconds, the river won and popped them from their sanctuary like a pair of bugs sprayed from a wall.

Danny's right arm felt as though it had been stretched to better than twice its original length. The pain and aching in his shoulders and hands made it very difficult not to scream. He had to look to make sure he still had a hold of the jacket. He did. In a way, the pain was good. He knew he was alive. He knew his body was still working for him. Below the water's surface, all was numb. He couldn't feel a thing below his waist.

The surf smacked him again in the face. Another turn in the river threw them once again nearer the shore. It was flattening out, no longer a narrow carved valley. His toe hit bottom. His shin cracked into a submerged object. He flailed his free arm against the tide. The water's rush began to slow. With all the torturous throbbing in his joints, Danny continued his never-ceasing struggle toward shallow water, pulling all the while the dead weight behind him. The water was now below his chest. He made it to his feet, and then fell back down. He crawled in the mud, dragging his precious cargo, inch by inch. Finally, almost completely out of the water, he fell prostrate on the sand, his lungs heaving, his entire body utterly exhausted.

Danny was flat on his back, his chest wheezing like a bellows, his lungs screaming for air. He felt the cold mud … sand oozing over his collar and down his neck.

He forced himself to roll over onto his stomach, then to his knees. He scooted next to Sam, panting over him, and gazed into the purple face of his lifeless brother. In that instant, he felt his mind divide in two. One half emotional, one pragmatic. Just the sight of his brother's face caused his heart to skip a beat, then jump into rapid contractions of pure dread. His heart pounded faster than the pace of his panting. But the pragmatic side of his mind stepped to center stage. He shook his head to dispel any negativity. It was up to him to do what had to be done. Each precious second might mean the difference between life and death for the kid.

He put his palm under the youngster's neck and straightened his head in line with his spine. In spite of his single-mindedness to administer CPR, Danny couldn't help but shudder when he caught a second look at Sam's face. The boy's lips were a dark blue, lips curled back exposing baby teeth in a ghostly growl. Black eyelids … black. A nose with no color at all, pale and ashen. A skeleton white.

Danny felt the tremors of sorrow bubble inside of him, but he pressed on. He pinched nostrils together with one hand, and pulled the boy's jaw up and out with the other. Then he blew his breath gently into his brother's mouth. He continued … again … again … and again.

The boy's chest barely moved. And he didn't cough or vomit water. He didn't move at all. Danny began heart massage, then went back to artificial respiration and then back to heart massage.

While pressing on Sam's chest, Danny mumbled encouragement to his comatose brother, babbling incoherent prayers. His voice grew audible and cried out across the flowing water, only to be snatched up and sucked away by the frosty wind.

Danny didn't notice the flashing strobe lights beaconing from the roadway 50 yards away. He didn't hear the car doors slam as half a dozen people sprinted in the boys' direction.

"Wake up, Sam," he admonished as he shook the kid gently by the shoulders. "Come on, Sam. Talk to me." The little boy's head rolled on his neck like a loose caster. Danny bent him over his knee and gave him several swift chops with his fist between the shoulder blades. The little boy didn't cough, twitch, jerk or anything.

"Sammy! Sammy! Listen to me, Sam. I'm not done talking to you." He held him up by his jacket at arm's length in front of him. The little boy's limp legs hung just above the shore, the toes of his favorite hiking boots making notch marks in the mud.

"Oh, Sam," Danny choked between sobs for breath. The terror of reality seized him. He had fought his emotional side when there had been work to be done. But now, mind-ripping deluge of emotional pain overtook him. Danny was engulfed by debilitating anguish that felt as though it would surely crush him.

He had his little brother close to his chest, hugging him with all his might. Through a cloud he saw people running toward him. All adults, all strangers. He could tell his sisters weren't among them. They would probably arrest him. Or they'd say they were there to help them. Sure they'd say that. Adults always say they want to help. It's just a code phrase for getting their way.

Danny was exhausted. He couldn't get away this time. He had failed. He hadn't accomplished anything he had set out to do. He had let his sisters down. And he had failed Sam in the worst way. That little admiring brother who always looked up to him. Danny pressed his tear-covered check against Sam's cold face and sobbed.

# 25

IT HAD BEEN a stroke of genius — giving Sandra the slip so easily. Clever at the very least. Her sister was so gullible; she had her objective and a one-track mind at this point. Lois didn't blame her. She didn't want anything bad to happen to the children either. But she had an entirely different agenda.

Barely thirty minutes out of Omaha, Sandra and Lois had to find a service station and check the oil in the sputtering Dodge. A high-paced puttering in the engine had become a tappity-tap, which soon became a heavy clicking noise accompanied by growing blackness spewing from the exhaust that easily contrasted in the white frosty air.

The sign at the edge of town said Valley, Nebraska. As they pulled under the dented canopy of a Phillips 66, a single attendant shoveled snow from the front door.

Sandra looked her older sister square in the eye. Her stare wasn't quite as fierce as back at the house, but it still conveyed a no-nonsense look. Most of all, whenever she looked at Lois, the overwhelming expression was unmistakable disappointment.

Lois tooted the horn. When the attendant came over, she rolled down the window and asked, "Could you please check the oil?"

"Sure," replied the middle-aged man as he bent over and looked in the window while wiping his hands with red rag. His face was cheery with bright eyes and a slight runny nose from the cold. As he looked in the car window, his expression changed from friendly

231

greeting to perplexed amazement as he caught a glimpse of the two women. The passenger was dressed in a thin cotton blouse, pink sweater and flimsy gray trench coat with her hair all tied up in a scarf. She looked as though she might well freeze to death even inside the car. The driver, on the other hand, appeared ready to attend a board of directors meeting at a Fortune 500 company. Outfitted in a smart dark two-piece business suit with matching navy silk blouse, pearl necklace and full-length gray fur coat, the woman kept her eyes straight ahead, staring through the windshield, puffing steadily on a cigarette.

The attendant went to the front of the Dodge and raised the hood.

"I've got to use the rest room, Sandra. Might as well do it here. Want anything?"

Sandra shook her head no.

"How long you been up, huh?" No response. Lois really didn't want her to start talking anyway. She knew that Sandra would really spill her guts and read her the riot act once she got started. Right now her mind was preoccupied. It was probably all she could do to keep from screaming because she didn't know where her kids were.

"Listen … let me get you some coffee while I'm in there," Lois continued. "I know we're on the right track. We're closer to them than you think. You'll see. A few more miles up the road is Fremont. We should stop at the police station there and see what they know."

Sandra just nodded, slowly — almost imperceptibly, while Lois started inside the station. A thought crossed her mind, and she went back out to the car, up to the front, where the attendant had his head buried in the engine.

"What's it gonna take?" Lois asked.

"At least a couple a quarts," he said, without coming out from under the hood. "Probably could use an additive, too."

"Whatever … here's a twenty. Put the rest of this in gas." She handed him the bill.

"Okay."

With that, Lois went inside the building and immediately lit up another smoke. A wrinkled-faced old coot in faded overalls sat in the corner spitting Skoal into a paper cup. A 13" black-and-white TV sat at a half-cocked angle on a dusty shelf with the picture rolling and the sound turned down. The place felt like a sardine can for automotive products. Every square inch of the place was full of something — quarts of oil with layers of fuzz growing on the tops of the cans, batteries stacked all over the floor, fan belts plastered about the walls. A reach-in soda pop cooler took up half the space in front of the register. The counter was loaded down with gum and mints, pork rinds and Cheetos, beer nuts and Slim Jims. With all the merchandise in the place, what got sold most were your two basic farming necessities — gasoline and Red Man chewing tobacco.

"You got a vehicle?" Lois said to the man in the corner studying his paper cup. He didn't even bat an eye. "It's worth a hundred bucks if you can give me a ride."

A glance flashed her way. He even put down his cup. "Were you talking to me?" He said in a wise tone as though he had scores of good-looking women addressing him every day.

"You heard me."

He leaned forward and stood up. He was shorter than she had thought at first; probably younger than he looked, too. His face had been knocked all out of whack, a Popeye effect. Either he was missing his lower dentures or been involved in an accident or fight that knocked his lower jaw halfway to his nose. He hardly moved his lips as he talked. "Where to?"

"Omaha"

"I can handle that."

"We got to go now."

"No problem, little lady. My truck's in the back."

The two of them headed out the side door away from the Dodge. They were only 30 minutes from Omaha, 45 at the most. The bank lobby would be open until three. Lois glanced at the clock above a moth-eaten mounting of a stuffed raccoon. The time was 1:20 p.m.

\* \* \* \* \*

"Dr. Denison's office. May I help you?"

"Yes, this is Detective Ron Gregory with Omaha PD. I understand that Dr. Denison performed an early morning surgery on a shooting victim. Has he come in yet? I need to speak with him."

"Yes, he's here. Just one moment."

The line hummed elevator music as the detective was put on hold. He made use of the time by reviewing again the patrolman's report made at the hospital from accounts of the victim's two friends and information gained from EMS personnel.

According to witnesses, four or five shots were fired after the three men were robbed. One round hit a Mr. Ralph Jameson in the abdomen. There was no provocation for the shooting, as the victims did what they were told. Only one person committed the robbery and shooting, a 15-year-old named Danny Stone.

The line clicked and a voice came on. "Detective Gregory, this is Dr. Denison. How may I help you?"

"Need to know how your surgery went last night with Ralph Jameson. What's his condition?"

"Not good, I'm afraid. He took one round in his lower abdomen. The bullet hit just about everything it could in that part of the body. He sustained a lacerated pancreas, perforations of the small intestine and a nick of the bladder. Luckily it missed the spleen and kidneys. He didn't suffer any tissue contamination, just lots of damage."

"Size of bullet?"

"Small caliber, probably a 25. Certainly a low velocity, the round stayed in his body. It was lodged in his small intestines. It's probably one of those cheap handguns that you couldn't hit an elephant with unless you were standing three feet in front of it."

"Has he awakened in recovery yet?"

"No, actually we didn't want him to awaken just yet. He's highly sedated. He'll be asleep for at least another 12 hours if …" There was a sharp end to the doctor's sentence.

"If what, Doctor?"

"If he makes it. Quite frankly, there's no way to know at this point whether he'll recover or not."

"I understand, Doctor, but help me out here. At this point, what's your professional opinion?"

"I can't give you a specific prognosis at this time."

"Off the record …"

"Okay, off the record, detective, but I'm just trying to be of help. There's nothing I can say that has any medical meaning until some time passes. Mr. Jameson isn't in real good shape. I went by to see him about an hour ago before I came to the office, and talked briefly with his wife. She said he drank and smoked a lot, and he's obviously overweight. I'd say, since you want an opinion right now, that Mr. Jameson's prognosis is very poor."

"How's his wife taking it?"

"Quite well. I was rather surprised. Anyway, that's all I can tell you right now, detective. We should know a lot more in 12 hours … or less."

"Thanks, Doc. Bye." Gregory continued to intently read the file and made additional notes even as he was dialing the office of the Nebraska Highway Patrol.

\* \* \* \* \*

"Hurry! Hurry!" yelled a tall uniformed cop as the mass of humanity surged down from the roadway toward the boys.

Two police cruisers with red and blue strobe lights pulsating sat on the roadway shoulder just above the riverbed. Another vehicle, a square-boxed emergency medical truck pulled up behind the squad cars. Danny watched through tear-streaked eyes as the occupants scrambled to the back of the truck, throwing open the rear doors.

Three police officers pulled up short in the sand 50 feet from the boys. They were followed by two weathered-faced men in blue overalls and denim jackets and a skinny fellow in a business suit. Danny still clung to his brother, the limp form held tightly to his chest. His eyes were wild, desperate. They gave him some space and approached no further.

"Help is here, son," said the largest of the policemen. "We're here to help you."

"Stay back!" screamed Danny. His voice cracked as he said the words. "Sure, you're going to help," he said sarcastically. "Why should you help now?" His nose was running; he could barely see through the tears.

"I know what happened," said the large policeman, trying to speak calmly through his pants for breath. "It's all over. We know where your mother is. We're bringing her here."

"Liar! You just want to take me in." He stepped back into ankle-deep water. He didn't care about the cold. He didn't even feel it.

The emergency medical personnel were now coming down the shallow slope to the riverbed with a stretcher in tow. Ranther took charge and took another step forward. This was no time for a discussion. If there was any chance to save the little boy, the opportunity was quickly evaporating.

"Come now, Danny ..." the sound of his name seemed to shock him for a moment. "The ambulance IS here to help. We ARE here to help you."

Danny's head began to shake involuntarily back and forth. "You can't help him," he choked. "He's dead." He choked out the last two words through sputters of spit and thick saliva. Tears came in waves. He sobbed unashamed in front of them. But he didn't lay the body down, and he didn't take his eyes off them.

Ranther's mind was racing. Okay, if the gentle treatment

wouldn't work, he'd do it by the book. The boy wasn't armed. If anything, he was cold, hungry and afraid, and ready to come in whether he admitted to himself or not. Ranther began walking, closing the distance between them.

"Stay back!" Danny screamed, but the huge deputy kept coming. He turned to run with Sam in his arms, but he tripped on a submerged root in the river and fell with a splat in the water. He had to let go of the limp body in his arms. He glanced over his shoulder. All of the men were coming, almost on top of him. With agility of a cat righting itself in the midst of a fall, Danny sprang to his feet and sprinted just ahead of their grasp.

Down the shoreline, his athletic legs carried him swiftly, boots slapped the water at the river's edge while leaving half-inch prints in the sand. The handcuff on his wrist flapped in the wind. Chief Cole's deputy, Luke, drew his service revolver and fired a shot in the air. Then he leveled it at the fleeing boy. Split second later Ranther parried the barrel skyward with an upper-cut blow to the man's forearm. The gun cracked a second shot that cut harmlessly through the frigid sky.

"What the ...? Are you crazy?"

"The kid's wanted for assault with a deadly weapon," Luke said meekly.

Ranther towered over the young cop and glared at him with a menacing stare that conveyed the message he wanted to get across. "He's unarmed, he's tired. I don't care what he's done. He ain't going nowhere, so don't be acting trigger happy." Ranther paused to make sure the point was properly received. "Got it?"

Luke nodded, then quickly broke eye contact with the Madison County Sheriff's deputy.

One of the overall-clad farmers took up the chase in earnest as the others fell back. He may have been tough and strong, but his legs were no match for Danny's who quickly widened the distance between them and disappeared behind an outcropping of bushes past a turn in the river.

The medics grabbed up Sam's cold, lifeless form and began in unison both artificial respiration and heart massage. Deputy Ranther stood over the scene as he watched the youth disappear from view. Both Chief Cole and Luke were running back to their squad cars. Ranther keyed the mike on his two-way radio.

"Base, this is Car 26. Do you have an ETA to Rogers for Sandra Stone, the mother of these kids we got here?'

"The Highway Patrol called in ten minutes ago," came the voice through the radio. "They said they should arrive by 2:15 p.m."

Ranther glanced at his watch. It was 1:50. He already knew the nurse aide's missing white Dodge had been spotted south of Fremont headed northwest on Highway 275. Sandra Stone had been taken into custody without incident, still dressed in house clothes and a flimsy raincoat, with no driver's license or ID. But she had nothing to hide and readily admitted who she was to the officer who stopped her.

Something inside told him she was combing the countryside looking for the children, too. When he had been contacted, Ranther asked the Highway Patrol to bring her to Rogers pronto. She was needed here ASAP. Her presence may help avoid a catastrophe. It looked like he already had one on his hands though. The little boy was being loaded into the back of the ambulance. His lips were blue when they placed him on the stretcher.

The fate of the little boy, however, was out of his hands. He was more concerned about the oldest one, Danny. Strong-willed and stubborn to a fault, this kid wasn't going to roll over and just give up. He had seen it first-hand, right in front of him while the boy was bawling his eyes out. There was no way that boy was going to just call it quits and surrender. Ranther prayed he wouldn't get himself shot by some local "John Wayne."

He said a little prayer for his wife Mary. She would never forgive him if he didn't bring in this boy safely and reunite him with his family. In the weeks these children had been roaming the countryside, the importance — the need — that his wife displayed about having children in their family finally hit home. He had never blamed her that she couldn't bear children. He had always been so absorbed in his work that he hadn't cared himself one way or the other. Now he knew the truth. The need inside her for a child in their home had bubbled to the surface. Maybe she had mentioned it to him before, and he just hadn't been listening. Maybe she had felt guilty or ashamed and never brought up the subject. But now he knew how she felt. He had to admit, he thought it was a great idea having children around his home, to teach, to be responsible for and watch grow up. They would have to adopt, but he was all for it. As soon as he got home, he would talk to Mary about it. He loved her more than anything else in the world, and he would do anything for her. The idea sounded better and better the more he thought of it.

A crackle came through this two-way radio. "This is HP Car Eleven. I have passenger S. Stone. We're entering Rogers' city limits at this moment. Over."

"Go to the City Hall on Main," replied Ranther. "We'll be right there." He hiked up his gun belt and hustled for the high ground where the cars were parked. As he neared the ridge, he saw Chief Cole waving to him frantically.

"Hurry," said Cole as Ranther jumped in the passenger door of the Chief's squad car. "I've already received a report of shots fired."

"Oh, God, no. I told Luke to keep that gun in his holster." Ranther had sweat beading up in his sideburns and under his hatband in spite of the cold.

"It wasn't Luke. Some hometown hero is acting like he's out to bring in our boy to collect some kind of reward … dead or alive."

Ranther groaned. He wanted to ask "why," but he knew. A local radio disc jockey had gotten hold of the story that Danny Stone was suspected of shooting a man in Omaha. The 10-hour-a-day radio station routinely broadcast an incessant barrage of market and commodity reports along with decade-old songs by Conway Twitty and George Jones. Ranther shook his head as the police cruiser sped downstream along the river bank. The radio announcer probably thought he had a real scoop on his hands, even though he took the story off the news wire. No doubt it beat getting excited over a change in pork belly prices.

"Luke, this is Cole. Come in."

"I'm here."

"Whatcha got?"

"The kid's hunkered down under the dredge at the sand pit. I can see Cecil Counterman's pick-up over on the far side. He's got someone with him. They're taking pot shots at the sand piles around the dredge so the kid can't move."

"Dammit, Luke. Get your ass around there and arrest those idiots. You'll be doing them a favor. If anyone gets hurt, I'm going to slap them with the most severe charge I can come up with."

"Roger, Chief."

"Poor kid probably thinks it's the end of the world," said Ranther in a whisper like he was thinking out loud.

Cole slammed on the brakes and whipped the cruiser into a U-turn, sped a quarter of a mile, veered down a shallow incline and emerged in front of a chain link fence on the rim of the sand pit.

"We'll have to walk from here." Even as the car lurched to a halt, Cole jammed the gear shift into park and reached for the handset to his radio. "Base, this is Cole. We're at the sand pit, south side. Send the Highway Patrol and Mrs. Stone out here." He paused for a split second, then keyed the mike again. "Vicki, better yet, you bring them out here ... and hurry. Out." With that, he tossed the handset on the floor and sprang from the cruiser already well behind Ranther.

# 26

DANNY HUNKERED DOWN. He was surrounded. Cakes of wet sand clung to his boots like lead galoshes. His clothes were a magnet for every kernel of silicone he touched, the freezing damp specks stuck to everything, draining the fading heat that remained in his body. Hypothermia was setting in, and his bones, encased in wet clothes, ached in the cold.

Zing! A rifle bullet kicked up a spray of sand which bit him in the cheek. He reeled, fell back, and rolled in the sticky dune. They were trying to kill him.

A gut-wrenching wave of fear swept through him. He wanted his dad … and his mother. He had just been trying to do what he thought was right. The helpless picture of little Sam passed through his mind, and again his eyes boiled with sadness, but tearless – dry in the face of confusion and danger.

In the past six months his entire life had been ripped apart. It made no sense. He didn't deserve it. His family didn't deserve it. For a moment he even wished he was back at the Jameson farm.

Just seconds ago, as he ran along the weed-covered river bank, the sand pit popped up in front of him. A peeled-back chain link fence provided access to the cratered landscape of gravel and chat hills, and mounds of smooth rocks — pea to quarter size. And sand, tons of it, in mountains better than four stories high.

It wasn't a matter of giving the authorities the slip — in the back of his mind he knew there was no way out. It was just that the mountains of sand, huge berms dredged from the river bed, along with the deep holes in the earth like void craters of a galactic moon, each sucked clean of dirt and gravel, comprised an inviting sanctuary.

He wasn't going to them. If they wanted him so bad, they could come in, find him and haul him out kicking and fighting.

Whap! Faster than a person could blink an eye. The bullet missed him, but he felt the velocity blast, a sharp snap of air past his ear. Barely three inches right of his shoulder the round smacked into wet sand with a "whop." The hole in the dune just appeared. It gave him a weakness in his knees and his bladder. He couldn't help it, crouched low in the gunk, freezing though he didn't realize it, he felt a warmth run down his thigh as he wet his pants.

"Come on out, boy." The voice was a high-pitched nasal twang. "Whatcha want … a cold coffin or a hot coffee?"

"Yeah, boy," came another voice, "hear you're pretty good shooting unarmed people. How good'ya shooting when someone kun shoot back?"

"Come out with your hands up 'n we'll get ya somethun' warm to drink … some food, too. Whaddayassay?"

Danny knew it was time to hunker down. Every time the brave talking stopped, the shooting resumed. At least it didn't come in volleys like they had semi-automatic rifles and were just blasting away. No, each shooter took his time, laying down individual rounds within inches of him. These crazy coots knew how to shoot. Probably able to nip the eye of a woodpecker at 300 paces.

But Danny had little room to hide. The two men talking to him were on a gangplank that ran from high ground on shore a hundred feet out over the river where it sat on a wooden piling. From there the operation of the dredge in the river bottom could be observed. Wherever he moved behind the sand pile, they could easily walk along the gangplank and relocate him. And each of them had rifles. They were in control. If he moved too quick to get out of the line of one, he could easily jump into the kill zone of the other.

Whap! The round impacted the wet sand with a startling thud as though a side of fresh beef was being struck with a baseball bat. Frozen silicone kicked in his face. Danny jerked and rolled. He dabbed his eyebrow and found his fingers covered with blood. Straight in front of him, the silhouette of a gunman, rifle pressed into the shoulder, eye locked down the sight, looked back at him. Danny lunged in the opposite direction and pressed against the ground.

He was virtually caught in the open. They could pick him off like an opossum waddling across an open road. He couldn't keep pressing his luck … what luck; he couldn't believe he'd thought of that word. Bad luck, maybe. The last three weeks had given him a lifetime of it.

He knew he had to use his head. Quit being bull-headed, always trying to slip, run or shy away from problems or responsibility. Now he'd have to face the situation in order to still be breathing in another hour. He could do that, of course. He had in the past. But he always waited until the last possible moment to come up with a specific plan.

These demented plow boys were playing cat while he was their mouse. Soon they'd tire of shooting into the sand dunes.

Danny tried to concentrate and formulate a plan. Hadn't he stepped forward and confronted the fat truck driver when they had needed a ride? Hadn't he intervened with Eddie and his drug-dealing scam? Not really, but he had intended to. One long stressful day of pushing crack on a street corner was going to be the extent of his drug-dealing career. You've got to be an absolute idiot to do that to make money. You don't sell, you buy … a one-way florist's special; an all-expense-paid trip to the mortuary. 'Cause if you don't get just plain shot to death by the competition, you've got a good chance of becoming hooked on the dope, throwing your ticker into deadly arrhythmia, and playing center stage at the local hospital while the medical staff watches you grow cold on an emergency room gurney.

The nasal twang voice brought him out of his mental deliberations.

"Talk to me, Annie Oakley. Hear you're a crack shot – can hit anything – 'specially if it's unarmed and standing five feet in front of you."

"Time to come out, Wild Bill. This time I'm hitting sompun 'sides sand."

There was only one thing he could do. They had him triangulated, he had only to move two feet either side of his spot behind the pile to be directly in the sights of either man. Even straight behind the mound, at the farthest point from the gangplank, they could still hit him if they wanted to; take pot shots at his extremities. Hit once, he'd be dancing around like a chicken with a broken wing. The thought was terrifying. Panic shot through him. He stood up and raised his hands. "Don't shoot. I'm coming out." As he stood up and stepped forward, he was immediately visible. Sunlight glittered in all directions from the handcuff that dangled from his wrist.

* * * * *

At the Rogers Police Station and Law Enforcement Center boisterous cheers of wild jubilation with hugs and kisses took top priority over a ride to the sand pit. Once he encountered the clan, Ranther had dropped the girls off in Vicki's care and supervision, before Luke picked him up for the ride to the river's edge where the two soggy, frozen boys had come ashore. A short time later, when Sandra Stone walked into the station escorted by a tall, lean Nebraska highway patrolman, the station house erupted in shrills of heart-felt joy.

"It's Mama!" cried Melissa, her recognition immediate, any hesitation non-existent, as she sprinted toward the door before Sandra even had one foot inside.

"Oh, baby!" She dropped to her knees and absorbed the full

rushing blow of the child flying into her arms. Sandra covered her baby daughter in kisses, stroking her knotted hair, pushing her out at arm's length so she could look at the little girl, then just as quickly pulling her back into her embrace. She saw the dirty baby face, the chapped lips and the snarled knotted hair of a camper who had been lost in the woods. But she said nothing about that, rejoicing in the moment.

Chrissy was right behind Melissa in the charge to the door, and she wrapped her arms about the woman's neck and nestled her cheek against her mother's cheek. The patrolman removed his sunglasses and watched the scene, glancing at Vicki with an understanding nod. Vicki's rotund face beamed as she put on her overcoat, then reached for a tissue on her desk and dabbed her eyes. No one was in a hurry.

"Mama's precious little girls, I've got you back ... I've got you back." Her eyes met Chrissy's, and then she hugged her close and kissed her cheek. "And I'll never let you go again."

Those few short phrases said volumes to the older girl. She knew her mother felt guilty, responsible for the ordeal they had endured. She also knew her mother was back to being her old self. Chrissy wasn't cold any more. She realized how smelly her clothes were. But she was warm now; the tears flowing from her eyes were torrents of happiness. "It's okay, Mom. Everything's okay now."

"Look, Mama," said Melissa. She reached down to pick up her doll that had fallen on the floor. "Mrs. Leatherwood is happy to see you, too."

"Oh yes, honey. And I'm very happy to see her." With that she gave the soiled dolly a gentle kiss on the forehead.

The two girls gave each other a quick hug, faces brightly smiling. Sandra stood up; her eyes searched the corners of the police station. Her glance passed over the patrolman who was wiping his sunglasses and the strange woman who stood behind the counter.

"My boys ... where are my boys?"

Vicki didn't have the heart, or the nerve, to tell any of them that the youngest boy was at this minute being rushed to the hospital in North Bend. She was glad the girls didn't know any of this as well, having been kept in a separate room from her dispatch desk until right before their mother had arrived. "Your oldest son is down by the river. The police chief wants me to take you down there right now." She looked at the highway patrolman, and he nodded affirmatively.

"Absolutely," said Sandra, concern now etched across her face. "Let's go."

* * * * *

"Just keep 'um high, and walk over this way. Slooooowly."

Danny crab-walked to his left around the sand mound he had been hiding behind. Just that second, a shot rang out and he dropped to his knees.

"Hands up, Cecil. You, too, Harold. Just lay those guns down. I mean right now."

"We're just trying to help."

"That's right, Luke. That kid's wanted. I suppose you know that?"

"I know that. I also know you two are under arrest."

"What for?" Cecil Counterman seemed truly shocked.

"Trespassing, for one," cited Luke "And shooting guns on private property, and …"

"For holy shit!"

"Now just come on off of there. Leave your rifles where they are. You won't be needing them for awhile."

Danny watched as the two red-neck heroes moved down the gangplank toward the high ground on shore. Luke waited there, at the end of the metal walkway, beckoning to them with his revolver pointed in the air for them to come on off.

Now was his chance! For a few moments he was no longer the center of attention. He ran in a crouch to his left, between mountains of iron-gray gravel and blonde water-smoothed rocks, toward the river, toward the engine house that powered and controlled the dredge. The building was conspicuous in a field of towering piles, a tin-covered shed on I-beam poles. Out the bottom of the shed ran a thick rubber hose, better than three feet in diameter that extended in a shallow trough until it disappeared down into the Platt River. The shed continued to shake and groan. The operator had high-tailed out of the place when the vigilantes started shooting, but he hadn't turned off the engine. Danny could hear sand swirling and grinding in the hose. Inside the engine house the dredge pump was connected with a grain auger and the sand continued on its way, up a metal tube several stories into the sky. Fresh wet sand gushed out of the top of the tube where it fell back to the ground and formed a high, growing inverted cone of sand.

Danny slipped into the engine house. The heat radiating from the working machinery was a welcome relief. He took off his denim jacket and soaked in the warmth. It felt like he had just lost 50 pounds. Sand coated the jacket with a quarter-inch layer; broken icicles hung from the hem. He stayed clear of the single window in the shed. They may look for him here, maybe they wouldn't. Well, surely in time they would, but maybe not immediately. He had a little time to formulate a plan. Probably his last. He had to make it matter, make it count for something. If all he did was surrender, everything they went through would be for nothing. He wasn't a hero, it wasn't anything like that. It was just that kids count. If they are honest and listen, they deserve to be treated with respect. He had done a lot of growing up in the past few weeks. He intended to be taken seriously. He intended that someone know why the four of them endured the life of runaways.

"It's what you learn after
you know it all that counts."

— *Anonymous*

# 27

THE WARMTH INSIDE the towering dredge house was intoxicating. Danny rubbed his hands near the whining engine, turned and pressed his back against the transmission cowling. Noise from the grinding mechanical dredge reverberated off the steel walls of the shack, pounding in his ears, and yet it seemed to seal him in a cocoon of security and protection from the outside winter frost, and the strangers he knew would soon be coming to get him.

The cold ache in his joints slowly subsided. He hung his jacket on a hood directly over the engine, and steam billowed from it as ice melted from the garment, dripped, then sizzled as it hit the hot engine manifold. He wanted to stay inside the warm, seemingly safe environment forever despite the grease and dirt around him. Let them come and find him; he was exhausted.

Yet he would not allow himself such a timid surrender. He hadn't done anything. For the first time, the sight of the flapping handcuff on his left wrist incensed him, and he pulled harshly on it as though it might pop right off. The metal dug into his skin. Danny flung his arm through the air, smacking the loose cuff on a pipe with a clang. He spotted a hammer and laid the loose shackle across the dredge engine. Several swift strokes sheared off the chain, and he tossed the loose cuff into the sand auger.

He didn't know how long he had been in the tower, certainly not long, but time was against him. Through grimy panes of window glass he saw the strobes of red and blue lights being deflected off mounds of sand. The beacons lit up the cloudy gray sky like a pulsating multi-colored rainbow. Suddenly the tower felt cold. An image of the freezing killer river passed through his mind. The thought of the snow-covered countryside made him chill.

The quiet, dank, smelly solitude of the dredge tower was finally broken with a boom that cracked through the dense artic air. A bull horn was calling his name.

"Danny, this is Deputy Ranther. I know you're up there. I'm from Madison County and I'm here to help."

It felt like the sound waves from the amplified megaphone were shaking the tower. The tin shack became an echo chamber pulsating with blaring words that bounced off the corrugated walls and pounded in his brain. The sounds were so crystal clear traveling through cold dense air that the deputy seemed to be hollering right into his ears. And Danny felt the gut-wrenching hopelessness of utter despair. Any accomplishments he had achieved in the past his mind systematically dismissed.

"Danny, your sisters are here. They are fine, and they want to see you. Please come down. I know you've been through a lot. We can take care of all of that; just come down."

Like put me in jail, Danny thought. The man was lying, he felt sure. The man would say anything to make his job easier. Danny covered his ears and violently shook his head. He didn't want to hear any of it. You know where I am, you want me, you come and get me, he thought. He felt a knot growing in his throat, and he spit to relieve the ache; the saliva hissed as it fried on the hot running engine.

A glance through the window confirmed his worse fears. There was no escape. Moving slowly, yet in unison from every side, police officers and townspeople were slinking around the sand mounds, converging on the tower.

Yet even with all the unknowing fear that his mind heaped upon him because of his youth and inexperience, the strength and resolve that he witnessed every day in his parents yanked him from any self-pity. He absolutely would not surrender. He stomped on the floor boards of the tower in frustration and anger. They could leave him alone or come and get him. He would not come out on his own.

Danny unlatched the lever that held the window shut, opened it and hollered into the winter air. "Come and get me." As soon as he spoke, he knew no one had heard him. The wind had died down, but the churning roar of the dredge smothered his words. He shut the window, then sat himself in the control seat of the dredge operator. The entire operation was controlled with a stick shift and transmission just like a pick-up truck. The dredge could be operated in low or high gear or reverse. Danny pushed in the clutch, dropped the shift control into neutral, and the whining churn of the incoming sand stopped. Then he pushed a red button on a control panel and the engine died.

With the constant noise of the dredge and engine subsided, he could finally think. He was the main event in town, a brief side show to break the monotonous daily routine of these people, but he really didn't mean anything to them.

He wished that just for an instant he could be reunited with his buddy, Freddie, or his girl friend, Rachael. That just briefly they could be talking about baseball or movies. He wanted so badly to see their familiar smiles and friendly faces.

He decided to leave the relative comfort of the tower. He was going to go out the top, through a trap door, onto the derrick 80 feet in the air that held the auger heads.

As soon as he was visible above the tower trap door, the bull horn began crying in earnest up at him.

"Danny … Danny! Don't go up there." The deep voice was laced with dread, and cried out at a higher pitch. If he had been listening, Danny would have heard the alarm and concern in the voice that called out to him, pleading with him to come back down. But Danny was not paying attention to the crowd below.

Step by step, his climb was calculated and precise. If they wanted to shoot him, he now offered his back to them. His warm dry gloves stuck to the ice-encrusted steel rungs, but he used his elbows in the climb as well. His feet kept slipping. He had to lock his heels over the rungs to keep from falling back. His knees were held in, close and tight. He was headed to the top. He would stay there until they came and got him or until he froze to death and fell.

Ranther told everyone in no uncertain terms to keep their guns down. He pulled Chief Cole to his side and asked, "When will the mother and the girls be out here?"

"Should be any minute," replied Cole.

Ranther tried again, pleading through the bull horn for Danny to reconsider what he was doing. There was no response. The teenage continued his steady assent to the top of the ladder and support apparatus.

What wind there was blew right through Danny's damp clothes. With no shelter whatsoever, his cheeks were already numb, his eyelids felt as though they were going to be glued shut by wind-borne sleet. Through whiffs of snowflakes he saw how small the tower looked perched on its massive steel I-beam legs. Four steel girders held up the small control booth for the dredge operation.

One beam supported the huge metal tube that ran down from under the tower and into the trough that led out to the river. The beams didn't sit directly on the ground. A circle about 30 feet in diameter and four or five feet deep had been cleared away of loose sand and gravel. The bases of the beams sat firmly on solid bedrock and were bolted into place by ten-inch shanks riveted directly into the rock shelf.

The higher up he went, the more the ladder swayed. Danny stopped on every rung to look down. One man started to get on the ladder that led up from the ground to the tower itself, but the man with bull horn pulled him back.

"Danny, now take it easy," cried the bull horn. "No one wants you to get hurt. Come back down."

"Come and get me!" They could hear him now.

Ranther gave Cole a pained expression and licked his lips. He glanced behind him to see if another car was arriving, but the road was obscured by mounds of earth and sand.

"Danny, give me a break, son." He tried to infuse some levity into his voice. The attempt was weak; his voice was strained. Ranther didn't have it in him to try and humor the boy. He was too nervous for that.

"I'm not your son … Get it straight … and save your breath… I'm staying right here."

"How'ya going to help your sisters up there, huh?"

Danny didn't answer.

"Your little brother needs you, too. Come on, whaddayasay?"

Danny pointed his finger down at the crowd and shook it. His emotions made a quick boil of both anger and anguish when the cop mentioned Sam. "You'll say anything, won't you, mister?"

"He's at the hospital now. He's getting the best of care. Don't give up hope." Ranther had to bring down the bull horn and clear his throat. The thought of how the little boy was faring brought a knot to his entire chest.

"He's dead," screamed Danny. "Just say it. Be honest. You're supposed to be real honest, ain't ya? So say it. Don't try and give me a bunch of crap." Danny adjusted his position on the ladder and wiped away tears as best he could with his frosty glove.

"Whatever, Danny. All I'm saying is there are a lot of people who need you, your mother for one. She's here in town, and she's being brought out here right now. So come on down. Make it easier on her when she gets here. I know she wants to see you."

"Shut up!" Danny hollered even louder than before. "You're lying! I ain't giving you nothing." He looked straight down at the steel beams and rock floor directly below. It hurt so much — just thinking of Sam made his heart ache. And now his mother. It had been so long since he'd last seen her. He didn't believe the policeman. The thought of her now made him even more sad ... and angry ... and confused.

If he wasn't careful and slipped on this ice-covered ladder, he wouldn't have to worry about them coming up to get him. Even now, he had to lock his arms over the rungs and hook his knees between them to keep from slipping.

But thinking of Sam just hurt so much. That little boy for seven years had followed him around with star-struck eyes, always trying to please, listening to his every word. He had failed the little guy. It was his fault. He had reached him in the river but hadn't saved him. Every time he thought of Sam the hurt was so great — he just wanted the hurt to stop.

Ranther again had the bull horn at his side, talking to Chief Cole. "Where's your dispatcher? I thought you said they'd be right out?"

"They should have gotten here by now," Chief Cole replied. He pulled his walkie-talkie from his belt. "Base, this is Car One. Come in, Base." No answer. He tried again, turned up the squelch all the way, but his only reply was the loud hiss of empty feedback. He walked over to where Luke had his neck craned toward the sky. "Go back to the road. See if Vicky and Mrs. Stone have made it out here yet. If not, backtrack into town until you find them. We need Mrs. Stone out here pronto."

"Right, Chief."

Danny moved up another foot on the ladder. If it weren't so cold, this might actually be a good place to be, just to think and sort things out. But it was getting harder and harder to hold on. His gloves were frozen again, and slick. His boots already slipped twice on the ice-covered rungs. His leather-soled boots provided almost no traction at all.

"Danny, come down. You're only going to get hurt up there. Please — come down before something bad happens," came the blaring cry from the bull horn.

"Where's my mother?" Danny hollered back. "She's here, ain't she? That's what you said." Danny moved up one more rung. "Well, where is she?"

"She's being brought out here from town," Ranther called back.

Danny heard the answer, but didn't believe it. It was just an excuse, a lie, a bid for time by the cops. He moved up the last and final rung. Directly in front of his eyes was the pole cap that held the guy wire hooks to the whole structure. He could go no higher, almost 100 feet in the air.

Chief Cole's handset squawked, "Chief, this is Luke. The HP and his occupants have slid off the road. Everyone's kinda okay. Vicki hit her head pretty bad, the squad car is down in the ditch. What do you want me to do?"

"Call the trooper a tow truck and leave him there. Get on out here with Mrs. Stone. And hurry."

"Come on down, Danny. Your mother will be here any minute," came Ranther's booming words.

Danny just didn't believe it. It all seemed so unfair — hopeless. Why had all this happened to his family? Had he done something wrong? He adjusted his position on the ladder and ignored the people down below.

Since the accident way back in the summer he had been the man of the house. The oldest, it was his responsibility to take care of the others, to get things done, to see things through. He hadn't measured up. The gnawing emptiness in his stomach was more than hunger; it was a catatonic, mind-weakening loss of hope.

Danny Stone clutched the ice-covered ladder and looked straight out over the winding Platte River through a gray misty sky.

Danny stood up on the ladder and held onto the guy wires.

"Danny!" screamed the amplified voice reverberating throughout the sand pit … "Come down! NO … don't jump!"

# 28

JUST A FEW minutes past 2 p.m. the farm-weary junk-hauling pick-up pulled in front of Lois' house. She handed "Popeye" a crisp hundred-dollar bill and got out without a word. The Thunderbird was loaded with all her luggage; there was nothing left in the house that held any meaning for her. She glanced again at her wristwatch. Time was still on her side.

Her neighborhood bank was a branch located in a shopping center inside an office plaza. Before she stepped from the car, she checked her appearance in the visor mirror. Then she checked her breathing. Just remain calm, she told herself. Just do it like before.

Two tellers staffed the windows. The only other bank personnel was a receptionist who opened new accounts and handled inquiries and an office manager whose primary function was to promote bank investments to regular customers, especially retirees.

Lois seated herself on a white leather couch near the receptionist's desk, waiting for assistance. The name plaque on the desk was unfamiliar. The usual receptionist Lois knew was not around. A strange face came out of a side office and walked over to greet her.

"Yes, may I help you?"

"Yes, I'd like to close out an account."

"I can help you with that." The woman's voice was all business with eyes that conveyed efficiency. Something else was in those eyes, a touch of scorn as though she measured each customer's request to quickly determine how much time it would take from her busy schedule. The woman's make-up was conservative, dressed in a two-piece dark navy blue suit with a coordinated powder blue silk blouse.

"May I see your driver's license?" Lois handed it across the desk. "And your account number ..." The bank employee was now deep into her computer screen.

"You have a considerable balance ... Ms. Devon." The woman turned away from her work and glanced at Lois. Her expression remained professional. "You say you want to close the account?"

"Yes, that's correct. A cashier's check would be fine."

"I certainly hope so, ma'am. We don't have that kind of cash here." She opened a side file drawer and withdrew a set of papers. "We sure hate to lose your business. Is there any particular reason why you are leaving us?"

"It's all very complicated really ... but nothing to do with the bank."

"We're here to help," said the woman behind the desk, no longer stiff and starched in her business attire. She became more relaxed and open as a soothing tone colored her voice.

Lois felt moistness in her palms. "Actually, the young lady who usually sits right there, where you are now, knows all about my situation." Lois wanted to stop right there, but the lady who in essence held her money just waited, obviously interested in hearing more. For several moments they just stared across the desk at one another.

"Yes, well ... you're referring to Cynthia Beckham. This is her day off. My name is Mildred Finch." Her arms were now on the desk, hands turned up. Mildred forced a smile.

Lois couldn't help it, her mind began to race, sputter with short-circuited thoughts. What was going on here? She had made a simple request. Why couldn't this overdressed bank employee just comply?

"Maybe you don't feel you are getting enough of a return on your money?"

Oh, that was it, thought Lois. She wants to sell me something.

"Ma'am, the return has never been a factor in this account. I've kept it in savings because I wanted it to stay liquid." Lois scooted her chair closer to the desk and cocked her head just slightly to the side. "Now, about the withdrawal."

"I understand … it's just the closing out I was concerned about, Ms. Devon. Even if you just leave a thousand or so in the account, then you'll have it here when you wish to use it again." Mildred went back to her computer screen and made several more keystrokes.

Lois felt a warm tightness spreading under her collar. She'd had a bad premonition about this final trip to the bank. Maybe she should just go. She had a large sum already. Why push it? Lois stared at the person seated across the desk; her eyes burned like lasers focused on Mildred's neck. The delay tactics increased the anxiety pulsating through her body. Her palms were getting sticky and wet. Please, she thought. Just give me my money. Lois wanted to swallow, but her throat felt tight, her tongue as arid as though coated with chalk.

"Mrs. Finch, please. I just want to close out the account. Could you do that for me?"

"Fine," Mildred said flatly. "I'll need you to fill out these two forms."

"What?" Lois said loud enough for one of the tellers to look up.

"Yes, ma'am. We're required by bank policy to get current phone numbers, home and work, current or new address, place of work … I'm sure it will only take you a few minutes to complete. And this second form must be completed for all transactions over $10,000."

Lois's agitation grew with each passing second. Something told her this newfound paperwork was all a stall tactic, a regular delay used to keep high-dollar depositors from withdrawing all of their money from the bank. "Why is it I've never had to fill out this form before?" Lois lifted up the federal transaction form.

"As I said, Ms. Devon. It's only for transactions $10,000 and over. I see you've had a lot of those in the last few months. Someone had to fill out that form; maybe the receptionist that was here did it for you ..." Mildred held down the scroll key on her keyboard and paused.

"My ... you've withdrawn almost $800,000 in just over five months. Are you sure I can't help you with some business matter?"

"No! And I'd appreciate it if you didn't ask again." Lois was now on the edge of her chair. The gall of this woman. What business was it of this bank clerk how much she took out of her own account, or how often? She swallowed to keep her composure, but her face felt flush. She wanted to give this employee a piece of her mind. She nibbled on her lip and began filling out the forms.

Mildred slipped from behind her desk. Lois' growing agitation and tense demeanor didn't go unnoticed. It didn't bother her personally, but she was concerned about the large and frequent withdrawals.

She stepped into a side office, pulled open a cabinet to the customer files and ran her fingers through the D's. She glanced through the window blinds and watched the woman at her lobby desk intently filling out paperwork.

Mildred picked up the telephone and dialed the police station down the block. She reached a personal friend who worked at the station, Detective Bill Reynolds. His regular duties involved juveniles and adolescent gangs, but he was always ready to help out where he could.

"Mildred, this is a surprise."

"I'm glad I caught you in."

"Is there something wrong?"

"Maybe, but not with me. I'm over here at the bank, the branch on Juniper just a few blocks from your office."

"I know exactly where it is."

"Well … I've got a customer here asking to make a very large withdrawal and close out her account. She's been a customer of the bank for sixteen years, and now she's acting rather strange."

"How much money?"

"Twenty-six thousand nine hundred dollars."

"That's a chunk of change."

"She acts like she's under some unusual pressure, and with all the street scams going on out there I … ah …. well, I'd hate to find out later she's had her arm twisted or fallen for some con game."

"What has she said about closing the account?"

"She doesn't want to discuss it … at all."

"No reason for leaving the bank after all these years?"

"None. Like I said, she's acting strange."

"What's her name?"

"Devon … Lois Devon. Lives on Magnolia."

"Okay, well, try to keep her there for awhile. I've got to go to court, but I'll send over one of the other detectives. I know you've got a feel for this sort of thing, Mildred. I trust your judgment. But tell me, why is a vice president of the bank closing out accounts at a branch office?"

"Filling in, you know how that goes. Mainly, I'm here doing a six-month review of the files. Thanks, Bill."

"Don't mention it."

Bill Reynolds took ten steps down the hall to the office of Detective Conner who was seated on his desk with a telephone receiver in his ear. Reynolds waited for him to get off the phone.

"Got something I need you to check out at the First National Bank branch on Juniper."

"What's it about?"

"A lady name of Devon, Lois Devon, is up there now wanting to withdraw the last of her money. The bank VP thinks something's fishy."

"Devon ... Devon. I've heard that name just today," said Conner as he got off his backside and grabbed a coat from a single hook on the door. "I'll check it out."

Mildred returned to the receptionist desk and watched attentively, yet patiently, as Lois completed the paperwork. Lois finished, looked up with eyes darting about the room, and pushed the papers across the desk.

"Thank you, Ms. Devon. We try to keep the red tape to a minimum." Mildred forced an ingratiating smile. "We sure do appreciate your business."

Lois said nothing, but Mildred saw her nostrils flare as she inhaled and let out an audible sigh.

Mildred continued. "Our money market accounts are guaranteed to pay 1/2 percent higher than other local demand accounts." Lois just stared, lips pursed. "You said you liked to keep your money liquid," Mildred said. "In addition, First National now has discount brokerage services for all customers whether your investment objectives are stocks, bonds or mutual funds."

"So?"

"Well ..." Mildred was caught short. Lois' thick tone oozed with no-nonsense frankness.

"Is the cashier's check ready?" Lois said, demanding, not asking.

"I could roll over your deposit into a new vehicle of your choice," Mildred said defensively.

Lois blew. "Gawd dammit ... I don't believe your gall. Give me my damn money or I'll have your bleached split ends in a clump in my hand." Lois stood and reached over the desk. Mildred jumped back at the last second and fell over her chair in a heap on the floor. Lois jumped around the desk and loomed over the prostrate banker. "Any other questions, Mrs. Finch?"

"No ... no," Mildred stuttered. She regained her footing and walked clumsily to her side office. "I'll get that cashier's check for you right now." Lois followed right on her heels.

Within minutes the check was ready. Lois read it over, letting her eyes stop on each number in the amount. Then she turned and headed for the door without saying another word. As she neared the door, she raised her eyes. A man in a dark overcoat stood directly in the entrance. Lois could see his eyes looking past her, and she turned and looked back. Mildred was standing in the middle of the bank waving frantically and pointing in her direction. Lois kept moving, but the man at the door blocked her way.

"Lois Devon?" he asked when she looked up into his eyes.

"Yes," she said. The word caught in her throat. She felt like she was about to choke. She hardly heard the word come out, but she knew she'd said it.

"My name is Detective Conner with the Omaha Police Department. I need to ask you to come with me."

* * * * *

The sounds came first — a high-pitched ringing deep in his ears that engulfed muffled voices. Then came the smell. A nasty, camphor odor made him swallow the dry pasty film that lay on his tongue. The smell also signaled his languid brain that he was awaking. With eyes still closed, he twitched his nose at the overpowering antiseptic aroma, then raised a hand to his face, rubbed his forehead and fluttered open heavy eyelids to an unfocused shadowy darkness.

Danny listened to the hum as his numb skin responded to the musty warmth that surrounded him like a wool blanket. He was lying in a strange bed, in unfamiliar surroundings. He couldn't place himself. A brief spark of panic ricocheted through his thoughts, but he was warm. Something about being covered — with crisp clean linen touching him — made it all better. Briefly, he allowed the encompassing sensation of warmth radiate through his body before he tried to make sense of it all. The absence of cold was relaxing. Something was good about this strange place.

A hand touched his upper arm, a soothing contact. He didn't try to see. The embrace made him relax even more and he waited for the voice.

"Danny … everything is going to be all right."

The sound of the words hung in the air, suspended in the room, a melodic serene tone that soothed his adolescent mind, descended and gently engulfed him and stroked his weary heart, a familiar voice from his very beginning, the first voice he had ever heard.

Sandra Stone squeezed her son's arm. "Danny, I know everything that happened … I'm proud of you, son. You've made me real proud of you, Danny." Her heart raced with joy, just the sight of him now handed her back her life. The fall had knocked him out, but the doctor said he was not seriously hurt. Several hours back with her children did more to snap her out of her depression than five months at the hospital. She was a mother once again.

Danny opened his eyes. The room came into focus as someone turned on a table lamp. His mother looked down at him with wet eyes that sparkled; light reflected from the lamp. She didn't say anything else; the ordeal had sapped her strength as well, but bent her head beside his and brushed her cheek against his. And hugged him.

His face was dry and rough, chapped, cold-snap weathered, but she pressed against him and kissed his neck. As she stood up, tears ran as little rivulets over warm cheeks.

"I feel fine, Ma." Danny reached across with his left arm and took his mother's hand. "Open the curtain," he said, trying to sit up in bed. "How long have I been asleep? How long have I been here?"

Melissa walked to the side of the bed and pulled herself up on the bed guard rail. "Eight hours, Danny. We've been waiting here in the hospital for you the whole time." Chrissy stood behind Melissa with a solemn face and touched his upper arm through his white cotton gown. She didn't have to speak to convey her feelings. Chrissy's eyes could tell a story, and he knew she was very glad to see him.

"The ambulunst people thought you had broken bones," Melissa continued as she held his hand, and he pulled her into the bed.

"Ambulance," said Chrissy.

"Really?... No, I feel fine. What happened?"

"We don't know," Sandra said, looking deeply into her eldest child's eyes. "We weren't there. But Deputy Ranther said you were high on the tower at the sand pit, and you jumped from it."

"I remember being on the tower ... I've never been so cold. Then I don't remember. Must'a blacked out."

"Oh, Danny. I saw that ladder. You could have slipped off that thing and been killed. There was nothing below that thing but a rock ledge."

"I'm okay now, Ma. Really. I remember being shot at, I remember that."

"Danny," Sandra put his hand in hers and bent low to speak directly to him. "Danny, I know how debilitating it is to lose hope. It's called depression. It happened to me. It seems like yesterday when your dad was torn from all of us. Makes you do crazy things and forget about important things. Will you ever forgive me?"

"Of course, Mom. I understand now. We just all missed you so much. Sometimes I thought you were never coming back."

She kept looking directly into his eyes. "Danny, we got there right after you came off the tower. Do you remember... did you slip off the tower?"

Danny sat all the way up in his adjustable bed. "No, Mom. I didn't slip."

"I wondered, Danny, but then, it makes me sad to think you might have lost your hope, since everything was going so bad, and have jumped to hurt yourself."

Danny was fully awake. His mother's immediate affinity for his thoughts, her acceptance of much of the weight of guilt, made him love her all the more. And love accepts burden in its own right. He didn't want her to feel unduly responsible for all that had come to pass. She was just being human; the nervous breakdown was part of it. Life can throw any family a curve ball just about any time it wants. Now he remembered feeling really low ... and scared. But he knew he wasn't about to throw in the towel; as bad as things had gotten he wasn't ready to quit. And he wanted his mother to be sure of that fact.

"No way, Mom. I knew I was in trouble being up on that tower. But I wasn't going to fall or let go. I made it to the sand pile, didn't I, Mom? I jumped to get down. I made it to the sand."

Sandra took her son's hand and raised it to her face and rubbed it over her cheek. "I remember when you did this with my hand the night your father died. You're such a dependable boy, Danny. I knew the sheriff's department and the highway patrol had it all wrong when they told me you shot somebody."

"They thought you shot Ralph," said Chrissy. "I told them it was Eddie. The sheriff said Ralph would live."

Danny listened. The events of the past day made some sense with the simple explanation.

"But that big tall sheriff's deputy didn't think it was you, Danny," Chrissy continued filling in the story, smiling slightly, telling him with her eyes that there were good people out there who wanted to help them.

"He's a real nice man," seconded Melissa.

"The man who stopped us along the river?"

Chrissy nodded.

"He was the one who called to me through the bull horn," Danny stated to the ceiling. "Where's he at now?"

"He's right down the hall," cried Melissa as she sprang from the bed and darted out the door. A second later she walked back into the bedroom leading the large man by the hand.

"He wanted to wait until you awoke before he left town, Danny," Melissa explained.

Big John Ranther approached the bed, his fingers gently twirling his Stetson in front of his waist.

"Yes, I wanted to meet you, young man. Considering all you've been through, I'd say you did a remarkable job, and I wanted to tell you so."

"Thank you, sir" Danny looked up at the rough, worn face with the sparkling blue eyes. He could see the decency and concern in the officer's gaze.

"It was darn near impossible to track you," Ranther continued. "It was apparent that you have a lot of determination and resourcefulness in you, young man. I think you can accomplish whatever you set your mind to, and I wish you all the best."

"Thanks again, sir."

"I just want to tell you, if I ever have a son, I hope he grows up just like you."

Danny's eyes grew moist. The lump in his chest was the best lump he'd ever felt, the compliment forced a smile out of him, and his picket-fence grin beamed for all to see.

"You're the best, Danny," Melissa said as she climbed the rail and jumped in the bed beside him once again.

"Well, I better be heading out," Ranther said.

"Where you going?"

"Got a little trip to Omaha to take care of." Ranther shook Danny's hand and headed out the door.

Sandra walked around to the foot of the bed. "Honey, your aunt has had her sticky fingers in all the trouble we've been having. She cashed an $800,000 insurance policy your father left for the four of you. I think that's why she took you to THAT farm. Anyway, Deputy Ranther had been closing in and would have already arrested her, except that he learned where you were, and first wanted to get you all in safe."

"She did all this to steal insurance money?"

"It looks like she did, Danny. I don't know why. She wasn't always like that. I can't answer why."

Danny lay back on the bed.

He could feel his toes and fingers. Even his ears didn't ache with that constant stinging brittle hurt any more. It was good to feel warm and see his mother and sisters again. For a time while he was waking, his exhausted mind had protected him with only pleasant thoughts of security and reunion.

But soon, reality came to the fore. If his mother and the girls knew all about Aunt Lois and Ralph, then surely they had received the bad news about Sam. Danny no longer thought of himself. He felt exposed and ashamed. They continued to look at him lovingly; Melissa was in the bed with him with her doll coiled up beside him with her head on his chest. Danny thought about asking them to leave the room. He didn't want to talk about anything else now; he felt so responsible. There was one event that ultimately made their long journey a disaster.

"The doctor says you can be released tomorrow," his mother said, sensing his sudden tenseness. She looked at Chrissy, who nodded and stepped closer to the side of the bed.

Danny closed his eyes and tried to let his mind go blank. "Danny," Chrissy said, "I want you to know that we never could have gotten through all this without you. I'm glad you're my big brother, Danny ... and I have some good news for you." Danny opened his eyes, but an expression of sadness remained etched on his face. He looked at Chrissy and searched her eyes.

"The sheriff's deputy told us all about it, Danny. You saved Sam. If it wasn't for you, he'd have drowned for sure."

"For real?" Danny came up in the bed with a start that pitched Melissa forward. "He's alive?"

"He's alive and conscious, Danny," said Chrissy.

"Where is he?"

"Just down the hall," Melissa said with a proud smile on her face.

Sandra stepped to the bed. Sam's in ICU and he's got pneumonia, but the doctor said it looks good. He's a tough kid, Danny. Takes after you."

"But he wasn't breathing."

"The frigid water protected his brain until the medical personnel were able to hook him up to a respirator."

Danny flew out of the bed, the lower half of his hospital gown fluttering around his knees. "We've got to go see him, Mom."

"We will."

"I mean now. I feel fine. I don't need to wait until tomorrow to get out of here." He darted to the closet, but found no clothes. "Where are my clothes?"

"You don't have any right now. We'll get you some." The girls laughed.

"Oh gosh, that's great news, Mom. Did he talk?"

"The doctor said he asked for you, Danny."

"Show me the way."

Melissa jumped in front leading the way to the ICU ward. Danny was right behind her, and then Chrissy and Sandra who knew it was too late to hold him back, followed by two frantic nurses who called in vain for Danny to return to his room.

At the end of a long wing Melissa stood at a door. "This is it."

They paused for just an instant. Inside, Melissa led him down a row of draped partitions and pulled open the green curtains as she reached the middle of the row.

There was Sam. An oxygen mask was fastened to his face, but he was awake, and his eyes sparkled when he saw his big brother.

Danny rushed alongside the bed and reached for his little brother's hand. For a time they just looked at each other. Sam appeared tired; his skin a pasty white. Sandra and Chrissy joined Melissa and Danny around the bed.

"Hang in there, buddy. You're going to do just fine," Danny said. Sam nodded slightly and tried to smile.

"I know how much you want to farm that land. I think you'll make a great farmer, Sam. I know you always wanted me to help you, too. I think that's a great idea. I know I'm in no hurry to see the city again. I think I like that old farm more than I realized before. Dad sure knew what he was doing."

Danny lifted Melissa up on the edge of the bed and put his arms around Chrissy and his mother.

"Sam knew it, too. I can't wait to get back home, Mom. I can't wait to get back."

"Yesterday is history,
Tomorow a mystery.
Today is a gift;
That's why it's called the present."

— *Anonymous*

Mr. Morris lives in Dodge City, Kansas, where he spends his free time catching ground squirrels and prairie dogs to feed to his two pet rattlesnakes, Buford and Dexter. This is his first novel.